AURUM
THE GOLDEN PLANET

AURUM

THE GOLDEN PLANET

SHARON JOSS

AJA PUBLISHING
USA

For my best beloveds

ONE

Renly Harkness stared in disbelief at his finished sketch of the beautiful Queen Fabienne. This commission was his fourth engraving for the young regent since she'd ascended to the throne nine years ago. He'd been twenty years old when he designed the platinum commemorative plate for her coronation, and the work had made him famous throughout the Universal Consortium of Planets. He had never travelled to Callisto-Prime, and never met the queen, but he knew her face nearly as well as his own. Nevertheless, the image he'd drawn did not belong to her.

It was Garrett's.

He tore the ruined sheet from his sketchbook and crumpled it in his fist. A headache bloomed at his temples. He closed his eyes and took a deep breath. The comforting aroma of turpentine and linseed oil, which permeated his studio, always calmed him. This room was his sanctuary; the one place where he felt safe, secure, and in control of his artistry.

Renly began again; starting with the woman's heart-shaped face and delicately arched brows. Again, his older brother's image stared out at him from the page.

He went to his workbench and selected an inhaler from among the many in his right-hand drawer. He shook it vigorously, and then inhaled; savoring the soothing mist expanding in his lungs. The sensation always refreshed him. His eyes settled on the holographic workstation. Perhaps he needed a different approach.

He powered on the imaging console, which responded with a low hum, and projected a larger-than-life image of the Queen into the center of his studio. Her three-dimensional image hung in the air, inches away from his fingers. The seemingly solid hologram illuminated her features from every angle, yet in spite of his intentions, the image he drew did not match the Queen's.

He wiped his sweaty hands on a bleached cotton rag he kept for that purpose, and set aside the sketchbook. He stood, stretched, and shook out his cramped hands; then stepped away from the workbench and moved toward the antique rosewood desk he used for correspondence. In the bottom left-hand drawer he kept a small decanter of golden liqueur, a personal gift from Fabienne. After pouring a half-inch of the royal whiskey into his empty coffee cup, he tossed it back in a single swallow. The golden liquid smelled like nectar and burned like fire. An uncontrolled shiver riffled down his spine. He craned his head this way and that, stretching out the tight neck muscles, then resumed his seat at his workbench.

Maybe he should work on something else. A new project. Admiral Zachary Cosgrove, the director of the North American Starfleet, had a narrow face and a forehead which rose well above the crown of his hairline. The face he drew above the uniform had Garrett's facial symmetry, broad cheekbones, and cold, arrogant eye set. A dozen more starts yielded the same results.

By the time he tore the last page out of the sketchbook, his sweaty shirt clung to him, and midnight had long since passed. Dozens of balls of furiously wadded paper filled the trashcan. Discouraged, Renly rubbed his face, set the alarms, and turned out the lights of his studio, then climbed the stairs to his apartment, opened a bottle of sixty-year-old Celestine Brandy, and drank himself into oblivion.

* * *

The nightmares began two nights later. So real, so loud. As if he was right in the same room with him. *Renly. I need your help. Renly, where are you?*

Every time his brother called his name, he jerked wide-awake and trembling; his sheets soaked with sweat, his mouth filled with the taste of dirt. The trauma of his childhood had somehow gotten twisted up with this new and haunting dream of Garrett.

He never did remember the face of the man who'd abducted him when he was nine. His only memory of those sixteen days was of the man's big gold teeth. But he never forgot the unmistakable, claustrophobic scent of moist earth that surrounded the coffin in which he'd been imprisoned. The despair of that time returned whenever he ventured outdoors. He never forgot lying in the dark, praying for someone to come. He prayed to God, to his parents, and to Garrett.

Only Garrett heard him.

Only Garrett came.

In spite of their ten-year age difference, he and his brother shared a psychic connection; everyone knew that. After his rescue, his parents and the police told him how Garrett had heard his pleas, and led the police to where the pedophile had buried him. And thank goodness, for it, because the man was never identified, never captured. Garrett saved his life. Garrett was his hero.

And now Garrett needed *his* help.

TWO

Leo Broussard had been the Harkness family lawyer for most of his life and accustomed to his godson's quirks, but when the master goldsmith answered his knock, he the change in Renly's appearance and demeanor rattled him.

Dark circles smudged the skin below his eyes and his hands shook with the palsy of an old man. All manner of strange tools and appliances covered his normally spotless workbench; the walls of the studio had been stripped bare of his artwork. A dozen or more large storage containers stood in one corner.

"What's going on, son?"

"I'm closing down the studio."

The smell the alcohol wafted over Leo. Renly had never been much of a drinker; booze was one of Garrett's many vices. He loosened his tie and set down his briefcase. "The studio is in the Trust, Renly. You can't sell it."

His godson paced nervously, his eyes on the floor. "You don't understand. He's in trouble. He needs me. I'm going to be gone for a while, and I need you to keep an eye on the place. Pay the bills for me. That sort of thing."

Damn that Garrett. "He contacted you?" They'd had no word for years. After Garrett used up all the Trust funds, he thought they'd heard the last of him. "What does he want this time?"

Renly fiddled with the tools on his workbench, not meeting his eyes. "I don't know, exactly. Took me some time to find him. Based on Starfleet records, he cleared Khirjahni customs on Aurum three years ago and never left. He's in trouble."

Leo snorted. "Of course he's in trouble. Aurum is an embargoed planet. When did he contact you?"

"He didn't, exactly." Renly looked uncomfortable. "I've been having these dreams." His voice trailed off. "He needs my help."

Here we go again. Leo didn't doubt the psychic connection between the brothers, but of the two, Renly's ability was far stronger, and he relied on his intuition for many of his business decisions. Garrett, on the other hand, exploited their connection as a means to manipulate Renly.

"I think you're overreacting." Every four years, the Arkady Universal Mining Corporation hosted the Gold Festival on Aurum; a three-week debauchery of gambling and excess, culminating the richest race in the galaxy. "Garrett is probably having the time of his life and ran out of money."

"I'm going there."

"What?" The announcement was so out of character, Leo scarcely believed his ears. Something else had to be going on here. Something Renly didn't want to tell him. "Did you and Sumi have another fight?"

"She moved out two months ago," he admitted. "But not because of this. She took a transfer to Singapore." He shrugged. "I didn't want to go."

Of course he wouldn't want to go. Agoraphobia was only one of several disorders, which afflicted Renly after the kidnapping.

The young man was a seething mess of neuroses. His fear of germs, crowds, and animals had changed him; kept him housebound. Getting out of the building was a good thing, but leaving Earth to chase after Garrett was just plain crazy. "Does Dr. Obote know about this?"

Color rose in the goldsmith's cheeks. "I don't need his approval to make a decision. Or yours either."

Leo recognized the mulish set of Renly's jaw. He tried a different approach. "Fair enough. Have you thought about what a trip into space would mean? You've never been in cryosleep. Or had a gastric lavage. You'll be gone for nearly a year. Have you thought about what that will do to your business?"

"I know." The pale young man looked sick to his stomach. "He needs me, Leo. He saved my life; I can't turn my back on him."

Leo ran his hand through his thinning hair. "I remember." Sadness washed through him in a wave. Between the kidnapping and his parent's fatal car accident two years later, Renly's childhood had been one disaster after another. Leo fretted often about the boy's mental state, but once he settled into this studio, his emotional problems, with the exception of his quirks and phobias, stabilized.

Garrett had always been the tough one. Nothing bothered that boy. Street-wise beyond his years, and not above exploiting anyone, even his own brother to get what he wanted. The only thing Garrett ever wanted or needed from anyone, especially Renly was money. What Renly earned as a master engraver wasn't nearly enough to suit Garrett's tastes. The idea of Renly 'rescuing' Garrett made no sense. There had to be a way to dissuade him.

"Aurum's a plague planet. Those genetic viruses are deadly to Terrans. Are you seriously considering that kind of risk?"

"The ambassador assured me the risk is only for people who travel to the interior. I'll be on the coast. Thousands of visitors attend the Gold Festival, and in forty years, they've never had a problem. I'm taking the utmost precautions. I'll wear gloves, and the hotel even offers special off-worlder accommodations. They have air filters in all the rooms."

"Look, son. Arkady Universal Mining holds exclusive access rights to Aurum. They decide who gets a visa. You don't travel in those financial circles. You'll never clear customs."

Renly nodded. "You're right. They turned me down, so I offered a gift commission to the Khirjahni royal family. The formal invitation and visa arrived yesterday."

* * *

On the day of his departure, Renly stared at the cluttered workbench inside his studio for the last time; trying to decide which of his tools to take with him. Sadness and longing washed through him, but to his own surprise, no panic. At least, not yet. The idea of leaving the security of this place and everything behind was almost unbearable, but he had no choice.

The nightmares were getting worse. The lack of sleep and his inability to work had him pacing the floors endlessly. Every time he closed his eyes, Garrett's voice echoed in his mind and the stink of moist earth haunted his dreams.

Now the day of departure had arrived. Renly regretted waiting until the last minute to decide which tools to bring.

Leo had offered to take him to the shuttle port and arrived an hour early. He understood Leo's concerns about him going after Garrett; he probably planned to arrive early to try to talk him out of it again. That wasn't going to happen.

Leo nodded to the instruments spread out across his bench. "Are you taking all that?"

Renly shook his head. "I wish I could." Apparently, there were weight restrictions even in space, and most of his luggage allowance was allocated to the precious metals he needed to bring for the royal commission. He'd packed six blanks of platinum and two more of white gold. He much preferred to work in white metal, but at the last minute decided to add a couple of yellow gold, just in case. He detested yellow gold, but he wanted to have it available if the monarch had a preference. More than twenty pounds, total. All that precious metal would mean he'd have to keep his pack with him.

"Chisels, right?"

He nodded. "Basically, yes. These are gravers." He picked up a slim vee-edge chisel and slipped the tang end into the ferrule of a mushroom-shaped handle. "When I attach the chisel into a graver handle, they become a burin. Engravers use burins to inscribe designs into metal."

The heft of the tool in his hand brought him comfort. The rosewood handle fitted into his palm with a perfection only achieved by decades of daily use. He far preferred the reliability and feel of his older gravers, but the newer ones held an edge longer.

"Why not just hire someone to find him? You'll be gone for months. You're at the top of your profession right now. I know people who specialize in this sort of thing. You don't have to go."

He stared into Leo's worried face, and knew instinctively that his godfather would never accept his motives for going to Aurum. Until he knew for himself Garrett was safe, the nightmares would never stop. Until he silenced Garrett's pleas, he would not be able to work. Drawing and engraving were the external manifestations of his creative soul. Like song to a nightingale, his art was his source of magic, and gave him more joy and satisfaction than anything else in life. No one could do what he could; or at least, not as well. Through his creative gift, he learned to cope with the nightmare of his childhood.

The urge to create kept him focused and distracted; his work kept the bad dreams away. Without his art, he might as well be dead.

"You're not talking me out of this, Leo." He turned back to the tools spread out on his workbench. The older ones were most reliable and offered a reassuring link to Earth, if only by memory. He didn't want to lose them, but couldn't bear the thought of leaving them behind for a year. Or more. He disconnected the graver from the handle and rolled it, along with the rest of the set within a segment of oiled chamois. The pungent scent of preserved leather tickled his sinuses. Reverently, he placed the suede-wrapped bundle inside his carry-all shoulder pack, where he'd already packed a small vial bottle of oil, two oilstones, sandbags, and a couple of chasing hammers. He wrapped six of his favorite graver handles inside a butter-soft goatskin. In an outside pocket of the weatherproof canvas bag he added a blank artist sketchbook and a number of graphite pencils.

Into the bag went half-dozen burnishers, two walrus bone rubbing sticks, various other scribers, and a calico pounce bag and added them to his satchel. These would leave little room for his sanitizers and first aid kit, but he would not leave them behind. He pondered instead, which items of clothing weren't absolutely necessary. He paused, realizing Leo had just asked him a question. "Excuse me?"

"The presentation medal you made for the Khirjahni King. You said you'd show me."

"Of course."

He reached into an inside pocket in his bag and pulled out a four-inch square flattened box, handmade of teak wood. He took off the lid, slipped the heavy platinum medal out of the protective flannel, and laid it on the worktable for Leo to see. He switched on the magnifying lamp, and positioned the light over the piece so Leo could appreciate the detail of the design. "It won't be finished until I can get a better sketch of him in profile. I haven't found many images of him available to work from."

Leo examined the medal. "Are those horns real or is he wearing some kind of headpiece?"

He shrugged. "The planet literature says some of the natives do have horns." Renly drew a shaky breath. "I'll guess I'll find out in about five months."

"He looks familiar."

Renly blushed and turned off the lamp, hoping Leo wouldn't recognize Garrett's profile. His hand trembled as he slipped the medallion back into the box. He hoped seeing the king's profile in person would help him make the changes he needed to finish the portrait. "I just hope he likes it."

With a grunt, he hefted the satchel by the thick strap and heaved it to his shoulder. He could barely stand upright. He considered leaving his vitamins and collection of antiseptic ointments behind, since he only planned to be there for a week, but decided against it. Better to bring his own than risk picking up a local bug.

He threw in two dozen pair of synthetic gloves; more than enough to see him through a week, and they didn't weigh much. And although the hotel offered filtered air, he couldn't possibly leave his personal air filter masks behind.

Instead, he removed his winter overcoat, bathrobe, and one of his spare shirts. His stay on Aurum would only be a few days, anyway. Just long enough to get Garrett out of jail or whatever jam he was in, and engrave the royal portrait.

Leo caught him with his gaze. "Are you certain you're prepared to go through with this? I'm not speaking to you as your lawyer here, Renly. I'm here as your friend. Don't do this. Your brother will never change. If he's gotten himself into trouble again, you can't help him."

Emotion welled in his throat. "When I was abducted by that awful man, and everyone else gave me up for dead, Garrett reached out to me and found me. He saved my life Leo."

"What if he's dead? What if you can't save him?"

Renly gazed into Leo's well-meaning face. "He's not dead." Renly patted his chest, over his heart. "I would know if he were. Look, I don't want to go, and I do realize you think I'm not up to this, but I am going. I *have* to. He came for me when everyone else gave *me* up for dead. *I owe him.*"

His lawyer gave him a sad, thin-lipped smile and nodded. "All right then. I guess we'd better get going."

Renly ran his hand across the centuries-old walnut surface of his workbench. Now that the time had come to leave his studio, it was like saying goodbye to his oldest and dearest friend. He'd done his best work here; even felt brief moments of genius and utter satisfaction in this room. His comfortable apartment upstairs had been his home for the last ten years, but unless he silenced Garret's voice in his head, this place was dead to him. *I am coming back.* He took a last deep breath, then hoisted his heavy carryall to his shoulder and staggered after Leo out to the waiting limo.

THREE

The crowd surged forward into the Aurum customs hall, carrying Renly along like a droplet of mucous in a large sneeze. He stayed well to the back of the crowds in the departure lounge, but the captain opened the doors on both sides of the cabin, and he instead found himself at the front of the stampede of sweaty, overdressed, impatient revelers.

Amidst the crowded customs hall, panic clenched his gut. He stumbled, and without the mob to keep him up, would have been trampled. Travelers from all over the galaxy pressed on all sides. The maelstrom of alien colors, shapes, and pungent perfumes made him dizzy. Worst of all, the penetrating smell of Aurum itself, which penetrated the overheated building with the heavy scent of sulfur, in spite of the face mask he kept clamped over his nose and mouth.

He shrugged into the smallest version of himself and kept his head down, avoiding eye contact; just as he'd done for most of the final ten days of his journey. It was second nature to him now; his only defense against jovial inquiries from well-meaning strangers who, after eyeing his modest and somber black suit, repeatedly inquired as to his financial holdings, recreational preferences, and sexual availability.

His fellow passengers all seemed to assume he was either a priest or some sort of undertaker. In particular, the party from Hepsilon VI did not understand the difference between engraver and embalmer. He'd taken to dining in his cabin, as the dining room hosted all sorts of festival-bound aliens who did not understand the concept of personal space. The thought of catching some alien virus and dying before they reached port killed his appetite, anyway.

Not even the double dose his anxiety medication seemed to dampen his sense of dread. His five months in cryosleep left him weak and short of breath. Not even the electro-stimulation of his muscles during the trip had been enough to maintain his strength. His heavy bag of gold, tools, and medications weighed nearly more than he could lift and carry.

Announcements echoed throughout the hall, repeated in a variety of languages both sharp and guttural. He'd opted to learn both Khirjahni and Th'Dorran, the major native languages of Aurum while in cryosleep, but the thrum of thousands of people and the acoustics of the room made the meaning of the words indecipherable.

At last, the line surged forward. Renly gratefully acknowledged the microchip implants made quick work of processing the mass of people, all of whom were bright-eyed with fever. Gold fever. It seemed as if every single person on board ship, from cabin boy to cabana queen, card shark to captain seemed infected, and the topic of gold and other precious metals dominated every conversation for the entire cruise. As the ship's purser so gleefully informed, the minimum net worth of each passenger was more than four *billion* Federation credits.

Since Renly had only secured his passage on the ship by virtue of his invitation from the Khirjahni royal family, he felt like a fraud. In spite of the luxury accommodations, even in his steerage berth, he found the trip to be a disheartening and exhausting experience. He found himself actually looking forward to the cryosleep on the return trip.

When he reached the customs counter, the agent instructed him to wave his wrist across the scanner. The identifying microchip, which had been implanted at the UCP space station, immediately set off an alarm. An armed security officer stepped up beside him.

"Mr. Harkness?"

His heart skipped a beat. "Yes?"

"This way please." The officer took his arm and he had no choice but to follow.

The officer led him to a windowless conference room inside the terminal. The stink of rotten eggs and stale cigar smoke choked the room. A round wooden table, flanked by eight chairs dominated the center of the room. In one corner, Renly recognized the UCF and American Alliance flags; the third flag was, he guessed, the flag of Khirjah. The twin suns on a lavender field, presumably to represent the famous lavender sky, a pair of dancing fish and some sort of goat, rendered in a primitive style. Accustomed as he was to designing national emblems as symbols of a country's strength, this childish scribble did not impress him.

Contrary to his expectations, the room was not without modern conveniences. Digital display panels lined the walls, flashing skymaps, images of the planet Aurum from space, the coastline, and presumably scenes of the countryside. Several displays cycled through images of various mining sites; a not-so-subtle reminder of the importance of Arkady Universal Mining Corporation.

He thought about removing his gloves, but decided against it. For whatever reason, they'd pulled him out of the customs line. He had done nothing wrong; perhaps this had something to do with his invitation from the royal family.

He pulled at the Nehru collar of his jacket. His clothes fit perfectly when he left earth all those months ago, but after so much time in cryosleep, he could barely believe this was the same jacket. He'd lost a lot of weight and muscle tone on the trip. Even the shoulders were too big.

The door opened, and a man in dark robes entered the room. He introduced himself as the Terran Ambassador, Robert Reinhardt. Renly shifted in his seat uneasily when Reinhardt excused the officer and asked him to wait outside.

"There is no cause for alarm, Mr. Harkness," Reinhardt began. "I never actually expected you would come here; but the situation in Khirjah has changed and I wanted to speak to you before you cleared customs."

Renly recognized the classic shape of the Ambassador's cheekbones as being of Slavic descent. A large nose, but good bones and well-balanced features. Plenty of laugh lines there, but the furrowed brow of a man with a lot on his mind. Renly estimated his age as somewhere in his early sixties. He guessed that whatever Reinhardt had to say, it wasn't good news.

"I'm afraid you've made this long trip for nothing. King Kehreru died unexpectedly six weeks ago. Khirjah is now under new rule. The new king is not interested in hosting a presentation ceremony for his predecessor. I apologize for being blunt, but there is no other way to say this. He has cancelled the audience."

Acid churned at the back of his throat and Renly tasted the bite of disappointment. All this way for nothing. "I had no idea," he choked.

"Of course not. How could you?" Reinhardt's weathered face appeared sincere. "I've arranged return passage for you on the *Platinum Queen*. It leaves in a few hours, and its next port of call is the

Farralon cluster. From there, you can book transport back to Terra."

A sense of relief surged through him, but only for a moment. Tempting as the idea was, he'd come to Aurum to find Garrett. To turn around and go back to without him wasn't going to purge Garret's image from his work or silence the madness of Garrett's voice in his head.

"Thank you, Ambassador, but my offer of a gift commission stands." Renly patted his too-heavy bag; relieved he'd brought the extra blanks and his tools with him. "I would be delighted to design a portrait for the new king."

Reinhardt gave him a doubtful look. "Why are you really here, Mr. Harkness?'

Renly's heart skipped beat. The Ambassador's challenge caught him off guard. "I'm here to do the kings portrait."

"No one spends five months in cryo to come to a tiny, backwards kingdom to paint a picture of the king, sir."

He squared his shoulders. "Engraving. I'm not a painter sir; I'm an engraver."

The ambassador waved him off. "Yes, yes. Master of a dying art, I've been informed. Arkady Universal Mining Corporation turned down your original visa application. I checked your bank records, Mr. Harkness. You aren't a corporate investor, and your net worth would not merit an invitation to attend the Gold Festival." Reinhardt smiled. "Let's be honest with each other. That's really why you're here, isn't it?"

"Excuse me?"

"The Gold Festival. The *real* reason you're here."

"Absolutely not." Renly debated how much to reveal to the Ambassador. Leo told him not to say anything about his search for Garrett until he was face-to-face with the king, but without Reinhardt's support, that meeting might never take place. Who knew how much pull Reinhardt had with the new ruler? He pulled a sketch out of his travel bag and handed it to the ambassador.

"This is my brother. His name is Garrett Harkness." He'd drawn Garrett's portrait from memory and aged the image to account for the years since they'd last seen each other. "He's a professional gambler. He attended the Gold Festival four years ago, but never left the planet. The Arkady mining executives keep telling me he left Aurum after the festival, but there are no records that show he cleared customs, no ships have his name listed on their manifests. No one has heard from him in five years. The Arkady people insist it's a mix-up, and say he's not here, but I don't believe it. That's why I'm here; to find my brother. I'm hoping my gift to the king will inspire him to request the local authorities to help me find him."

"I see." The ambassador stared at the drawing for a moment. "My brother served in the IPF. Career pilot. His ship disappeared on a training mission just outside the chromium sector. That was twelve years ago. They never found his ship or his crew. I know what it's like." He raised his eyes to Renly's. "To wonder and never know."

"I'm sorry for your loss."

Reinhardt sighed aloud. "All right. I will relay your offer to the king. I can't make any promises, or guess how long you might have to wait for an answer. His Highness is pretty busy these days. He may not respond before the end of the festival. He may not respond at all."

The thought of being forced to leave Aurum without finding Garrett was unacceptable. "Could I search for Garrett without the king's permission?"

Reinhardt shook his head. "I doubt you'll have much luck. The population here at the capital is only about five thousand. I've lived here twenty Earth years. I believe I know all the Terran ex-pats who live here." He handed the sketch back to Renly. "I don't recall ever seeing this man. If you're hoping to find your brother, and he's the gambler you say he is, he'll be at the festival. Unfortunately, the Gold Festival is Arkady's private party. Nobody gets in without an invitation, not even the locals, except as paid workers."

Renly shivered with a sudden chill. "Maybe he left the city."

The ambassador sighed. "The planet of Aurum does not have a large indigenous population, Mr. Harkness. Summer temperatures here are roughly equivalent to spring in Iceland. In spite of the presence of massive geothermal aquifers, and the warming influence of the seas along the coast, there is only a narrow temperate climate zone between the 45th parallels, which can support native life. Only the coastal regions are safe for Terrans. In addition to frigid temperatures, the interior of this planet is host to dangerous predators and a slew of genetic viruses, most of which are particularly malignant to us Earthlings. If your brother wandered outside the habitable zone or into the interior, he's dead. I'm sorry."

"I'm not leaving" Renly answered. "Please tell the King my offer still stands. If he changes his mind, you can reach me at my hotel."

FOUR

Edward Duprees walked into the smoke-filled bar at the Aurum Galaxy Inn Hotel at mid-day. The hum of conversation hushed when he paused in the doorway, just long enough for the patrons to recognize him as a regular. His mood soured when he realized Richard Blaylock had arrived ahead of him. No doubt the ambassador notified him of Renly Harkness's arrival as well. In spite of his antagonism for the man, he could not ask him to leave. Technically, Blaylock was his superior, but for the duration of this year's Gold Fest XVI, Edward was the Executive Director; responsible for every aspect of Arkady Universal Mining interests on Aurum. Richard Blaylock's arrogance was the reason they were being forced to deal with the escalating Harkness issue, although after their long association, he knew Blaylock had a different perspective.

He stopped at the bar and asked Jiala to bring him his usual, then crossed the busy saloon to sit with Blaylock.

If the other man was unhappy to see him, he didn't show it, and greeted Edward warmly enough. Blaylock liked to say he was a big picture man, where Edward prided himself on his attention to detail and people skills. Had Blaylock informed him of the Harkness issue instead of dealing with it himself, Edward was certain he would have been able to persuade the artist not to come looking for his brother.

After Ambassador Reinhardt informed him of the goldsmith's arrival, he retrieved the transmissions between Renly Harkness and Richard Blaylock from the corporate archive. The correspondence clearly documented Blaylock's condescending tone in his communiqués to Renly Harkness, bordering on contempt. Blaylock had been the Executive Director of the last Gold Festival. Like it or not, Blaylock would insist on being part of this meeting. Might as well accept it.

"I assume you're here for the same reason I am, Richard, but I would prefer to handle things my own way. Please let me do the talking."

"Of course. I wouldn't have it any other way," Blaylock answered mildly.

"Reinhardt thinks he's harmless. Suggested we go ahead and give him a pass to the festival. I'm inclined to agree."

"Absolutely not. Giving out free passes sets a bad precedent. This is not a roadside carnival; it is the richest event in the universe. Think about your responsibility to the company. To our stockholders. Our guest list has been carefully cultivated and screened. We're the hottest ticket in the galaxy. Once you start making exceptions..." His hand waved the air imperiously.

Edward resented the lecture. Of course Aurum was the jewel of the company's holdings. The planet possessed the largest deposits of rare and precious metals in the galaxy. Embargoes were of course, illegal; but the company got around that encumbrance by allowing public access once every four years. Visas were issued only to major stockholders, their most influential backers, celebrities, and the super-rich.

"He's a native Terran, Richard. Never been off the planet. He probably has some romantic notion about the universal applicability of Earth laws. And now he's finagled his way here with a royal invite. Who knows what King Hakaroah will do? My guess is he'll ask us to handle this anyway, so now that Harkness has arrived, we ought to make the offer ourselves. The last thing we want is to air our dirty laundry in front of the new Khirjahni ruler."

"Don't be ridiculous, Edward. As usual, you've overstated everything. These Khirjahni don't care what happens to off-worlders who wander into the forbidden zone. Why do you think it's *called* the forbidden zone?" Blaylock gave him a disgusted look.

Edward sipped his sixty-year-old scotch, savoring the smoky, peaty burn as the liquor warmed him. Blaylock had the maddening ability to put him on the defensive in almost any situation. *He's just waiting for me to screw up.* Once again he'd been backed into a position of cleaning up after a mess made by Richard Blaylock.

"As always, I value you input, Richard, but I'm going to give him access to the Festival. I'll get Wayne to escort him around the park." Wayne was getting too wrapped up in the racing stables, anyway. Territorial. Obsessive, even. Babysitting the artist for a few days would get him out of the trainer's hair.

"Not the Gold Ball."

He glared at the older man. "Give me a little credit, Richard. Of course not the Gold Ball."

"Good." Blaylock nodded toward the doorway. "There's our boy, I'll bet."

Edward nodded, and waved the serious-looking young man over. "Mr. Harkness? Please join us."

The grey pallor of cryosleep identified the narrow-shouldered Terran more persuasively than any nametag. The artist wore a black, oversized silk jacket with Nehru collar, ill-fitting slacks, and shiny leather city shoes. Probably a fashion trend on Earth these days, but funereal and out of step at the festival. He shivered as he approached; a classic sign of new arrivals to the chill climate.

"Edward Duprees, Mr. Harkness. May I call you Renly?" He introduced Blaylock, noting the man wore synthetic biohazard gloves. *Oh boy, another one of those.* He kept his face impassive. He motioned to Jiala to bring another round, but Harkness declined the offer, asking instead for bottled water. Not a good sign. The Terran stared at the bartender with an expression of terrible fascination.

He enjoyed the off-worlder's discomfort. After living on Aurum for more than a decade, he recognized the shocked gaze of all new arrivals when they came face to face with Khirjahni aboriginals for the first time. A curl of massive horns, like a prize-winning ram, emerged from the crown of hair above Jiala's eyebrows and circled around each side of her head along her ears. Above the broad, flattened nose of an ex-boxer, the thick skin of Jiala's forehead puckered, giving the locals a solemn expression. Unusual at first glance, but not unattractive. In a few days, he wouldn't notice. Had it been so long since he'd lived among Earthlings? Had he changed so much? *Wait until he meets his first mandragon._*

"Don't worry about Jiala, Renly. You can't catch anything from the locals."

"At least not through *casual* contact," added Blaylock.

Edward cut Blaylock a sharp glance. Blaylock returned it with an innocent smile. *Asshole.*

Harkness reddened and looked away. His shaking grew visibly worse.

It didn't take a genius to figure out the man was practically falling apart. But before he had a chance to say anything, Blaylock barreled in, assuming control of the conversation.

"Ambassador Reinhardt informed me of your arrival this morning.

Clever of you to go through the royal family for a visa."

A flinty look came into Renly's expression. "You know why I'm here."

Score one for the scarecrow, Edward mused. Maybe he had a bit of grit after all.

"Why don't I believe you?"

Renly's expression hardened. "You never even tried to him."

"It's not that, Renly," Edward began, but Blaylock cut him off.

"Drop the act, Harkness. We both know why you're here. You think I don't know your game? We all know you're here for the gold. Every off-worlder on this planet has gold fever. Why would a goldsmith be any different? "

The Terran stiffened. "I work with precious metals every day. I don't care about the mineral content of this planet. All I do care about is finding my brother. Something you haven't managed to do in four years."

"Hold on a minute, Renly," interjected Edward. He glared at Blaylock to back off. "In spite of what you believe, we *have* made every effort to find your brother. I give you my word; he's not on Aurum. I understand your concern, and your skepticism, but on behalf of Arkady Universal, I want to apologize if you have been given the impression that you could find him if you came here."

Renly said nothing, but Edward could see he wasn't about to give up. "I understand you plan to appeal to the royal family for assistance. I'm afraid that puts you in direct conflict with our company's best interests."

"Are you threatening me?"

Edward leaned forward and tapped his finger on the table top for emphasis. "Aurum isn't Earth. The Khirjahni don't care for off-worlders much. They don't give a damn about you or your family. Part of Arkady's agreement with the Khirjahni government is to refrain from bothering them with our off-worlder problems. With the recent change in leadership, Arkady Universal is at a delicate point in our contract renewal negotiations. Complaining to the king about your missing brother is only going to upset everyone."

"His name is Garrett. Garrett Harkness."

"A professional gambler," Blaylock interjected.

Edward swallowed his impulse to slap the smug expression off Blaylock's face. "I'm not without sympathy for your situation, sir. However, for all intents and purposes, the Arkady Corporation *is* the law enforcement authority here on Aurum, especially where off-worlders are concerned. We will not allow you or anyone else come here and set off an intergalactic incident."

"Hey, I'm not trying to cause an incident." Renly put his hand to his chest. "My brother is alive. We have a psychic connection; I sensed his presence as soon as the captain touched down on Aurum. I'm not trying to make trouble, but I'm not leaving until I find him. With or without your help."

"Don't be ridiculous," Blaylock taunted. "You will never find him on your own. Aurum is nothing like Earth. How would you even begin?"

The young man frowned. "Talk to law enforcement, I guess. Check the morgues and hospitals. Maybe the hotels?"

"Let me explain something to you about Aurum, Renly. The Khirjahni are a simple people. Fishing folk and tribal herdsman whose cultures have blended over the centuries. Half the population mass is right here in the capital. The other half live in small villages scattered along the coast or as nomadic tribesmen on the steppes. They're a law abiding and peaceful people. There is no police force. No morgue. No hospital." Edward gestured to the overhead chandeliers. "The only advanced technology on this planet came from Arkady Universal. The only off-worlder power source they've adopted is lithium batteries. If they had their way, these people would still be lighting their homes with candles and oil lanterns. In 60 years, we've put in plumbing, roads, and even a communications satellite, but they still don't appreciate anything we've done for them. Tell you the truth, they put up with us as long as we keep to ourselves. So if Garrett is on this planet, there are only a few places he could be. Either here at the hotel or in the Festival Village. And Garrett Harkness is not in any of those places. I give you my word."

"He might be using a different name. He'll be at the casinos or at the track."

Edward exchanged a glance with Blaylock, who nodded, conceding the point. "All right, for the sake of argument, let's say I believe you." He pulled a thin card out of his inner pocket and handed it to Harkness. "This is a guest pass to the Festival. I've arranged for an escort to accompany you anywhere in the village you'd like to go for the duration of the festival. The racetrack, casino, shopping, wherever you want. Look for your brother, by all means. You find him; the company will pick up the tab for your tickets back to Earth. In return, you agree not to petition the king. This is a one-time offer. Agreed?"

"What if I don't find him?"

"You will have to accept he's not on Aurum. You leave on the last transport with the rest of the visitors and that's the end of it."

* * *

In the relative sanctuary of his hotel room, Renly stripped off his gloves and cracked the seal on an imported bottle of purified water. The chilled water tasted flat, and he shivered in the frigid room. His personal thermostatic device indicated the room temperature was only fifty degrees. He searched the room for a communicator to call the front desk and complain, but found no telecom equipment whatsoever. No satellite monitors, no display units, not even a refrigeration unit; not that this place needed one.

Outside his window, the lights of the landing port reflected dimly off the salt flats in near-total darkness. They'd flown in over the ocean, and docked the shuttle at the customs depot, but other than an expanse of empty landscape, he had no sense of the local landscape. As the festival goers boarded transports to the village some twenty miles south, the ambassador offered to drop him off at the hotel. From what little he'd gathered on the short drive, there wasn't much to see; mostly bare dirt and grey, wind smoothed rock. Reinhardt told him the off-worlder hotel served mostly pilots, their crews, and Arkady executives working the festival or visiting the coastal capital, three miles to the west.

"Open forests and rocklands border the coastal areas of the temperate zone, rising to the great steppes," Reinhardt explained. "Think of the central plains of America before the settlers crossed, or the African savannas before the resettlement in the 23rd century. Now multiply the total area of those biomes by a factor of five. Forty percent of the inhabitable land on Aurum is highland prairie. Another fifty percent is volcanic mountain ranges. Other than the ocean, surface water is hard to find; it's all below ground, in aquifers. They use geothermal power to heat your room at the hotel, but if I were you. I'd ask for a couple extra blankets. The Khirjahni aren't sensitive to the cold like we are."

He closed the drapes and debated going down to the front desk to complain about the chill. The day had stretched long; he'd barely had a chance to catch his breath. The thick woven blankets covering his bed looked warm and inviting. The nubby fabric felt soft as cashmere, and appeared hand-loomed. He admired the primitive designs incorporated into the weavings. Unlike the crude design on the flag, these reminded him of aboriginal art he'd studied on Earth. The muddy purple and brown colors probably came from organic dyes. He hoped they were hypoallergenic. He added two extra blankets he found in the wardrobe to the bed.

He slipped off his shoes and hung his few clothes in the simple, narrow wardrobe. On Earth, such dark wood might be called ebony, but no one on Earth made wood furniture any more. He slipped into the low bed, regretting that he'd brought no robe or slippers. Tomorrow he would speak to the concierge and ask them to adjust the temperature in his room.

He turned off the lamp beside the bed and pulled the covers over his bare shoulders. The hiss of air purifiers soothed him as he settled into the comfort of the bed. For the first time since leaving his studio, he felt a sense of accomplishment. He was finally *here*, on Aurum! He'd actually made the trip into space and survived. Not only that, but the Arkady execs had decided to co-operate and had given him exactly what he'd wanted all along.

He could feel Garrett's presence so strongly; almost as if he were in the next room. He hoped Garrett felt his presence, too. *I can do this.* Tomorrow, he would find Garrett and they'd head back to Earth. As he drifted off, he imagined the reunion. This time, he would be the hero, and they'd finally be even. He knew exactly how Garret would feel when he showed up to rescue him…

FIVE

When Wayne Strickland awoke, he was alone. Not even a warm spot in the bed beside him to indicate the girl had only just left. He checked his chronograph. Well before dawn, but she would already be at the stables.

He threw the covers off and swung his legs to the floor. Damn her. If he didn't know better, he'd think she was avoiding him. He ran his hand through his rumpled hair. A headache pounded at the back of his skull and his mouth tasted of tequila and stale cigars. Too much booze last night, and not enough sleep. He'd try to catch a few winks at the stables later this afternoon.

She promised to come over last night but never showed. He tried to remember the last time she shared his bed. Ever since the festival opened, the days seemed to stretch endlessly. Yesterday seemed like a long time ago.

His communicator beeped just before he stepped into the shower. Ed Duprees rarely called him this early. "Hey Ed."

"Good, you're up. I need you to play the host a guy at the festival."

He suppressed a groan. Three years ago, Duprees finally put him in charge of the racing stables. Back then, the Barn Manager title meant he shoveled shit, but he found a way to turn things around for himself.

He didn't shovel anything anymore. Now things were about to pay off big time, and he didn't want anything to jeopardize his plans.

"You've got me spread pretty thin already, Mr. D."

Duprees went on as if he hadn't spoken. "Keep him busy for a few days. You know the drill; kill him with kindness. Wear him out."

His cheeks grew hot. "Ya want me to babysit this guy?" The familiar prickling of his skin stopped him from saying anything else. He choked back his outrage. Years of anger management reprogramming had helped him recognize his own warning signs, but sometimes the old attitudes slipped out.

"You don't like this job any more; we can always use you back in the mines."

"Sorry, I'm still waking up. There's no problem." Edward Duprees had been a lowly shift supervisor in the mine when he arrived, fresh off the prison planet. They shared a common appreciation for gladiator sports, and from there, a weird sort of professional friendship grew. Wayne made sure his crew always exceeded their quotas, and took a hands-on approach for solving internal problems in his team, which made Edward look good. Edward's rapid promotions and reputation for getting the job done moved him rapidly into the highest levels of Arkady management, and he made sure he brought Wayne Strickman along with him. The fact was, he'd tied himself to Edward's star. If that made him Edward's bitch, fine. But only until he made his nut. And that day had nearly arrived.

He took a deep breath. "Who is he?"

"An artist. Renly Harkness. Claims to be looking for his brother, but he's here at the invitation of the royal family. The old family. With Kehreru out of the picture, I don't want to risk making a stink before we get on an even footing with the new king. We don't know how Hakaroah will react if there's an incident, and Blaylock is just waiting for me to make a mistake, so I want you to handle this. The brother is a pro, so if he's here, he'll be in the casinos."

"Or the track." He could park the artist in the clubhouse while he took care of business. He needed to get hold of K'Sati; and get the list of winners from her. She had an uncanny talent for picking them, and he wasn't done with her yet. Not by half.

"All right. What do ya want to do about the brother?"

Duprees snorted. "I am not convinced there is a brother. The only thing I care about is making sure the festival runs smoothly. If there's any trouble, I want you to take of it. Quietly. Understand?"

"Absolutely." The UCP inspectors got the same treatment whenever they showed up for their unscheduled inspections of Arkady operations. "Ya know ya can always count on me."

* * *

Wayne smashed his shoulder against the door of the girl's room at the stable. The flimsy lock gave way with barely a protest, but the room was empty. The air was stale; she hadn't been here in hours. *So where had she spent the night?* The shirt she'd been wearing the last time he'd seen her lay on the floor in a corner. He checked her bedding. No fading body heat warmed the tangled sheet of the narrow cot.

So where the hell was she? She knew better than to avoid him, but sometimes they needed a little reminder. He pulled his bowie knife from its sheath at his belt and used it to slice the shirt to ribbons. The Terran half-breed, K'Sati wasn't the first woman he'd bedded on Aurum, but she had an independent streak, just like Earth women. Until he discovered her uncanny gift for picking winners at the track, he'd been ready to give her the boot. Even so, a man shouldn't have to put up with that kind of disrespectful behavior. Good thing the big race was only a week away.

He strode purposefully through the stable, checking each stall, but found no sign of her. Chances were better than even the girl was down on the track with Ruben, but he didn't have time to chase after her this morning. Nearly time to drive into town and pick up Renly Harkness. He stopped in his tracks. Only half the stalls had been cleaned. She wasn't far. He decided to make a quick check of the tack room.

No stable girl. Instead, he found the Terran junkie, Jason Brown.

Brown came sniffing around sometimes; usually with his hand out. K'Ruhi, the farrier, vouched for him, but Wayne knew better. This guy was always up to something.

"What are you doing here/"

Jason jumped, and shoved something into the pocket of his pants. His skin shone with a greasy sweat. With a shaking hand, he grabbed a tin of leather cleaner off the shelf of a rustic bookcase. "K'Ruhi asked me to fetch this."

"Turn your pockets out."

Jason tried to shove his way past, but Wayne pushed him hard up against the door jamb. The guy cringed and Wayne savored his terrified expression. What a wuss.

He laid his forearm across Jason's neck, effectively pinning him. "I said turn out your pockets." The guy smelled of sour sweat and fear. He looked like he'd been living pretty rough lately. Nice clothes, but wrinkled and grimy.

Jason struggled weakly, but Wayne had no problem controlling him. His fingernails were dirty, as if he'd been working at the stables. Fat chance. He made a mental note to start checking the stables more thoroughly at night.

"Get off me," he gasped.

Wayne rabbit-punched him hard, twice, just below the ribcage. All the fight went out of Jason; he crumpled to the floor. Thus incapacitated, Wayne patted him down. In one pocket he found a half-dozen paper packets of dream dust; in the other, a sizable handful of solid gold coins.

"Well, well." He stepped back to examine the coins. All bore the UCP assayer's stamp, which certified the purity of the gold. "I didn't realize selling dream dust was such a lucrative occupation. You've got yourself quite a little nest egg here. Thanks." He slipped the coins into his own pocket. This would come in real handy at the track today.

He tore open the packets of dream dust and scattered the brown powder across the floor.

"What are you doing?" Jason demanded. "That is my money. My property. He scrambled across the floor, pinching up tiny grains of dust and depositing them into his palm.

Wayne grinned. "You're just lucky I'm in a good mood. This is *my* barn, *my* stable, and *my* tack room. Everything in it, including your sorry ass belongs to me. If ya don't like it, I suggest ya leave."

"You don't understand. That money isn't mine. I owe a guy; if I don't pay him by ten tonight, he'll hurt me."

He sounded like he was about to cry. *I'll give you something to cry about.* "Tell ya what. If you're not out of my sight in ten seconds, *I'll* hurt ya. Mess ya up big time. That what ya want?"

Jason scrabbled to his feet and ran; hunched over, clutching his precious dream dust in both hands. *Pathetic.*

Wayne patted the outside of his pocket, pleasantly heavy with gold. Now all he needed to do was find K'Sati. So far, she'd picked the winner in seven of the last eight races. With another twenty-five or so qualifying heats still to run until the Final, he planned to keep a much closer eye on her. He didn't much like this new attitude of hers. Time to end this nonsense. His future depended on it.

SIX

K'Sati tossed another forkful of straw into stall number fourteen, and spread it across the floor, stomping down the vegetation to make sure there was plenty of padding to cushion the feet of the occupant. Bits of straw and dust tickled her nose; she sneezed several times in succession. Behind her, the number fourteen traggah, Neatfoot, snorted a response, and pushed her big head over the half-door leading from the paddock.

"No laughing, you," K'Sati reached up rubbed the animal's long striped nose. She drew back the bolt and opened the half-door giving the large animal access to her stall. "In you go."

Seeing her favorite charge dig into her grain bin so eagerly warmed K'Sati's heart. After losing her qualifying heat in the Gold Fest prelims yesterday, Neatfoot had sulked; even refused her dinner last night. As the traggah chomped the special blend of grains K'Sati fed to all the Arkady Stables racing stock, she stroked the animal's wide warm side.

"I am glad you have your appetite back."

The traggah pulled her head out of the feed bin and gazed at her with expectant eyes. The question was unspoken, but K'Sati didn't need to use her empathetic abilities to understand the question.

"No, dearest. No racing for you today."

The traggah sighed deeply, and returned to her breakfast.

K'Sati kept her thoughts well shielded until after she left the stall and put the pitchfork back in its proper place in the tack room. No point in getting Neatfoot upset again, but the traggah had lost her last race for the Arkady Racing Stables. She wouldn't run again until released back into the wild after the end of the festival.

"Where were you last night?"

She jumped. Wayne must have been hiding behind the tack room door, waiting for her. Her stomach flipped uncomfortably. *Only a few more weeks.* Once the festival ended, all the Arkady people would leave and he'd go with them.

"You surprised me."

"I missed you." Wayne's gloved paw slid down her bare arm.

She stiffened to his touch, but said nothing. He was big, even by Terran standards, and accustomed to taking whatever he wanted from any of the stable girls. Most were half-breeds, like her, who straddled two cultures without being accepted by either. After he tired of a particular girl, he'd find a reason to fire them. In spite of her efforts not to attract his attention, his eye had settled on her anyway.

His grip around her wrist tightened. "Is Golden Boy running today?" He liked that she bruised easily. She did not welcome his touch, not anymore, but could not seem to stop it. Any resistance on her part only made things worse. It excited him. Aroused him. Only her meekness, her absolute acquiescence seemed to pacify him. Lately, she found doing as he wanted ever more difficult.

"Not today." She kept her tone even. All the Arkady Mining executives were quite taken with Golden Boy, who was faster and had the greatest desire to win of any traggah she'd ever known. When

Wayne discovered her affinity for the traggahs and realized she could pick which traggahs would be most likely to win on any given day, he brought her to the attention of the Terran training master, Ruben. Ruben made her an assistant trainer and depended on her intuitive abilities to improve the care and training regimen for the traggahs. It took a while to convince him, but now even Ruben agreed that Golden Boy was the closest thing to a sure winner; the first the Arkady Racing Team had seen in decades.

Wayne also used her knowledge of the traggahs to bet on the races. By company rules, gambling by employees was not allowed, but Wayne told her several of the Arkady Mining executive had given him money to place wagers for them on Golden Boy winning the Final.

"Why not?" An edge of warning crept into his tone. The grip on her wrist grew painful.

"I am taking him to the farrier. That hoof needs to be looked at."

"Ya said that yesterday."

Tears of pain pooled in her eyes and he let her go. She turned her back to him but refused to rub her throbbing wrist. Instead, she selected the green bridle for number 19, and the brown for number 12.

"Ya told me 14 would win her heat yesterday. The beastie didn't even place in the top five. Mr. Duprees is very disappointed, and so am I."

Even after all these years of racing, the Terrans did not understand the traggahs drive to win. If they did, they would know Neatfoot had run her best race yesterday. "They tell me are ready to run, and in their hearts, I know they mean to win." She eased her way toward the door.

"I noticed ya fed her real good this morning."

The menace in his voice made the hair along her arms stand up. "Until they are released back into the wild at the end of the festival, they all get fed the same."

"Yeah, but she won't be in Final. No point in wasting expensive feed on a loser."

She stared at him in disbelief. He had to be joking. There was so much about these Terrans she still didn't understand. "No traggah wins every race."

"The company doesn't care about every race, they care about the final." He leaned closer and whispered, "I asked you where you were last night."

She clutched the bridles to her chest. He fairly radiated heat. He was starting to scare her. Last week, someone had sliced up her work boots. Wayne claimed innocence, but he wore that big knife sheathed at his belt, and she could think of no one else who would have done such a thing.

She stopped sleeping in her quarters to avoid him. He had not been around at all yesterday, so it had been several days since he'd lain with her. She could not evade him forever, but now that the daily racing had started, Ruben had kept her much busier than usual, which was good. Wayne would not dare go against the training master. "Ruben told me to keep an eye on Golden Boy. I fell asleep in his stall."

He grabbed her by one horn and shook it playfully, even though she repeatedly asked him not to. "So why isn't he running today?"

"I do not decide when he runs. He will run when Ruben decides he is ready." The Arkady stable had seven other traggahs competing. Silverbeard and Stripe would both run today. This year, Arkady's fleet of traggahs looked like the strongest herd they ever trained. Neatfoot's unexpected early loss made everyone jumpy. The corporation expected to sweep the top four spots. Ruben wanted to hold off running the favorite until the final heat. That way they would know just how fast he needed to run to make the final without ruining the odds.

Wayne clamped his heavy paw down on her already bruised shoulder. She fought the feeling of suffocation she endured every time he came near her. Could he see not he was smothering her? She appreciated how difficult it must be for the young traggahs when they were brought into the stables after living free on the broad plains of the steppes. Even her old life at the temple had seemed less cloying than this Terran.

He pulled her close and put her hand on his erection. "I told you, I missed you."

Perhaps this was how all earthmen acted. He seemed oblivious to her reluctance. "I must go. We have two races to prepare for today."

He wrapped his hand around her neck, and her pulse protested as his grip tightened. "No more losers, understand? They don't win, they don't eat."

She nodded, terrified he was serious; certain Ruben would never agree.

His fingers dug into her throat. He pulled her closer, his breath hot in her ear. "Good. Tonight we'll celebrate the double win. Just you and me."

* * *

Hours later, K'Sati left the track and walked up the hill toward the stables. Behind her, Silverbeard plodded like an olding, his head down, and his ears at an unhappy cant. Even Ruben, the training master had turned his back on them. He refused to listen when she'd tried to explain that Silverbeard had been kicked just before the start, and then thrown off his stride twice by other riders who'd crowded him in the straightaway. She couldn't understand Ruben's reaction. Silverbeard had not lost on purpose.

She tried to assuage Silverbeard's wounded pride, but the inborn desire to win instilled all traggahs with a fiercely competitive nature.

Every traggah lived for the joy of leading their herd across the steppes. Racing with a rider on their backs was almost second nature to them. For two years, they raced these traggahs daily. Daily racing not only fed their need to run, but prevented them from dwelling too much on any one loss. Once they heard the roaring crowds, they fed on the excitement, and became mad with the will to win. Stripe had won his heat with ease. Silverbeard had been the last to cross the finish line in his. For a wild traggah, being last meant being left behind. Being last meant being eaten. To lose was to die.

She stopped outside his stall and stroked the lathered fur of his neck. She could sense his unhappiness like an itch he couldn't scratch. Anger, too. "I will brush you down and you will feel better. Soon you will be running free on the steppes with your friends." She sent him images of the herd racing across the plain, but he shook his head abruptly and pawed at the ground.

Wayne approached her, his face dark with anger. "What's he doing here?"

"I am putting him in his stall." She slid open the bolt to his stall but he grabbed the traggah's lead rope out of her hand.

No ya don't. He's lost his stable privileges. That piece of meat cost me a bundle today. The only thing he deserves is a bullet through the brain. Take this one and 14 over to security. Tell Harvey I said to put them both down."

Her heart caught in throat. Traggahs were the heart and spirit of the Khirjahni people. To cause harm to any traggah was taboo. "You cannot be serious!"

The slap came out of nowhere, and nearly knocked her down. Silverbeard whistled and stamped angrily; she held her hand to her glowing hot cheek.

"Don't tell me how to run my stable. If those animals can't win,

I'm sure as hell not going to feed them. And I don't see any point in releasing the losers back into the wild. Taking those two out of the gene pool will make the next generation faster."

Silverbeard reared, jerking the rope out of Wayne's grip, whistling his displeasure. Traggah heads emerged from every stall, each whistling an answer. Wayne stepped back; K'Sati snatched the rope from him.

"Easy." She stroked Silverbeard's neck to calm him. Her face burned where Wayne slapped her. She sent soothing thoughts to all the agitated traggahs.

Wayne pointed at her as he backed away. "I want it done by sundown."

She hustled the still anxious traggah into his stall. "He does not mean it. I will never allow him to harm you, I promise." She soothed him with a remembered prayer from her childhood. *We are herd, my beloved. Though the rahgs may chase us through the forest, and the longteeth hunt us on the plains, I will never leave you. Though the wind and cold surround us, and craggons seek to snatch us from above, I will stand beside you. As brothers and sisters we stand together. You are mine and I am yours. We are herd.*

* * *

As the shadows lengthened, and the twin suns neared the horizon, K'Sati began to panic. Her appeals to the training masters at each of the six largest racing stables fell on deaf ears. None of them would agree to take the Arkady traggahs. Not one of them offered to help.

Time was running out. She would need someplace to hide Neatfoot and Silverbeard until she could talk to Ruben. In a flash of inspiration, she remembered the farrier's paddock. She had to bring Golden Boy over there anyway. Most off-worlders couldn't tell one traggah from another. Without their numbered bridles, K'Rui's paddock would be an ideal place to hide the traggahs.

She gathered up Neatfoot, Silverbeard, and Golden boy and trotted them over to the farrier's paddock. After removing the bridles from Neatfoot and Silverbeard, she released all three traggahs to join half-dozen others already in the pen.

She trotted over K'Rhui's workshop, but couldn't find him. She called his name, but received no answer. Perhaps he'd been called away to one of the other stables. She didn't want to leave the traggahs there without telling him. He might ask Wayne about them, or bring them back over to the stable. She remembered K'Ruhi sometimes drank after work with his friend Jason.

Jason had the dream powder sickness, which affected some Terrans, but the traggahs all liked him, which spoke well for his character. She rounded the barn and found him sitting alone in the last of the fading sunshine outside the storage shed where he occasionally stayed. In one hand, he held a large jar of brown porridge; in the other, a spoon. The heady smell made her want to gag. Jason called the thick slurry, which the Th-Dorrans called *makiri*, hooch. Made from fermented grains, it was a favorite of dirt-eaters.

"Well, hullo K'Sati," he slurred. "What can I do for you?"

"I'm looking for K'Ruhi. I've put Golden Boy and two others in the paddock to get their feet trimmed." She hesitated to tell him more. "Do you know where he is?"

He shook his head. "What are you all wound up about? Have another run-in with that boyfriend of yours?" He patted the seat next to him.

She shook her head. Jason didn't work for Arkady stables. He claimed to be a horse expert on Terra, but he had nothing to offer in the care and training of traggahs. As far as she knew, the only reason, the Arkady team tolerated him was because K'Ruhi sometimes needed an extra hand and the traggahs all liked him. K'Sati once asked Neatfoot why the traggahs liked Jason so much, but the only answer she ever got was that he smelled good. Probably because he always smelled like _makiri_.

"Just tell him to come find me before he does anything."

"No worries, pretty girl."

"And don't tell Wayne you saw me."

Jason held up a finger in front of his mouth. "Your secret is safe with me."

She ran.

SEVEN

Renly came downstairs for breakfast the next morning and the Khirjahni concierge handed him two messages. The first, from Ambassador Reinhardt, informed him that His Royal Excellence, King Hakaroah of Khirjah had granted him a brief audience that afternoon. Renly debated cancelling the interview, but decided against it. The Arkady execs hadn't stipulated he couldn't *meet* with the king, only that he couldn't ask for assistance in finding his brother. His offer of a commission for the royal family was still on the table; he could think of no reason not to go through with the meeting. Renly carefully folded the note and slipped it into his jacket pocket.

The other message was from the Arkady executive, Edward Duprees, telling him his man, Wayne Strickland would be waiting for him at breakfast. As soon as he walked into the dining room, the bear-like Strickland introduced himself as his personal escort for the day.

"Hey Renly." Strickland's big paw engulfed his. "Wayne Strickman. I'm the Barn Manager for Arkady Racing Stables."

Having grown up around polo stables, Renly could not imagine a more unlikely barn manager. Wayne wore his black hair pulled back tight into a braided tail that reached halfway down his back. His broad cheekbones bespoke of past scarring, badly derma braded, but did not detract from the classic profile and strong jaw of the man's face. A high forehead and piercing eyes gave him an air of keen intelligence unmatched by his speech pattern.

"Mr. Duprees asked me ta show ya around the festival for the next few days."

Yellow gold buttons decorated his ear cartilage in the fashion of many of the ex-pat Terrans he'd seen so far, and more gold flashed on his powerful fingers and a pair of heavy wrist cuffs. Anyone who'd been around horses knew better than to wear jewelry, and the ostentatious display ruffled his sense of propriety. As a goldsmith, he appreciated the value of gold more than most, yet he noticed the Arkady executives seemed hold it in no special regard. He noticed even the smallest Khirjahni coins were of pure gold, but the Khirjahni wore little in the way of personal adornment.

After a breakfast of seamed grains and fruits in the hotel dining room, Wayne drove him out to the festival site in his lithium-battery-operated Personal Vehicle. Unlike the PVs on Earth, this one seemed to be without heating controls. Once again, Renly regretted not bringing warmer clothing. He shivered in his light jacket as he surveyed the alien landscape. Not a city or a building in sight. Only low rolling hills covered in some sort of grey-green grass, and a few stretches of open forest populated by wind-sculpted trees.

Wayne warmed to his role as tour guide, seemingly unbothered by the chill. "This is one of the few roads on the whole planet," he announced. "Aurum was discovered centuries ago, but until the Arkady Universal Mining Corporation began mining operations sixty years ago, they had no paved roads."

He gestured to the featureless landscape. "Doesn't look like much of a problem."

"Do not let the lay of the land fool ya. This area is full of rahgs.

They hunt in packs and eat anything that moves."

"What's a rahg?"

Wayne paused before answering. "They're like wolves; they hunt in packs. If anything happens to the car, don't leave the vehicle, and don't ever, ever leave the road. Too easy to get lost out here. The Khirjahni won't allow us to put up transmission towers, and the high metal content in the soils and rocks produces subspace magnetic fields, which interfere with satellite transmissions."

"Why not just use aerial transport?" They were probably heated. Faster, too.

"We do, at the mines. But not inside the habitable zone. The risk of being attacked by those damn flying lizards is too great, unless we stick to the coastline. Real territorial, and big enough to damage or bring down about any ship. They go after anything that flies into in their territory. In case ya haven't noticed, they got no birds on this planet. Craggons won't tolerate anything in their airspace."

He gripped the armrest tighter. "I was told they live in the forbidden zone."

"Relax. They don't come out this far. But just so ya know, the forbidden zone covers most of the interior of this planet. That's why Arkady set up mining operations are well outside their territory. Workin' the mines is like living in deep freeze, but at least ya don't have to worry about craggons or that damned dragon pox. Don't worry. You're perfectly safe."

"If I don't freeze to death, first," he grumbled. "Isn't there a heater in this thing?"

"Sorry. This is a company runabout. I live at the corporate housing near the stables. I don't leave the festival grounds too often, and hardly ever come out this way. Won't be much longer. Been here so long, I kinda forget about the cold. What ya need is a set of these robes." He fingered the dark blue fabric. "Spun from traggah wool. Light and warm as anything."

"Traggah. Some kind of sheep, right?" No doubt the same weave as the blankets on his bed at the hotel.

Wayne gave him an incredulous look. "I guess ya haven't seen the racing program. I thought ya knew. It's well, hmmm. It's kind of like a cross between a buffalo, and a wildebeest. They're big and fast. Ya wouldn't believe how fast. Faster than a horse, by a long shot."

His teeth began to chatter. "Where can I pick up a set of those robes? I'm freezing my ass off here, Wayne."

Wayne grinned and pointed to a cluster of buildings in the distance. "We're almost there. That's the site of the Gold Festival."

* * *

What Renly assumed to be a cluster of buildings turned out to be an enclosed city, complete with hotels, casinos, shopping, and even indoor parks. When they cleared the security station and stepped inside; Renly breathed a sigh of relief. Not only was the air soft and warm as a summer afternoon, but the filtered air bore not a trace of sulfur stench he'd endured since leaving the hotel. He breathed deeply, savoring the spicy scent of roses massed outside the monorail depot.

"Now this is summer," he marveled. Skylights and clerestory windows provided plenty of natural daylight, while the lush garden-like plantings lent a tropical atmosphere. The sound of fountains and music and laughter blended together in a pleasant hum.

"Nice, isn't it? All the buildings at the festival site are geothermically heated. We also got dozens of greenhouses where we grow fresh produce year-round, including all kinds of exotic fruits and vegetables. And we got huge freezers and refrigerators filled with imported meats and the best exotic provisions. Our guests are used to the best, and won't accept anything less."

"This is the central plaza," Wayne motioned to the general mall area around them "We got shops offering the finest jewelry, clothing, and art gathered from every corner of the universe. But if you want to shop for robes, the booths in the central market offer the best aboriginal crafts."

Quaint storefronts ringed the cobblestone marketplace, displaying elegant jewelry, massive gems, and above all, fanciful whatnots of gold and platinum, safely protected behind walls of thick glass. The marketplace design suggested a colorful reinterpretation of a fantasy bazaar, complete with turreted pavilions, brightly colored pennants, and the enticing aroma of roasting meats. Even the street vendors wore appealing costumes out of tales of the Arabian nights, with flourishes of tinkling silver bells and yards of gossamer scarves. The market was busy, but not crowded. After the stress of the trip and his arrival in Aurum, Renly began to relax.

Wayne led him through the tent city maze in the plaza to a pavilion displaying bolts of bright, hand-woven fabrics. Over the shopkeeper's protests, Renly insisted on a set of black robes without any ornamentation.

"But sir," the Khirjahni saleswoman protested in lightly-accented English. "You are too young for such a dark costume." She eyed the cut of his Nehru jacket. "And too thin, I think. Look at this deep blue. Or the mauve here. The color matches our twin suns Oratei and Ahipu."

"No, the black is fine. Thank you." He'd been disappointed to discover the robes had to be custom fitted. He posed uncomfortably as she took his personal measurements. "When will they be ready?" Renly made a silent appeal to Wayne, but man stood across the way speaking to a veiled woman at the wine seller's.

She assured him they would be ready the following day.

After he paid for his robes, Wayne took him to the hotel district, where they checked the reservation lists at the three largest hotels. At each hotel, they checked the registry and he showed the engraving of his brother to the desk personnel, the concierge, and the doormen. With each shake of the head, his hope of finding Garrett began to fade.

By late afternoon, they still had two more hotels left to check. They hadn't even set foot in the casinos or the track. Not wanting to miss his meeting with the King, he reluctantly asked Wayne to take him back to the hotel.

On the drive back, Wayne tried to console him. "Hey, don't get discouraged. If he's here, we'll find 'im."

"I don't think we're looking in the right place. We're not going to find him at the hotels." Renly couldn't escape the feeling that they'd wasted the entire day. Yesterday, he'd been certain he'd find Garrett at the most expensive hotel at the festival, but now he wasn't so sure.

When no one at the hotels recognized Garrett's picture, Renly started thinking more about what *kind* of trouble Garrett might have gotten in. Whenever he'd asked for help in the past, it was because he had a big score he was sure was going to come through and didn't have enough money to buy in. But he'd wrangled an invitation to the gold Festival four years ago. He must have had more than enough to buy his way in.

"What happens if someone gets into trouble," he asked. "What do you do with them? Where do you put them?"

Wayne laughed. "What kind of trouble? This is the Gold Festival. Our guests are the most powerful people in the universe. Ya can't lock up a billionaire. A lot of business gets done here. Far as I know, we rarely have a problem. Long as everyone plays nice, they let it go. Our security guys keep an eye out, and if there's anybody complains, they step in, but usually it's just the case of someone having too much of a good thing, if you know what I mean.

The more he thought about it, the more convinced he became that they would find Garrett at either the casinos or the track. Maybe he owed someone money. Garrett knew how to keep a low profile. He might be staying in a room under an assumed name, or with a friend. Of course.

"I want to start at the track tomorrow. If Garrett is here, I'm pretty sure I'll find him there."

Wayne looked pleased. "Works for me. Your brother like bettin' the ponies?"

Renly shrugged. "We grew up with horses. He played polo for a while; thought about going pro, but never did."

"What time you want to start tomorrow?"

A distant memory of watching Garrett practicing in the early mornings came to him, and he took it as a sign. "Let's start early."

"You're the boss."

* * *

The audience with King Okanga Hakaroa took place in the throne parlor of His Majesty's residence in the capital city of Khirj, along the rocky shoreline of the Merkehle Sea. Instead of a castle or magnificent estate, the royal lodgings consisted of a rather modest, two-story, terra cotta and stone home with a walled garden close to the central marketplace. Like the other Khirjahni homes in the neighborhood, the royal residence was built around a central courtyard; no windows faced the cobblestone streets. The only obvious difference between the royal estate and its neighbors was the pair of guards stationed at the front gate.

After Renly gave his name, Ambassador Reinhardt emerged from the house to escort him inside.

"You will only have a few minutes with him. His English is excellent, so don't worry about your Khirjahnese. Your name will be announced, and you will enter the parlor, and stand no less than two body lengths from him. He will remain seated. You will bow slightly from the waist when introduced, but you will not address him directly unless he asks you a question."

"So how am I supposed to make my offer?"

"Apparently, he knows your work," Reinhardt stopped him just outside the parlor, and gave him an appraising look. "Did you really design the medals for the 2448 Olympics?"

He gave a small nod. "Not exactly a topic one brings up in casual conversation."

* * *

"Though I come from far away, I come in peace."

Renly bowed slightly at the waist. Reinhardt had coached him in the proper Khirjahni greeting. "I am but one of many. I am herd." A faint scent of pineapple mingled with the prevailing sulfur, and through an open window, Renly caught a glimpse of the royal garden.

King Hakaroa motioned him closer. The massive carved chair on which he was seated was decorated in an organic design of whorls and spirals placed incised in such a way that mimicked both ocean waves and the curl pattern in the young king's horns. Renly admired the hand-rubbed patina that only comes from long wear. The king and he were probably close to the same age.

His Majesty cut a striking figure, with his high forehead, a topknot of shiny black hair, broad cheekbones, and tribal tattoos. For the first time in many long months, Renly felt an itch to draw him. In the very best sense, the young king had a memorable face; a warrior's face. A charismatic face; one that inspired trust and could rally a nation. He wore a simple costume of rough spun breeches fastened at the ankle, and a dark leather vest studded with polished brown shells resembling scales. As he waited for the king to speak, he debated whether to use an inlay to depict the regent's tattoos, or whether he should omit them.

"While I appreciate your offer to redesign the national emblem of Khirjah, I have no desire to have the image of good King Kehreru simply replaced by mine. I wonder, Mr. Harkness, if you would be willing to consider a different sort of commission."

He glanced nervously at Reinhardt, but the Ambassador only nodded encouragingly. "What do have in mind?"

"I want an image which will convey the essence of our land and culture instead of just another portrait of the current ruler. Something timeless and meaningful to those beyond our borders, yet relevant to our people as well."

Renly bit back his disappointment. He had always been so careful in his choice of subjects. Portraits and the human profile were where his artistic strengths lay. How would he even begin to design a logo for a plague planet? Monsters and microbes? An open pit mine? Something like this could turn out very badly for his career. Ambassador Reinhardt was giving him the high sign as the king and his aides waited for his answer.

"I will do my best."

The king beamed and thanked him. The audience was over.

The Ambassador handed him an envelope as they walked out to the Ambassador's PV. "Compliments of King Hakaroah. A royal invitation to the Gold Ball."

He shook his head. "You take it. Edward Duprees gave me a pass to search the Festival grounds. I was over there all day today."

"Excellent. Any luck?"

He shrugged. "It's only the first day. They gave me an escort, and

I've got full access to everything. I'm checking the race track and casino tomorrow."

"I don't suppose they mentioned the Gold Ball."

"I'm not much for parties. Besides, I think I'll have better luck finding Garrett at the track."

Reinhardt shook his head. "That is the King's personal invitation. He gave it to you. Your will attend as the Royal Family's representative. This is not something you can turn down without giving insult. Go. The Gold Ball is the pinnacle event of the festival; only the highest rollers are invited to attend. It may be the only place you'll find him."

EIGHT

The first race started at mid-day, but at Renly's request, Wayne picked him up early. They arrived at the track a few minutes before second sunrise. Even at that hour, spectators lined up along the rail, watching the traggahs and their riders warm up on the course. Pastel colors of sunrise glowed softly through the transparent dome overhead, but the stadium lighting more than compensated for the hour. After the freezing commute, Renly appreciated the relative warmth of the climate-controlled venue. The designers of the festival site seemed to have anticipated everything.

Wayne got them both coffees, served in mugs emblazoned with the Gold Cup logo.

He cupped his hands appreciatively around the warm porcelain. Hostesses wandered by, offering complimentary fresh-baked pastries and finger foods. It all smelled so good, he nearly forgot about his resolution not to eat the local cuisine. The hotel catered to the Terran palate, but the menu options were limited and uninspired.

He focused his attention the faces of everyone around him. The sound of hoof beats and smell of straw and animal sweat triggered powerful memories of his childhood days spent watching Garrett practice out on the polo grounds at first light.

More than anything, he'd wanted to join Garrett and his friends out on the polo field. You are much too young; his parents told him, and his pony, Brownie wasn't a proper polo pony. They would not even allow them to practice on the empty field. So he and Brownie practiced in the paddock behind the barn. Even after he demonstrated their proficiency, his parents would not lift the ban. He would have to wait until he was twelve to join the older boys on the field. Until then, his time on the field was limited to the rest period between chukkers, when, along with the rest of the spectators, he was allowed to stomp divots back into the grass.

The ground shook. A trio of bulky creatures thundered past, and Renly jumped back from the rail.

Wayne chuckled. "Them's racing traggahs. Fastest four-legged beast in the galaxy. "

The jockeys brought their mounts around for another go, and Renly got a good look at them. Other than hooves and a thin mane, traggahs bore little resemblance to a horse. Wayne had been correct; traggahs looked like a cross between a buffalo and a large, long-legged antelope. A disproportionately large head and graceful, muscular neck rose above powerful shoulders. Their well-balanced body colors varied from rich mahogany to an ash grey, alternating in white and darker stripes in a handsome pattern down their faces, throats and underbelly. The attractive striping continued on the animals' legs as well, which stood high as a man's shoulder.

His overall impression was one of speed and power, but as he studied the animals dodge through the trees and leap the obstacles of the steeplechase course, their apparent bulk did not hamper them one bit. The traggahs appeared every bit as agile as a goat.

Indeed, the ram's curl of black horns around their ears and the creatures' long beards added to their goat-like appearance, softened somewhat by a broad nose and face, and large, expressive dark eyes.

"No kidding."

The earth rumbled beneath Renly's feet as they thundered past him down the track. The horned men astride were a far cry from the diminutive jockeys of Earth. These were big men; and they had their hands full trying to control their mounts as they thundered toward the jumps. Renly recognized them as Khirjahni.

"No Terran jockeys?"

Wayne flexed his gloved hands. "No Terran in his right mind would want to get that close to one of these; all the animals on this planet carry diseases. Besides, Traggahs won't allow any but Khirjahni on their backs, and they're too big to try to force 'em to think any different." Wayne tapped his forehead. "The Khirjahni say they got some mystical connection with the herds. Fine by me."

"They don't race anywhere else?"

"Nah. The locals won't let us export 'em. They're the Khirjahni sacred cows. We spend two years pampering and training and feeding 'em, then we have ta release 'em back into the wild after the festival. What a waste." Wayne made a sound of disgust. "Thrillin' to watch, though. You a bettin' man, Renly?"

He shook his head. "No, but my brother and I grew up around horses. He's the gambler."

Wayne nodded and showed him the betting windows. "We accept off track betting here, so your man could be placing his bets elsewhere, but he would have to be in one of the casinos. Still, most of the betting action happens here. Even rich folks like the experience of a day at the races, so you might want to station yourself nearby. Behind us is the clubhouse. That's the best place to see the action, once the races start."

"Thanks."

He pointed to a cluster of buildings on a small rise outside the stadium. "That is the stable yard. I'll be there if ya need me, or I'll meet ya in the clubhouse after the last race."

"You're leaving? I thought you were my chaperone."

Wayne waved his hand dismissively. "Ya don't need me and I got things to do. You know the drill now. Talk to anyone ya like, as long as they're wearing an Arkady uniform. Don't bother the guests or I'll hear about it."

Surprised and pleased at being allowed to wander around without an escort, Renly thanked him, and returned to scanning the faces of the bystanders along the rail. He showed Garrett's picture to anyone wearing the Arkady logo on their uniform and asked if they'd seen him. So far, no one had.

The warm-ups ended, and the trainers, jockeys, and their mounts headed back to the stables. The crowd began to thin. Garrett had not come for the morning workouts. With the start of the first race just two hours away, he couldn't shake the hunch that his brother had to be nearby. Like any gambler, Garrett would make it his business to know the trainers and familiarize himself with the fastest stock. Perhaps the stables.

He decided to take a quick look. Once outside the filtered air of the festival site, the stench of sulfur hit him like a blow. In spite of the dual suns and his brisk pace, the outside temperatures reminded him that his new traggah-wool robes he'd ordered were ready. He made a quick mental note to pick them up later and promised himself he'd make the stable check a quick one.

Six different racing teams appeared to share the eight rows of stables; with the Arkady team being the largest. As he turned down the first row, his stomach tightened as he sensed Garrett's presence growing stronger with every step. *He's here! I knew it!*

As he passed the first stall, a traggah put his big head over the half-door and whistled, nearly knocking him over. Renly backed away, intimidated by the size of the creature, more than twice the size of a an earth horse. The traggah seemed to be whistling *at* him.

Within moments, a dozen more traggahs had stuck their heads out as well, and their sharp whistles echoed loudly across the quiet stable yard. Some began bucking and kicking at their stable doors.

He froze. These huge animals were nothing like horses. As he turned to leave, he ran smack into a small Khirjahni woman and knocked her flat.

He helped her to her feet, noting as he did, dark bruises at her wrists. "I-I'm sorry," he stuttered. His apology was drowned out by the noise of the traggahs.

She gave a single cough, and the commotion quieted.

He stared at her. "Wow. How did you do that?"

She frowned at him for a moment, then her eyes widened and she gave him a wondering smile. "Oh, you're an empath!"

"What?"

She circled him as if he were an oddity. "You can sense them. You are able to hear their thoughts."

"What?" Her eyes were her best feature. Mottled green and brown like those of the other Khirjahni he'd met, but she also had a light blue ring the iris.

"They can hear yours."

He shook his head. "I'm sorry. I don't know what you're talking about." Khirjahni, although her horns appeared to be much smaller than others he'd seen.

"You are looking for someone. They want to attract your attention." She moved over to one of the stalls, and petted the excited occupant's long nose gently. "They want you to notice them. They cannot understand why you are ignoring them."

She was just a little thing. Early twenties, perhaps.

He frowned. *How could they...?* Sure enough. From the open half of every stable door, peered a traggah with their ears pricked forward, staring at him with a bright-eyed intensity he found disturbing.

"I have never seen them react in this way to a Terran before."

"What did you mean when you said they could hear my thoughts?" She didn't look like Jiala or the other Khirjahni women he'd seen. Her bone structure was more delicate, more feminine. She didn't have the heavy brow ridge or a thick neck.

"I have never met a Terran empath."

"I'm not an empath. Not really. I don't think."

"My father was Terran. I always wondered if my gift came from him or the Goddess."

He shrugged. "Some people on Earth have the gift. I wouldn't say I was one of them. It only works between my brother and me."

The traggah in the stall behind him whistled loudly. Almost like a laugh. He backed away.

When she smiled, her whole face lit up. "Traggahs instinctively yearn to bond. He will not hurt you. What is your name?"

She stroked the traggah's neck affectionately. She had no fear of the great creature, which could have squashed her easily. He held out his open palm, holding still as he remembered doing for the ponies he'd known so long ago. "Renly Harkness."

She cupped her hand beneath his open palm and brought it closer to the animal's wet nose. "This is Silverbeard," she said. "I am K'Sati."

As soon as he touched the animal's nose, he knew it wouldn't hurt him. The tension eased from his shoulders and he reached out to stroke the muscular neck. "So silky."

K'Sati smiled. "We shave them for racing. In the wild, their coat is long and warm. We use their wool for making cloth, but they are nothing like the sheep you have on Terra. Traggah are brave; their hides are tough and thick enough to protect them from predators. Even longteeth. Only craggon hide is thicker. Not even arrows can pierce it."

In spite of her rugged boots and scruffy clothing, she seemed intelligent. Her English held but a scant trace of accent. Well educated, he guessed. She wore knee-high boots and worn clothing. "Are you one of the jockeys?"

She smiled shyly. "I'm an assistant to the training master at Arkady Racing Stables. These," she gestured to the dozen or so interested traggahs. "Are my herd. We are bonded. I can sense when they are ill or when they are ready to run. With my help, the head trainer can decide how best to train them."

The traggah nuzzled his hand, seeking attention. Renly silently rejoiced in his forethought to have brought so many pairs of gloves. At this rate, he would need them.

"Silverbeard likes you. Do you not hear him in your mind?"

He shook his head. "I don't think I'm an empath like you think."

She cocked her head at him. "Why are you here? Off-worlders are not allowed in the stable areas."

"Oh." He showed her his guest pass and pulled Garrett's picture out of his pocket. "I'm looking for this man. Have you seen him?"

She studied the image of Garrett, and then shook her head. "Sorry."

"He's my brother. He came here for the festival four years ago, and disappeared. I came here to find him. When I came to the track this morning, I got the feeling he was close by. When I didn't find him at the warm-up, I thought I'd have better luck at the stables."

"Why the stables?"

Such a lovely, expressive face. Not classically beautiful, but she had a spark about her. "We grew up with horses." An innocent sincerity. "Um, back on Earth. He's a professional gambler."

The spark dimmed as she handed Garrett's picture back. "Ah. Then your best chance to find him is at the betting windows."

"Of course." He wondered if gambling went against the Khirjahni belief system. She certainly did not look happy he'd mentioned the subject. "Sorry to disturb. I'll leave you to your charges."

* * *

By the time he got back to the track, long lines the betting windows were every bit as mobbed as he'd feared. He stationed himself against the wall at one end of the elegant wagering pavilion, grateful to be out of the chill of the stables, but suffocating amidst a sea of furs, heavy perfumes, and the sparkle of gold and jewels worn by men and women alike. No wonder the Arkady Corporation kept such a limited guest list. He had never seen so much obvious wealth in one place in his life.

The noise and the cackle of shrill laughter did nothing to quell his discomfort at being in the midst of so many strangers. He remembered one of the tricks Dr. Singh had taught him; how to maintain his calm in overwhelming situations. He concentrated on only one person at a time. The crowds interfered with getting a good look at all the betting windows, but he found a spot where he could observe people in the two or three betting lines closest to him. He kept his attention focused on the men, and as each approached one of the betting windows, he concentrated on comparing their jaw lines, brows, and cheeks to his memories of Garrett's. Face after face; profile after profile, but none of them resembled Garret.

Near the end of the day, in the mad rush before the last race when the crowds at the windows were heaviest, he caught sight of a familiar face. By the time he realized who he was, the guy had already stepped away with from the window.

Renly waved wildly. "Paul," but the gate announcer's voice drowned him out. "Paul Hite! Over here!"

The dark-haired man turned and Renly saw the recognition dawn in the face of his brother's best friend. Without a word, Paul turned and began to move away from him through the crowds. With his heart beating madly, Renly fought and shouted his way through the mass of people across the hall. By the time he got outside, Paul was nowhere to be found.

Even in his frustration at losing Paul, his hopes soared. *He's here!* If Paul was here, so was Garrett.

NINE

Renly's initial excitement at seeing Paul Hite wore off quickly. Four more days passed without another glimpse of him. Wayne rechecked the master list of Gold Festival attendees, but Paul's name wasn't on the list. He even showed him the crew manifests for the ships transporting festival passengers. Once again, they went through all the hotel and casino records, but found no sign of anyone named Paul Hite. Wayne pointed out that seeing his brother's friend did not mean Garrett was on Aurum.

Renly spent hours scanning the security images, searching for Paul's face. He made several sketches of Paul from memory, but they all ended up looking like Garrett. Without an image, he was the only person able to recognize Paul.

With no other leads, Wayne told him he was free to keep searching on his own.

Frustrated and punchy from lack of sleep, he spent most mornings in the operations center, scanning security images from the casinos; afternoons he spent at the track. Every evening, he cruised the casinos, but with no success. Garrett's presence; so strong when he first arrived, seemed to fade with each passing day.

* * *

The royal family arranged for his transport from his hotel to the Gold Ball; held in the Midas Ballroom Conservatory, adjacent to the Amalthea Hotel. Wayne told him the Amalthea provided the best security of all the hotels in the festival village, and constructed to provide guests with virtually inaccessible private vaults for their valuables. The jewelers and gold buyers stayed here, secure in the knowledge their merchandise and their purchases would be as safe on Aurum as anywhere in the universe.

Despite the plain and box-like design of the hotel, the Conservatory was a charming birdcage of iron and beveled crystal panes built in an old-Earth Art Nouveau style. With the suns setting behind the western horizon, millions of twinkle lights lit the ornate building like treasure chest full of diamonds.

The royal family sent a car and chauffer to his hotel, along with a formal suit of clothes in the Terran style. Renly balked when he read the label on the inside the jacket, indicating the garment had been custom tailored for His Royal Highness, Okanga Hakaroah, but the chauffer convinced him to wear it. The jacket hung loosely on him; too big in the chest and shoulders, but the sash hid the ill fit. The King's suit was clean and far nicer than the suit he'd brought with him, and he supposed one didn't turn down the King's wardrobe, when offered. The deep purple sash was a bit much, but the Terran woman who took his royal invitation assured him he looked splendid. His hopes of finding Garrett faded when she gave him a green and gold eye mask and helped him put it on.

"It's a tradition, dear," she told him. "Everyone but the mandragons wear them."

He stepped into the main ballroom and stared in wonder. Polished onyx floors reflected the twinkle lights of stars and half-moon shining through the cut crystal ceiling. Women in brocade skirts and shapely bare legs seemed to drift in mid-air across the night sky mirrored beneath them. The room swam with glitter provided by the guests; each bedecked in layers of sparkling gems.

Couples moved gracefully across the dance floor; he estimated no more than three hundred guests. Even so, with everyone wearing masks, finding Garrett would be difficult. He noticed the bar on the other side of the room and made his way through the crowd. Tremolians he recognized from the cruise ship; their colorful costumes sparkled with jewels and tinkling golden bells. A group of humanoid types with bright blue hair and skin clustered near the window. By ignoring the obvious non-Terrans and women he eliminated a third of the guests. The Arkady executives all wore black robes emblazoned with the company hologram: an image of a golden planet surrounded by rings of glittering silver.

He sat at the bar and the tender set a glass of champagne in front of him. From here, he could get a pretty good look and anyone ordering a drink, but after all the disappointments of this week, he wasn't expecting too much. Ambassador Reinhardt insisted this event was the best place to find Garrett; he hoped it was true.

A man slipped onto the stool next to him and muttered his order Khirjahni.

The language classes he'd taken on board the ship had seemed like a good idea at the time, but since the official language of the Gold Festival was Terran English, he hadn't much chance to use his newfound skill. "*Doh cassa English*," he asked, hopefully.

The man turned to him and gave him a ghastly, golden-eyed, toothy smile. His swollen face was covered with iridescent brown scales of varying sizes. The man's snout and large misshapen jaw jutted forward like an animal's. His narrow lips did not cover the neat row of pointy brown teeth along the gum line. "Of course I speak

English. I'm American, same as you." The graveled voice scraped like an iron rasp across stone.

He gasped. The guy was not wearing a mask.

The creature's expression faded somewhat, but he shrugged it off. "Oh boy. Lucky me, I must be your first mandragon." He laughed; a choking bark. Long black claws grew from the tips of his gnarled brown fingers.

"Y-you're human?"

"Surely you've heard of dragon pox." He spoke carefully, as if he had trouble getting his mouth around the words.

A nervous shiver ran down Renly's spine. The guy had a Boston accent. With a trembling hand, he pushed away his empty glass. "They told me the coast is safe for off-worlders."

"I guess I got nothing to worry about, then." The thickened skin on the man's face masked his expression. He raised his hand in a mock toast.

Renly tried not to stare. The bones of the mandragon's skull face had been reshaped and elongated. His entire facial structure seemed impossible. Dragon pox indeed. A wave of dizziness washed over him, and he grabbed the bar. Why hadn't anyone else in the room noticed?

Wayne had mentioned the mandragons. Gold prospectors who lived in the forbidden zone. Dirt-eaters, he called them. Based on Wayne's description, he assumed they were not welcome in civilized company. "I thought-- I mean, why are you here?"

"Are you kidding? The Gold Ball is on our honor. Look around. There's a lot more like me here."

Confused, he took another look at the crowd and realized the man was right. People he assumed to be wearing costumes looked just like the man standing next to him. *Mandragon*, he corrected himself. "I'm sorry, I don't understand. Why is this event is in your honor? Don't you have the dragon pox?"

"Take it easy, man. I'm not contagious. Name's Sully." The creature took a sip of his beer. "They aren't kidding when they tell you it's an aggressive genetic virus." The words barely rose above a coarse whisper. His grossly thickened skin masked his expression. He could not smile. "

Renly fought his primary instinct to run in favor of satisfying his curiosity. "How did you catch it?"

"I'm a prospector in the Crags of Corrah. All of us are."

Renly frowned, his thoughts churning. Was this what the Ambassador had meant about finding Garrett? He didn't want to believe it. "Is the disease reversible? I mean, no offence. "

Sully shrugged at his reflection in the mirrored panel behind the bar. "None taken. I don't think about it all that much anymore. The benefits outweigh the risks."

"How can you you can you say that?" The urge to draw Sully's strange face filled him with both yeaning and revulsion.

"When I leave here at the end of the festival, I'll have more gold than Midas. I'll be richer than I ever dreamed, and that's saying a lot. I'll buy me a new face. Ten new faces, if I want."

"I thought all the gold belonged to Arkady Mining Corporation."

The Mandragon nodded. "They like to think so. But their mineral rights are limited to the lands outside the 45th parallels; what you call the temperate zone. They're not allowed to mine on either Khirjahni or Th'Dorran lands. But the Forbidden Zone straddles the lands between the two countries, and the Crags of Corrah are host to the richest deposits of gold ore on the planet. The Th-Dorrans and Khirjahni don't care if a few crazy Terrans want to try to pull a little gold from the craggon caves. Once every four years, Arkady hosts the Gold Ball for us prospectors. We come down from the mountains and auction off our gold to the highest bidder. We have a little fun, chase a little tail, and bet on the races. Those of us who make a killing leave this stinking planet at the end of the Festival as rich as kings. Those that don't, go back to the hills for another four years."

Something clicked. A connection he'd missed. A feeling of certainty washed over him. He reached into his bag and pulled out the engraving he'd done of Garrett. "Have you ever seen this man?"

Sully studied the portrait, and shook his head. "Doesn't ring any bells."

"He came to this festival four years ago; he hasn't been heard from since." The pupils of Sully's unnatural yellow eyes were elongated, like those of a reptile. A chill swept over him.

"Maybe you should do yourself a favor and let him be."

"Now you sound like those mining executives."

Sully tilted his beer and poured the amber liquid down his throat in a single long swallow. "Let me give you some advice, Terran. You will see a lot of guys just like me here tonight, so listen carefully to what I have to say. Only a desperate man prospects for gold in the Forbidden Zone. Once you go, there's no turning back. Gold fever changes a man. After a year or two, we are not the same. After four years, we're not considered human any more. We can't return to Earth. The things we used to care about don't matter anymore. Family, friends, home. It means nothing to us."

Renly had no answer for that; only the conviction that the disease must have affected Sully's mind somehow. Garrett wasn't one of these creatures. No way. Garrett had called him here for a reason. Even as he disbelieved Sully's characterization, he remembered Garrett had always looked after Garrett's interests first.

"If your brother went up into the hills looking for gold, he did so knowing what he was doing, and believe me, he doesn't want anyone, least of all his family, coming after him."

* * *

After Sully moved off, Ambassador Reinhardt appeared at his elbow with a fresh glass of champagne. "Glad to see you changed your mind about coming."

He told the ambassador about seeing Paul, and his fading hopes for finding Garrett.

Reinhardt seemed sympathetic. "I feared as much. I saw you talking to Sully."

"You think that's what happened to Garrett. You think Garrett is one of those mandragon creatures."

The ambassador held up his hands. "Not at all. I am an optimist. But I think you now understand now what the Arkady executives believe happened to your brother. If I were you, I'd make the most of this opportunity and reassure yourself that he is not one of our honored guests this evening."

For a moment, his vision blurred. The idea of Garrett as one of those animals like Sully nauseated him. No. It couldn't be. The very idea made his skin crawl. "I don't know what I'd do if he was one them. I don't think I could stand it." He felt faint.

"Have you seen the preview?"

"No, I just got here."

"Come with me." Reinhardt took him by his arm and guided him into another great room; this with a circular stage set in the center. Armed security guards stood kept the curious from reaching out to touch the waist-high piles of stacked gold ingots from the forbidden zone. On a second stage, eight huge nuggets of raw ore, each the approximate size of a bowling ball was on display. Six of the nuggets appeared to be pure, solid gold; one was equal parts gold and clear rock crystal, another embedded with bits of turquoise and small rubies.

Stunned by the beauty and sheer volume of gold in the exhibit, he could only stare in wonder.

"The prospectors smelt their gold into ingots and bring them to the Arkady assayers for a receipt, which becomes their minimum bid from Arkady Mining. If the winning bid for the whole lot doesn't top the Arkady price, the mandragons walk away with Arkady's money in their pockets. If the winning bid goes over the Arkady price, the miner receives the greater price. The nuggets are sweepstakes prizes. They're put up for bid separately. As specimens, they usually go for far more than the ingots."

"Good grief. No wonder everyone kept insisting I was here for the gold."

Reinhardt nodded. "Sixteen tons of it."

"They pull this much out every four years?"

"Or more. Compared to what the company pulls out of their mines every year, this is a drop in the bucket, but Arkady doesn't spend a dime pulling this out of the ground. They're not permitted to mine in the forbidden zone, so this how they get around it."

"That is a lot of gold."

A few minutes later, Renly recognized Edward Duprees step onto the stage and announce the bidding would be starting in a few minutes. At the same time, a procession of mandragons entered the room and took up positions closest to the stage, as if building a proprietary, protective wall between the guests and the gold. As the audience stepped back, the auctioneer stepped up and opened the bidding.

Renly eased himself to the back of the room. The auction itself didn't interest him. Reinhardt was right; he needed to assure himself that Garrett hadn't somehow become one of these lizard men. While everyone else's attention focused on the bidding, he examined each of the mandragons as closely as he could. When he assured himself that Garrett was not one of the mandragons, he breathed a huge sigh of relief.

The noise and excitement of the auction approached a fever pitch. He had no desire to stay. This time of night, it would be quiet over at the stables. He hadn't been back since that first time, and he'd felt his brother's presence most strongly when he'd been there. This time of night it would be quiet. Maybe he'd have better luck.

He slipped out the door and headed toward the stables.

TEN

The brisk walk up to the stables invigorated him. The king's suit kept the chill night air at bay, and he appreciated the sudden silence after the excitement of the gold auction. The stars and moon lit up the night sky much more brightly than in his memories of Earth. While Aurum certainly lived up to its reputation as a primitive and bleak planet, he also appreciated the stark beauty of the empty landscape. In the distance, the famous Crags of Corrah rose steep and jagged as black fangs against the diamond points of the star-studded night. The sulfur-tainted air, so unpleasant when he first arrived, did not bother him quite as much. He no longer needed his kerchief to buffer the stench.

As he neared the dimly lit stables, sounds of angry voices reached him. He froze, uncertain what to do. He did not want to walk in on an argument.

A traggah whistled, and a woman's voice yelled angrily, "Stop! Stop it!"

He raced around the corner of the barn and found the stable girl, K'Sati and one of the traggahs facing off against two men kicking a third man on the ground. "Hey!"

With a last vicious kick, the two attackers took off running, leaving their victim lying motionless in the dirt. The commotion woke up the traggahs, who began whistling and stamping in their stalls.

He rushed to the man's side and rolled him over, while K'Sati attempted to calm the excited traggahs.

Renly stared onto the swollen and bruised features of Paul Hite's face.

"Oh no, it's Jason," she gasped. "Is he all right?"

"Jason?" Paul's pulse beat thready and erratic beneath his fingers. He shook his head. "You're mistaken. His name is Paul. Paul Hite. I think he needs a doctor."

"Wait here," she told him. "Let me put Neatfoot in her stall, and I'll help you carry him."

He patted and shook him, but Paul did not respond. A curious sense of exhilaration filled him. *I've got Paul!* I've really got him! This time, he wouldn't slip away from him, either. Garrett couldn't be far.

K'Sati returned a moment later, and together they managed to carry him to a shed where she said Jason was staying. She lit a battery lamp and they settled him onto a cot shoved up against one of the bare walls. Trash, rotting food, and empty vodka bottles covered the floor and almost every surface of the small room. The place stank of stale sweat and vomit, but Renly detected no sign of Garrett.

"How do you know Paul," he demanded.

She gave him a puzzled look. "His name is Jason. Are you saying he is your brother?"

"No, but they're friends. His real name is Paul Hite. He will know where to find my brother. How do you know him?"

She shrugged. "He helps K'Ruhi out sometimes. He comes and goes."

Renly's heart skipped a beat. "Who is K'Ruhi? Is he Terran?"

"No, K'Ruhi is the farrier. He is Khirjahni."

"What about his friends?"

She shook her head. "I cannot say. He is not a close friend. He comes around only occasionally, and stays for a few days. He had taken Neatfoot from her stall. When I stopped him to ask where he was taking her, those men came up and began beating him."

Renly loosened his tie and unfastened the top button on his shirt. The answers he needed would have to wait until Paul regained consciousness. "What about that doctor?"

"We have no Terran doctors here. The closest healer is at the Temple of the Mother in the Stonewood Forest." She knelt beside Paul and examined him. "I am not a healer, but I learned much when I served the Mother. I do not detect any broken bones, only bruises." She leaned close, listening to his breathing, and checked his eyes.

What should we do?"

She gave him an embarrassed expression. "I do not believe he is badly injured. I believe he passed out from drink and dream dust. His hands bear no wounds or scratches. He did not fight those men. His fingernails are black and curled. He shows the early signs of dream dust addiction. He is not in pain."

"That figures." He nodded at the empty bottles littering the confined space. "I guess I'm not surprised. He hasn't changed much since the last time I saw him. What *is* dream dust, anyway? Some kind of narcotic?"

"A hallucinogenic. From the forbidden zone. Highly addictive to Terrans." Her eyes looked huge in the lantern light. Worry lines etched her forehead.

"Are *you* all right?"

She shook her head and looked away. "I cannot remain here with you. I am meeting someone."

Oh. At this time of night, that probably meant one thing. He wondered if she was married, or whatever the Khirjahni called pair-bonding. Or maybe meeting her lover. Whatever the case, she didn't look very happy about it. "Of course. Thanks for your help. I'll stay with him until he wakes up," he assured her.

She appeared relieved. "I will come back in the morning. He must answer for taking Neatfoot from her stall tonight. She is my responsibility."

After she left, the tiny room seemed to darken and feel claustrophobic. Renly could not sit still. He wanted to slap Paul out of his stupor, but would not allow himself to do so. He needed Paul's cooperation to find Garrett, and if that meant letting him sleep it off, he would wait. He slipped out of his jacket, rolled up his sleeves, and slipped on a pair of synthetic gloves, glad he'd remembered to bring them. He cleared the trash and clutter from the shed, filling a nearby trash bin with the worst of the litter, as well as dozens of empty packets he assumed once held dream powder.

Paul's abnormally thick, blackened fingernails disgusted him. They did look like claws. Mandragon claws. K'Sati seemed to think they were a sign of dream dust addiction, but the mandragons he met all had similar blackened claw-like nails. Was it the drug or dragon pox?

By the time he cleared the worst of the litter out of the room, the sky was beginning to lighten with the hint of first sunrise. Renly took a seat on the only chair in the room, and waited for Paul to wake up. Instead, Paul went into convulsions.

* * *

"You gotta help me, man. I'm dyin'." A sheen of perspiration dampened Paul's skin, soaking his clothes. Another wave of trembling and dry heaves shook his bony frame and he curled himself into a fetal position.

His condition seemed to be getting worse, not better. And through it all, Paul refused to tell him where to find Garrett. "Can't you see I'm sick? I've got dust sickness. I'm gonna to die if you don't get me something."

Paul's whiny voice grated on his nerves. In spite of his obvious discomfort, Renly found it difficult to dredge up any sympathy for him. "Tell me where Garrett is and I'll get you what you want. Come on, tell me."

"Get me what I need and I'll tell you."

They'd been going back and forth on this point for more than an hour. Enough already. "Fine. We'll do things your way. I'll help you get your dream dust, and you tell me where Garrett is."

"You can't get dust on the coast. You'll have to find me some tranquilizer patches…" Dry heaves prevented him from saying more.

After the wave passed, he helped Paul to his feet, but the man could not stand on his own. Paul began to cry.

He began to worry Paul might die of withdrawal after all. He had to do something. "All right. Tell me where to go. I'll get you what you need."

Paul was still crying when gave him the directions. "I don't have any money. Those guys took everything I had."

"Why did they beat you up?"

A sly, well-remembered expression crossed Paul's wan face. Even as kids, he never trusted Paul. "I was robbed."

"Sure you were." Renly stood and slipped on his jacket. "I'll be back as soon as I can."

Paul smiled weakly. "I'll be waiting."

ELEVEN

"Golden Boy isn't here," K'Rhui told her.

K'Sati felt the blood drain from her face. K'Rhui had to be playing a joke on her. "I put him in the paddock yesterday, but he is missing now." Wayne would kill her if anything happened to Golden Boy. "Paul said he would tell you."

"Who?"

"Jason! Where is he?"

K'Rhui shook his head. "Jason left early this morning."

"That cannot be. I saw him last night. He was in no condition to—when did he leave?"

"I did not see him leave. He left me a note."

She didn't wait for him to finish; she ran back to the stable to check Golden Boy's stall.

Empty.

His numbered bridle and custom saddle were also missing from the tack room. On the floor beneath the saddle stand, she spied an empty dream dust packet. *Oh no!*

In a panic now, she raced out of the tack room and back to the shed where she's left Paul and his friend Renly. The door was open;

Renly stood out front with an angry expression on his face.

"Where is he?" But she already knew the answer. "You said you would stay with him!"

"He told me he was sick, I-."

She waved at him impatiently and dashed for the paddock; relieved when Neatfoot and Silverbeard whistled a greeting to her.

Renly caught up with her, out of breath. "What are you going to do?"

She slipped a bridle over Neatfoot's head and led her out of the paddock. "I'm going after Golden Boy. Your friend Paul has taken him."

"That's crazy."

"Golden Boy is running his preliminary race is tomorrow. I must get him back before anyone discovers he is missing." The thought of what Wayne would do to her if he found out terrified her. According to K'Rhui, Paul probably took Golden Boy less than an hour ago. Her gift told her the direction. The road led toward the Stonewood forest.

"Wait, I'm coming with you."

She stared at him, wondering if he meant truly meant it. Terrans never ventured far from the coast. But on her own, she might not be able to take Golden Boy back from Paul. "Have you ever ridden a traggah?"

"No, but I grew up on horseback. I'll figure it out."

The determined look on his face convinced her. "Okay, you can ride Silverbeard."

Silverbeard, however had not bonded to the Terran, and she needed move quickly. In the end, she persuaded Silverbeard to allow Renly to ride him, even as he put his ears back and protested bitterly about the extra weight in Renly's pack.

"Leave the pack; it is too heavy." Neatfoot danced beneath her, eager to be off.

"No way." He patted the canvas carryall slung across his shoulder. "My whole life is in here. I'm not leaving it."

He could ride, a least. She understood that much by how he sat astride the traggah.

"Let's go!" She dug her heels into Neatfoot's ribs and they were off.

TWELVE

"What do you mean she's gone?" Tension began to build in Wayne's shoulders and neck. Conversations with K'Ruhi always tried his patience. The farrier was a man of few words. Wayne suspected the man possessed below average intelligence. "Where did she go?"

K'Ruhi frowned. "She did not say. They were in a hurry."

"They? Who did she have with her?"

He shrugged. "A jockey, I think. No. A Terran."

"Well which is it? Terran or jockey?"

K'Ruhi's face lit up. "A Terran jockey!"

"There are no Terran jockeys, dip shit."

"He was Terran," K'Ruhi insisted. "A jockey. On Silverbeard; er, number twelve."

Wayne fought to control his rising temper. "Are you saying K'Sati and some Terran rode out of here on traggahs?"

"A Terran *jockey*. No saddle."

Impossible. No Terran in his right mind would climb on to one of those beasts; might as well ride a rhino. Wayne choked back his frustration. This couldn't be happening. He unclenched his fists. "How long ago did they leave?"

"Three, maybe four hours."

Wayne rubbed his jaw and fumed. She'd decided to go defy his orders to have the traggahs destroyed, and decided to release them back into the wild. He'd only been half serious, but she had no sense of humor about her precious traggahs. Stupid bitch probably figured she could do the deed and get back with no one the wiser. *Wrong.*

Chalk up another day without K'Sati's list of ringers. He should never have let her out of his sight. This disturbing new pattern of excuses and lies meant only one thing: he couldn't trust her any more. His mood darkened.

Fine. He would get her good when she came crawling back. Oh how he was going to enjoy making her pay for this. And so would whoever else was involved. *Who the hell did she get to go with her?*

The training master, Ruben, came running up; an expression of panic on his face. "Several of the racing traggahs are missing," he announced, breathlessly.

Odd. Even more strange that Ruben would come running to tell him. The training master rarely ever acknowledged his presence. "Yeah, I already know." He and Ruben both reported to Ed Duprees, but Ruben knew he'd worked his way up from the mines, and never let him forget it.

He was one of those men who took pleasure in pointing out other people's mistakes. A snitch. Trainer or no, Wayne never understood why Edward hired him.

"I don't think you understand the nature of the problem," Ruben panted.

The training master sure had a high opinion of himself. He waited a full beat before responding, and was pleased at how cool and professional he sounded. "Like I said before, I am aware of the situation, and would appreciate it if ya would give off and let me do my--."

"One of the missing traggahs is Golden Boy."

"What!" *Impossible!* He whirled to face K'Ruhi with an accusing stare.

The farrier shrugged, his expression confused. "I, I didn't get a good look--."

Of *course* she would take three traggahs; the two she was releasing and one to get back. A fast one. *The fastest one.* Golden Boy.

The whole company expected Golden Boy to win this year's Gold Cup. All the senior executives already put a lot of money on him, knowing the odds would be best before he won his first race. If anything happened to Golden Boy... they'd ship him back to the mines and forget about him.

Unless he got Golden Boy back, he was good as dead. If he could keep a lid on this thing a little bit longer, she'd be back with Golden Boy in a few hours and Ruben would look like a fool. He clenched his teeth into a smile for Ruben's benefit.

"Relax. I asked one of the stable girls to take them out for a little exercise, that's all. Everything is under control, Ruben. Ya got nothing to worry about." He would kill that little half-breed bitch for this. He would kill her and dump her in the rocklands for the lizards to eat.

"Exercise? Well, I'm glad to hear it." Ruben offered a thin-lipped, phony smile of his own. "I already notified Mr. Duprees. He asked me to tell you that he and the rest of the board are waiting for you in the clubhouse conference room. They want a full report in the next ten minutes. If you run, I think you can make it."

THIRTEEN

Renly huddled low over the racing traggah's neck, his heavy bag clutched in front of him, clinging to the animal's sparse mane. Silverbeard had enough power to bolt out from beneath him. The animal was wider and more powerful than any horse he'd ever ridden, and he hung on with grim determination, lest he fall and be trampled to death. Within moments, the stables and festival grounds had disappeared far behind them.

His heart pounded in an echoed rhythm of hoof beats and the explosive breathing of their mounts. They dashed down a hard-packed dirt road through low rocky hills at exhilarating speed. Silverbeard huffed like some massive steam engine made of muscle and sinew. Renly's body responded automatically to the movement of the racing animal and soon he settled into the relentless rhythm of the magnificent beast beneath him.

Ahead of them, K'Sati rode Neatfoot with a casual ease he envied. He imitated her body position, shifting his pack behind him, lowering his head along his steed's muscular neck. Silverbeard's stride lengthened and his gait evened out. The traggah's ears pricked forward, as if to say, 'thanks, that's better'.

He caught himself grinning like a fool. Never in a million years would he have ever imagined he would end up riding an alien creature through the wilderness of a distant planet to rescue Garrett. He'd even surprised himself. He'd done it without even thinking.

After a while, the hills flattened out and the road descended in to a valley. They encountered no one else. He began to wonder if they were riding in the right direction, but he'd been to the festival site often enough to know that this was the only other road from the festival village. He realized Paul must have lied to him; and wondered again why he wouldn't say where Garrett was. Wouldn't even talk about him. The sting of Paul's lies made him more determined than ever to catch up to Paul and make him talk.

In the distance, he spotted a line of trees, and hoped that was their destination. They should have caught up to him by now, he thought. He couldn't imagine that his brother's friend had more than a couple hours head start. Renly tried to calculate how many miles they'd covered. Their pace had slowed to a ground-eating lope, but neither traggah seemed tired in the least.

By mid-afternoon, his muscles began to cramp. The odor of traggah sweat filled his nostrils; sores developed where his legs rubbed against Silverbeard's ribs. Without the shelter of the rolling hills, the raw bite of wind buffeted them, biting him through his thin clothing. He was glad for the heat of the animal beneath him, but the winds whipped the moisture from his skin. His lips grew cracked and dry; his eyes gritty.

His thirst grew. Fifty feet ahead of them, K'Sati rode with single-minded intensity; her eyes glued to the approaching forest. He called out to her about stopping for water, but the wind whipped the words from his mouth and whisked them off into the desolate prairie like silent ghosts. They passed no restaurants, inns, or any sort of buildings.

The land around them seemed empty of life; human or animal.

Finally, as they approached the line of trees, K'Sati sat up on Neatfoot, and both animals slowed to a brisk trot.

"When we reach the stone forest, there is a small spring where we will stop for water. But for only a few minutes. Golden Boy is just ahead of us."

"How do you know?"

She looked at him, as if startled. "Open your thoughts. Are you not aware of his presence?"

Warily, he shook his head. "No."

She nodded toward his mount. "Look at Silverbeard's ears. He and Neatfoot both sense Golden Boy. Traggahs are born with an innate sense of their herd clan. This is how they find each other in the wild. Neatfoot, Silverbeard, and Golden Boy are all born to the same herd. Even at the stables, we keep them together. After racing season, when they are released, they can find their way back to their clan by instinct, no matter how far away they are. You have that same ability. If you open yourself to Silverbeard, you will become aware of Golden Boy, just as I do."

He shook his head. "I don't think it works that way for Terrans. The only person I'm *aware of* is my brother."

The wind colored her cheeks with a rosy glow. She had wrapped her hair in a colorful scarf on the ride, but wisps of her dark hair caressed her brow. The Khirjahni were a handsome people. The urge to sketch her made his fingers itch.

* * *

Up close, the forest appeared different from his earlier impression. The twisted trees grew in a widely scattered formation, providing broken shade, but little protection from the wind. Beneath the trees, the packed red earth of the road transitioned into a fine sandy gravel. Only the merest bits of grey-green plants and weeds fought for existence beneath grey woody brush. The stunted trees appeared to be some sort of conifer, based on the needled leaves and oddly-shaped cones. Beneath the heavy sulfur smell, he caught a familiar light scent he couldn't quite name.

K'Sati pulled Neatfoot to a halt and slid to the ground with admirable grace. "This way."

He eased himself off Silverbeard and groaned as his feet hit the dirt. The traggah snorted and shook himself with vigor, obviously happy to be relieved of his rider. Renly stretched out the kinks in his legs and groaned as the circulation returned like pins and needles to his numb feet. He followed K'Sati down a narrow footpath, while the traggah crowded him from behind.

Sheltered beneath a natural stone formation, the spring was about the size of a swimming pool. Both traggahs pushed ahead eagerly, wading knee-deep into the shallows to drink where the water burbled to the surface. Renly watched uneasily as K'Sati scooped handfuls of clear water from an elevated trickle into a stone trough, which seemed to have been carved from the stone for that very purpose.

The water seeped across a mossy, lichen-covered rock face before dripping into the stone basin. Long strands of bright green algae rimmed the edge. The hotel and festival grounds provided sterilized water. No one said not to drink the local water; the subject never even came up.

"Is the water safe to drink?"

She gave him a questioning look. "For Terrans?" She shrugged. "I do not know. This is the only place for water."

Renly had never experienced such thirst in his life, but only a fool would drink unsterilized water on a known plague planet. Fleetingly, he wondered if Paul had brought his own water, but his thirst betrayed him. He cupped his hands into the basin and drank. He refilled his hands with cold sweet water until he could hold no more.

Other than the rocks around the spring, he saw little few other landmarks. "Why do they call this place the stone forest?"

She gestured toward the trees. "Stonewood. The wood of these trees is very heavy and dense, like stone. In the old days, before the Khirjahni and Th'Dorrans signed the treaty, the Khirjahni used dead limbs of the stonewood trees as weapons."

Renly glanced around at the forest floor. "I don't see any dead limbs."

She shook her head. "You won't. The trees are too hard to cut for firewood, but the dry wood burns for days. It makes excellent charcoal. Most of the areas closest to the coast get picked clean on a regular basis."

With a tentative grip, he tested the pale reddish bark of a nearby sapling. Solid as an iron bar. Even a thin twig resisted all but his most strenuous attempts to bend it. He crushed a few of the pine-like needles between his fingers. The faint aroma of pineapple filled his sinuses. Neat.

When he reached into the branches to pick a pinecone, something bit him.

"Augh!" He jerked his hand away, but the blue-skinned lizard refused to let go. He smacked his gloved hand against the tree, trying to knock the creature loose. Again and again, he banged the lizard against the trunk until it finally let go and skittered away.

K'Sati grabbed him and dragged him away from the tree. "Get away from there!" She ripped the bloody glove off his hand. "Oh no!" She sounded frantic.

A cold, heavy sensation snaked up his arm. "What was that?"

"Bhok-Bhok. Tree lizard." She put his bloodied hand to her mouth and sucked vigorously, then spat a yellow gob of *something* onto the pale sand beneath their feet.

Oh shit. "Am I going to get dragon pox?" His legs trembled.

She shook her head. "Only craggons carry the pox. They live in the mountains."

Relief flooded through him. "Thank god."

She dragged him over to where the traggahs were eating grass. "Tree lizards are poisonous," she told him. "How do you feel?"

His legs refused to cooperate. He slumped to the ground. "I think I'm going to throw up."

She grabbed Silverbeard's bridle and dragged him over. She shoved his wounded hand into the traggah's mouth.

He jerked his hand back. "What are you doing?" His hand was on fire. His entire arm throbbed painfully.

She slipped her hand into Silverbeard's slobbery mouth and pulled it out; dripping with grass-clotted saliva. She slathered traggah drool all over the bite area.

His tongue felt too big for his mouth. "Wha-?" His vision began to narrow.

She peered into his face. "Traggah spit has antiseptic qualities. Can you ride?"

Her voice sounded like it was a million miles away. His throat began to constrict. He couldn't breathe.

"Get up, Terran, or I will leave you. I must get Golden Boy back."

He heard nothing more.

FOURTEEN

K'Sati stared at the unconscious Terran at her feet. Mother of stars, whatever gave her the idea to bring an off-worlder along? Of course the trees were infested with lizards. Everyone knew that. What was she going to do now?

She looked up the path. Golden Boy was *so close*. Maybe ten minutes ahead of them. He wasn't running any more. If she left now, she could catch up to them and trade traggahs with Paul. It would be dark soon; easy enough to sneak Golden Boy into his stall before morning. He would win his race and no one would ever know.

The unconscious off-worlder began to gag. She rolled him onto his side and he vomited up water in great wracking sobs. There was nothing she could do. Even if she took him back to the stables, he would die before they got there. And Wayne would be waiting for her. On the other hand, the Terran would slow her down if she brought him with her.

He choked on his own bile and gasped for air.

"Come on, get up." She hauled him to his feet.

"I hate this place," he mumbled.

She leaned him up against Silverbeard, but the traggah skittered away, refusing to cooperate. She slapped the Terran's face. "Can you ride?"

His head lolled to the side. "Never should have come."

Too heavy for her to hold upright, he slid to the ground. His lips were turning blue. She checked his hand. Three bites. His arm had swelled, and the sleeve of his jacket was cutting off the circulation. She grabbed the sleeve and ripped the seam apart up to his armpit. She winced at the sight of it. The arm had doubled in size and was hot to the touch. "Come on, get up. We have to *go*."

His eyes rolled back in his head.

He was dying. He would die no matter what she did. But the idea of leaving him for the scavengers she would not do. She would have to take him with her. If she tied him to Silverbeard's back, she could leave them at the gate of Temple of the Mother, where they had the proper herbs to purge the poison from his system. She would still have time to catch up with Paul in the rocklands before he reached the steppes. Once they reached on the high plains, she would never catch them. Golden Boy was too fast, and he loved to run.

She coaxed the Silverbeard to his knees, and settled him to the ground. *Stay.* She sent him an image of what she wanted.

He snorted and put his ears back unhappily, but stayed down.

She dragged the Terran's limp body over to the traggah. He clutched his heavy shoulder pack with one hand and refused to let go. His muscles had locked into spasms now; she couldn't loosen his grip without breaking bones. With no other choice, she eased him and his bulky satchel across Silverbeard's back. She ripped the rest of his jacket into strips and used them to tie him to the animal.

She patted Silverbeard released him to stand. The traggah groaned and lurched to his feet, protesting with irritated whistles. Already, the unconscious man listed to the side. They wouldn't get far like that.

This would be so much easier if Renly would just open up to the animal.

"Wake up, wake up!" She slapped his face.

His eyes opened, but held no spark.

"You must hang on or you will die. You must help yourself. Are you listening?"

She slapped him again, and he nodded. He shifted himself into a better position on Silverbeard's back. The traggah shook himself and his ears came forward. A good sign.

"Renly." His alien name sounded strange to her ears. "Listen to me." She gripped his chin in her hand and forced him to face her. "You are an empath. Stop shutting them out. Open your mind. Traggahs have a need to bond. This one wants to bond to you. He wants you to recognize him. Say his name, Renly. Say it in your mind."

"Gah," he said, and was gone.

Silverbeard gave a little buck.

No! He needs our help. You must carry him. He is herd to me.

The herd usually abandoned the hopelessly sick and injured. She felt the question in Silverbeard's mind, but for the moment at least, he'd stopped bucking. She leapt onto Neatfoot's back, and pulling Silverbeard by the reins behind them, set off at a trot through the stone forest.

* * *

An hour later, pre-dusk for second sunset deepened the shadows around them. They still had not caught sight of Paul and Golden Boy. K'Sati sensed them ahead of her in the gloom, but she couldn't push the traggahs any harder. The trees were treacherous at night, and if she went any faster, Renly would topple off his mount. They would be at the Temple of the Mother soon. It would take her only a moment to tie Silverbeard to the front gate and ring the wayfarer's bell. With a bit of luck, she would be able to sneak up on Paul after he bedded down for the night, and steal Golden Boy back without a confrontation.

Even in the failing light, she recognized this part of the forest. These woods had been her playground as a child, and in a way, they seemed to welcome her home. By the time the lights of the temple appeared ahead of them, night had fallen completely. She hesitated. When she left this last, she swore she would never return. Seven years was a long time. No one would recognize her, now. She had no reason to be wary, yet caution made her nervous.

As they rode up to the temple gates, her heart soared with relief.

Golden Boy stood in the visitor paddock with another traggah, dining on the sweet hay the acolytes grew just for that purpose. She choked back a sob of relief, and urged Neatfoot forward.

At the entrance to the temple, two young acolytes came running out to greet them. She put them to work getting the unconscious Terran pulled off of Silverbeard.

"He has been bitten by a tree lizard," she told them. "More than three hours ago. Call the Temple Mother."

The girls shouted out for assistance with the unconscious off-worlder. None were turned away from the Temple of the Mother. More young women streamed out of the temple, and K'Sati led Neatfoot to the paddock. If she left with Golden Boy now, she would have him back to the stables by dawn. No one would ever know.

Renly began to struggle against the girls. "Where's Paul?" he was barely coherent. "Paul!"

Using Neatfoot's bulk to shield her from the women, K'Sati moved to the paddock gate. She recognized the voice of the Queen Mother immediately.

"Your friend Paul is here as our guest. He is sleeping right now. You may speak to him later, when you are well. Come now girls," she clapped briskly. "Bring this poor man into the healing room and prepare him for the rites."

K'Sati slid the bar to the paddock aside and opened the gate. She slipped Neatfoot's bridle off and the traggah eagerly joined the others gathered around the feed trough. Golden Boy didn't resist when she slipped the bridle over his head and seemed happy to see her.

She turned to leave the paddock, only to come face to face with the Queen Mother herself and half-dozen priestesses.

K'Takiweah nodded, looking extremely pleased with herself. "I thought I recognized you, K'Sati." Her eyebrow lifted in that way that K'Sati remembered so well. The temple mother's cruel mouth twisted in a false smile.

K'Sati began to tremble.

"Welcome back, little blaspheme. I always wondered what happened to you. I am so looking forward to getting reacquainted. I cannot tell you how happy I am that you've decided to return to us."

The priestesses took hold of her and K'Sati knew Golden Boy would miss his race.

FIFTEEN

The delicious aroma of warm porridge awakened him. Renly opened his eyes. He lay on a thick pad on the floor of a whitewashed room. A young Khirjahni girl of about nine kneeled next to him, wafting steaming hot cereal beneath his nose.

She was the first Khirjahni child he'd seen since landing on Aurum. She wore a simple, rough-woven shift belted with a braided cord. Tiny goat-like horns emerged from a halo of short brown curls. At this age, her graceful neck looked no different from a human child.

Her eyes widened when she noticed him staring at her.

"Where am I?" He scooted himself into a sitting position, but settled back down again when the room began to spin.

She smoothed his forehead with her small hand. "Your fever has passed."

The porridge smelled delicious. "Is that for me?"

She nodded at his bandaged left hand. "Are you in pain?"

He flexed his fingers experimentally. "Not enough to complain about."

She handed him the bowl and a wooden spoon. The warm cereal settled his stomach. "Where am I?"

She gathered her shawl around her and stood. "You were brought to the Temple of the Mother for healing after being bitten by a tree lizard. Deadly, even for Khirjahni. No one thought you would live, but yesterday, you began to wake up."

Yesterday? "How long have I been here?" He realized he was naked beneath the blankets and his face grew warm. "Where's my pack? My clothes?" For such a young girl, she seemed remarkably composed.

"Three days." She motioned to a simple cupboard beneath a barred window. "Your pack is there. Your clothes were ruined; but you are welcome to help yourself to whatever you need from what you find."

He nodded, and scraped his spoon across the bottom of the bowl to get the last bite. "Thank you."

"You may thank the Queen Mother in person. She would like to speak to you as soon as you are dressed." She bowed and left him alone in the whitewashed cell.

The realization hit him like a blow. *Three days.* He'd missed his return flight. The festival would be ending soon, although he was certain there were still a few days left before the final closing ceremony. Whatever happened, he didn't dare miss the final transport leaving Aurum.

As he unwound the bandage on his hand, he struggled to recall his last memory. He remembered stopping for water with K'Sati. He examined his hand and frowned. Three sets of bites marked the ugly purple and green flesh. He remembered nothing of being bitten, or any lizard.

Paul. They were chasing Paul. What happened? He searched for Garrett's presence in his mind, but felt nothing. After months and months of his brother's voice in his head, only silence answered him now.

Renly struggled to his feet, using the wall to brace himself against a spell of vertigo. He rubbed his jaw; they must have shaved him while he slept.

Using the stuccoed walls for support, he made his way over to the wardrobe and found his carryall untouched; everything, including the gold and platinum bars all as he had packed them. He found a pair of faded brown traggah wool trousers and a homespun sleeveless tunic. Damn these Khirjahni; didn't they ever get cold? He wrapped a blanket around his shoulders and wished for the robes he'd bought.

His Corinthian leather dress shoes sat on the floor of the closet, covered with dried mud; the leather split and separating from the sole. A total loss, but his socks had been laundered. Still, by the time he got himself dressed and washed his face in the standing basin, he felt almost himself again.

His room opened into what he guessed was a dormitory hallway, lined with heavy wooden doors. The sound of murmured conversation led the way, and eventually he emerged into a central room, which appeared to serve as both a meditation room and classroom.

A dozen young women in pale green robes kneeled on thin mats facing an older woman seated on an elevated dais. The room appeared to have been designed like the hub of a wheel, with hallways leading in various directions. The pale walls had been painted in a manner of aboriginal cave paintings; depicting stylized the horned Khirjahni people living and travelling amid herds of traggahs.

The women bowed their heads, as if in prayer, all but one, who sat cross-legged on a raised dais with her face turned upwards to a magnificent domed ceiling covered in a frieze of trompe l'oeil clouds amid a peach-colored sunrise of the twin suns of Aurum. The style of painting on the walls compared to the much more modern style of the friezes on the ceilings made Renly wonder who had built the shrine, and whether or not any of the art depicted was truly aboriginal or Terran.

A soft gong sounded in a distant part of the building, and the Mother's eyes turned immediately to his.

"I am glad to see you well, Terran." The coldness of her voice and the stony glitter in her eyes spoke differently. "Your traggah has been tended to, and the acolytes have prepared food to take with you. The day is still young; you will easily reach the coast before dusk."

Renly stepped into the room, as most of the young women rolled up their mats. They kept their eyes to the floor, he noticed.

"Thank you for saving my life," he began.

She flicked her hand with a casual nonchalance. "The Mother of All saved you; I am but her instrument. Had you arrived much later, not even the Mother could have saved you. You Terrans are such a fragile species." She leaned forward, and stared straight into his eyes. "You bear the marks of the tree lizard now. Be thankful. No other Terran has ever survived such a bite."

"Where are K'Sati and Paul?"

Something flickered across the cold woman's face. "Gone. Back to the coast, both of them." She smiled coldly. "No one thought you would live."

* * *

The temple Mother did not come to see him off, but several of the Priestesses did, joined by a crowd of acolytes and orphans. The stable master brought Silverbeard out to him and stood by with an almost paternal air, as Renly repeatedly tried to mount the unwilling traggah. The younger children laughed hysterically at his frustrated efforts. The priestesses hid their smiles behind their hands.

After ten minutes of wrangling with Silverbeard, he admitted his defeat, and told them he preferred to walk a bit, to stretch his legs.

The stable master rolled his eyes. "To reach the coast by dusk, you must ride. There are more dangerous creatures than tree lizards to worry about after dark."

Renly didn't stick around to hear any more. He dragged the now perfectly-docile traggah behind him and walked out of the temple down the path to the well-marked road leading back to the coast. He tried several times to get onto Silverbeard's back, but the creature refused to stand still long enough. The one time he managed to get mounted up, the traggah promptly bucked him off and whistled his satisfaction as Renly cursed him with every word he could think of.

Even so, he found himself glad for the animal's company, and found that he could keep half his upper body warm by walking close to the animal's thick neck as they walked. By switching which side he walked on, he was able to keep warm enough to keep his teeth from chattering.

In spite of his questions, no one at the temple would tell him what he wanted to know about K'Sati, or Paul, or Golden Boy. It bothered him more than a little that Paul and K'Sati left without him. Of course K'Sati would have headed back to the coast with Golden Boy. He wondered if the traggah won his race.

But why would Paul go back to the coast? K'Sati had been terrified he was headed toward the forbidden zone. Why would he suddenly turn back? And she would not have been able to force him to return with her if he didn't want to. All she wanted to do was to swap traggahs with Paul and return Golden Boy to the stables. Even in his drug-addled state, Paul had to be aware that Golden Boy was scheduled to race, so why take him instead of one of the others?

Why was Paul heading into the forbidden zone anyway? Renly turned the idea over in his mind. Only one answer seemed possible: Garrett had to be in the forbidden zone. It was the only answer that made sense.

Beside him, Silverbeard snorted and shook his head, almost as if he wondered the same thing.

And come to think of it, why had no one come looking for him? Surely both K'Sati and Paul would have reported his accident to the authorities. He could have died! How strange that no one bothered come check on him; not Wayne; or even the ambassador. He'd been gone for four days! Why wouldn't K'Sati and Paul say something about him being bitten by some stinking tree lizard when arrived back at the stables? *What is wrong with this place?*

Leo's words came back to him. *Aurum is a plague planet.*

He held up his injured hand, which was now beginning to throb. He wondered what kind of lizard germs were already multiplying in his system. The Khirjahni obviously shared their genes with traggahs. Their horns were practically identical. And the mandragons...

Renly stopped short. *Oh god. What if I turn into one of them?*

No. He forced himself to remain calm. Everyone told him dragon pox came from the craggon caves, high up in the mountains of the forbidden zone. What if they were wrong? No one had said anything to him about the after effects of lizard venom.

And Garrett. Why couldn't he feel Garrett anymore? Had the venom done something to him? Or had something happened to Garrett while he'd been unconscious?

His stomach growled uneasily, but he'd already eaten the lunch they'd packed for him at the temple. All of the women and children spoke excellent English, something he would not have expected, this far from the coast. Still, he couldn't help wondering why the temple Mother and her priestesses seemed so eager to send him on his way.

* * *

After hours of walking, the light began to change. Not full dusk yet, but more the promise of dusk, and they still hadn't gotten through the damn forest. Silverbeard began to get skittish, shying at every leaf flicker and noise in the underbrush. A couple of times the traggah tried to bolt, and had half-dragged Renly a dozen yards before he'd regained control of the animal.

He kicked himself for not letting the stable master tie him to the traggah. If he had, he'd be back to the coast by now, probably having a nice hot bath at his hotel. Only the lure of the hot bath and hot meal had kept him going this long, but he was beginning to think they were lost. Surely they should be through the forest by now. Had he somehow gotten off the main road?

As the day lengthened into evening, the sounds of animals scampering around them in the underbrush grew louder. Renly picked up the pace, but keeping his own rising panic under control was almost as difficult as restraining the two-ton traggah dancing nervously beside him. Renly realized that if Silverbeard got spooked, or decided to bolt, he would not be able to stop him.

A large animal seemed to be following them in the thick brush beside the road. To his left and a little behind, he guessed. A cold sweat rolled down his back. Silverbeard's nostrils flared, and the whites of his eyes showed his fear. Renly began to trot alongside the nervous traggah, but his stamina faded quickly.

They'd only gone a few hundred yards further when he caught the scent of woodsmoke up ahead. Silverbeard surged forward, and Renly hung onto the traggah's neck, half-running, and half dragged along beside him.

They rounded a turn and the road widened before them, opening into a clearing. A cluster of low buildings stood before them; a barn, a few sheds, and more important, a sweet two-story structure with lights glowing through shuttered windows, and the heavenly scent of something savory wafting across the clearing.

The traggah whistled shrilly; his call answered by two more from inside the barn. Lights at the front of the house illuminated the courtyard. The front door of the house opened, and Renly spoke to a lone figure silhouetted in the doorway. *"Hello,"* he called out in Khirjahni. *"I am lost. May I shelter in your barn tonight?"*

The man hefted a three-foot long club in his hand, and replied in excellent English, "We do not host dirt-eaters. Show yourself!"

Renly stroked Silverbeard's tense neck. "I mean you no harm! I'm coming from the temple. Got bit by a tree lizard."

The man lowered his club and nodded. "Ah. The Terran. We hoped you would survive. Come, we will get your traggah bedded down and fed first. Then you may tell us all about your ordeal over dinner."

SIXTEEN

The old Khirjahni, Okoro, and his silver-haired wife, Rima, welcomed him into their home. The house, which also served as Okoro's studio, looked to have been built by hand. With its massive exposed beams and stone walls, the place had a rustic feel. The couple lived in one large room, with sleeping quarters in an open loft above. A simple screen separated Okoro's workspace from the kitchen and living area.

Renly grinned delightedly when he realized Okoro's art so closely resembled his own; the only real difference between them seemed to be their choice of mediums. Where he worked in precious metals, the old man worked in the local stonewood.

His art hung from every wall; plaques of the highly-polished coffee-colored wood, etched in a style similar to those he'd seen at the temple. Some bore the whorled tribal images and designs he'd seen on the Khirjahni King's sculpted throne. When asked, the old man blushed and told him the of chair's history.

"My father carved that throne from a huge knot at the base of one the ancient stonewoods, but the effort took more than half his life, and he died before he finished. I was a young man, then; I did not wish to spend my life as my father had, dedicated to a single work of art. The Arkady Mining executives were in negotiations with our old king, Kehreru. Part of our arrangement with the mining executives included shipments of the custom blades and saws I needed to speed up the work. Using Terran tools enabled me to complete the work my father started, in only a few more years. Had I used the tools of my father, I too would have died before I finished."

Eagerly, Renly showed him his tools and the precious metals he'd brought with him, including the portrait of the old king.

"I know the portrait doesn't look like him," he apologized. "This is my brother's face. We haven't been close for years, but he's been on my mind lately. His image creeps into all my portraits." He shook his head sadly, as he realized his last chance to find Garrett had disappeared with the lizard bite. "I don't know what to do now. I can't work anymore." He slipped the metal disk back into its box. "I'm sorry. I don't know why I told you."

Okoro stopped him. "Let me show you something." He took a key out of his pocket and unlocked a cupboard built into a nook beneath the stairs. Inside the drawer were many small items wrapped in dark blue felt. He unwrapped one and handed it to Renly.

The octagonal medallion weighed heavy in his hand. Gold, by the heft of it, with the portrait of a handsome man engraved on the face. Unlike any of the work hanging on the walls of the studio, this piece was as fine an example of a master engraver's art as any Renly had seen. The clarity of detail and the perfection of the technique transcended the planet's culture. Or any culture.

He choked back his emotion. "Where did you get this?"

"That is my work. Of my son, Okarhi. I completed that portrait the day he went off to war. He is wearing the traditional garb of all Khirjahni soldiers: the boots and battle coat of craggon hide lined with traggah fleece, a shirt of softest traggah wool, woven by Rima's own hands, and the necklace of craggon teeth he took from his first kill."

"Craggon?"

The old man nodded. "You Terrans call them dragons. In the old days, a Khirjahni boy ascended to manhood only when he and his mates killed a craggon. The leader of the group is given the long fangs as a measure of his bravery."

Renly peered closely at the necklace around the warrior's neck. Like King Hakaroah, the young man's facial symmetry and regal bearing made him made for a riveting image. "The whole necklace is of long fangs."

The other man smiled sadly. "By horns, you have the right of it. He was a brave and reckless boy."

"I thought the Khirjahni were against killing."

"True enough, in times of peace. Today, the Khirjahni are a blend of two peoples; the coastal H'aack fishing people and the ancient nomadic Khirjahni tribesmen; descended of the sacred traggah herd of the high plains. With the arrival of the Arkady Universal Mining Corporation some sixty cycles ago, King Kehreru agreed to sell mineral rights beyond the 45th parallels to Arkady Universal. At that time, many of the Khirjahni gave up the nomadic life to join the H'aack fishermen in the coastal cities and take advantage of the new technology and comforts made available by the Arkady shipments. Like the H'aacks, the Khirjahni live a cooperative lifestyle. Few Khirjahni still follow the herds, but we retain the belief that we are all of the same clan. Our leader is chosen by popular acclaim.

But our traditional enemies, the Th'Dorrans, and some off-worlders as well, ridicule us as a nation of followers. They consider us cowards. Th'Dorrans believe in the law of tooth and claw; their people are ruled by the domination of the strongest; their king is determined by bloody duel.

The Khirjahni are not cowards. The rite of a young Khirjahni man taking on a craggon, the sacred beast of Th'Dorrah is a ritual shared only between the Khirjahni and our ancestors, the traggahs. Only a herd can defeat a craggon, and only the Khirjahni bear the horns of the sacred traggah. The horns are blessing and a sign of our bond with the Mother of all. No Th'Dorran army has ever bested the Khirjahni."

"I don't think I've met any Th'Dorrans. Are they like the mandragons?"

The old man shook his head. "Th-Dorran lands are on the far side of the planet, separated from our people by the forbidden zone. They claim they are descended from the great craggons in the mountains, but those tales are merely superstition. Only their temper and taste for blood give them any semblance to craggons. Mandragons are off-worlders like yourself who become infected with dragon pox, as you call it. The virus lives in the soil of craggon lairs. Only off-worlders are susceptible; only gold prospectors living in the forbidden zone contract the virus.

Renly studied the handsome graven image in his hand. Every detail, right down to the coarse weave of the fabric peeking out from beneath the sleeveless coat had been captured in the high-relief engraving. The son's noble facial structure echoed his father's but his high forehead reflected his mother's serene and dignified countenance. "This is a wonderful portrait." He handed back the engraving.

"He was killed in battle; in the last great war against the Th'Dorrans. Ultimately, the Khirjahni prevailed, so his death was not without merit." Okoro unwrapped a shield-shaped plaque of polished platinum. "This is the portrait I did for King Kehreru at the end of the war. For his coronation."

The image was of Okarhi.

Renly gave the old man a questioning look.

Okoro unwrapped a dozen other Khirjahni portraits, of both men and women; all bearing the likeness of Okoro's son. "Like you, I became haunted by the face of my beloved son. After a time, I stopped doing portraits, but I cannot destroy these." The old man caressed the surface of his son's portrait. "His body was never returned to us. Perhaps if I knew where he was buried, I would be at peace, but I think you understand how it is to not know and be haunted by the not knowing."

"I am sorry for your loss."

"In Khirjah we say, *be at peace. He runs with the great herd.*"

"Be at peace. He runs with the great herd." He met the old man's knowing gaze. "My brother came to Aurum four years ago and disappeared. I came here to find him. The other day, I spotted one of his friends. When I confronted him about my brother, he tricked me, and ran off with one of the Arkady racing traggahs. K'Sati and I chased him into this forest, but then I got bit by one of those poisonous tree lizards."

"You mean K'Sati Apai."

"You know her? She dropped me off at the temple, but they went back to the coast. Golden Boy had a big to run." Renly helped Okoro rewrap the portraits of his son and place them in the cabinet.

He nodded. "We spoke to her as she passed by on her way to the temple. You were unconscious. She asked about your friend, and we told her he had passed by less than ten minutes ahead of her. But she has not come back yet. Neither of them has passed this way."

He frowned. "That can't be. At the temple, they told me they both left the next day. Golden Boy had a race to run. Maybe you didn't see them. Maybe they didn't stop."

"This is the only road leading through the forest from the temple back to the coast. All travelers pass this place. Other than the spring at the edge of the forest, we have the only water and shelter for miles. Our traggahs would have alerted us to them. They would have stopped."

Renly shook his head. "Why would they tell me she'd gone back to the coast?"

The old man and his wife exchanged a weighty look.

"What? Tell me."

"K'Sati was raised by the temple. We knew her as a young acolyte. She would come here to speak to our traggahs; and she could really speak to them. They would whistle excitedly every time they saw her!" Rima's eyes shone with the memory. "She could charm the lizards right out of the trees, just by sitting quietly. Oh, you should have seen her."

"She was a wild little thing. As she grew older, she hated the idea of spending the rest of her life confined within the temple. She ran away many times before she came of age. Until she stopped by with you last week, we had not seen her in many years." Rima looked worried. "She was reluctant to go back to the temple, but you looked near death. She had no choice."

"I do not imagine K'Takiweah would allow her to leave," Okoro added. "Her ability to communicate with the traggahs is a blessing from the goddess."

He remembered the cold woman from the temple. He instinctively disliked her. "Would she do that? Keep her against her will?"

"She has not come back this way. Nor has the young man she was following. Yesterday, four men from Arkady Mining came through here on lithium-powered sleds, asking about her and the missing traggahs. We told them to check at the temple."

* * *

Renly lay on the narrow pallet Rima made up for him in front of the fireplace, exhausted, but unable to sleep. Memories of the past and his recent dreams and experiences merged into worrisome thoughts and unanswered questions.

Why hadn't the temple Mother or any of the priestesses told him there were people looking for him? They had no reason not to tell him. He had seen no one on the road. If they had stopped at the temple, what had they been told, and where were they now? Perhaps Okoro and his wife misunderstood. Or perhaps, K'Sati and Paul took a different route back to the coast. A shortcut. That was why Okoro and Rima hadn't seen them.

Of course Wayne would have been told about his accident when they arrived back at the stables. And it made sense that Wayne would come on sleds to carry him back to the coast. But why would Wayne bring so many people, if all he was only planning to pick him up at the temple? That didn't make sense, either.

Wayne and his men *had to be* searching for them. Searching for Golden Boy, at any rate. The only reason they hadn't found him was because someone at the temple had said he wasn't there. The temple Mother must have lied to them too, just as she'd lied to him. She'd deliberately misdirected them.

They were looking in the wrong place; they would never find him. He might as well be lost.

Like the body of Okoro's son was lost.

Like Garrett was lost.

Long-forgotten memories he'd tried so hard to forget began to surface.

As a kid he'd always hated that Garrett and his best friend Paul got to do whatever they wanted just because they were older. It wasn't fair that he was restricted to playing in the yard or the stable.

Sometimes, the boys from Garrett's class would ride their bikes over after school and hang out behind the stables. Renly discovered that as long as he kept out of sight, he could eavesdrop on them and imagine he was one of them. They talked about girls and played dice and cards and drank. When Garrett received his Personal Transport Vehicle for his sixteenth birthday, the boys stopped riding bikes. They stopped coming over, and the only time Renly ever saw his brother was when he tried to follow him, which Garrett hated.

Garrett attended the local university, and after much sneaky trial and error, Renly gradually discovered his various hangouts. Paul didn't go to college; he lived in a not-very-nice part of the entertainment district. In spite of the squalor and dreariness of the neighborhood, Garrett and all his friends always ended up at Paul's. Paul knew people. Dangerous people. Renly found himself irresistibly drawn to Paul's house, just like Garrett and his friends. Exotically dressed women and men with neon tattoos and diamond-studded teeth paraded in and out of the house at all hours.

Renly made himself a hidey hole outside Paul's kitchen window, in the oleander bushes bordering the house next door; a perfect vantage point for observing people coming and going, but after they went inside, he couldn't hear what they said. The second spot was less secure; a shallow lair he'd hollowed out beneath an overturned cast-off sofa in the back yard. Close enough to the kitchen window so he could hear everything in the kitchen and back bedrooms, but difficult to get in or out of without being seen.

When Garrett caught him one day, on his bike a block away from Paul's place, he had a fit. Renly tried to tell him he wasn't doing anything, but of course Garret didn't buy it. His brother whipped him with his belt until he cried like a baby, and made him swear never to spy on him again. He told him if he ever caught him anywhere near the place, he would make him very sorry.

But he couldn't stay away. He told himself he wasn't spying. He told himself he was worried about Garrett, but that wasn't it. He pretended to be worried about Paul and his friends making Garrett do things he shouldn't be doing, but that wasn't it either. It was the thrill that called to him, and even as he knew he shouldn't be there, he couldn't stop himself. Paul's house became a magnet for him; a drug he could not ignore.

The weekend after Garrett moved out of their parents' house, Renly rode his bike over to Paul's and hid in the oleander shrub, watching the people come and go. Garrett was there! He was living there!

They were having a party; personal transport vehicles filled the street outside. A group of men showed up and left guards at the front door. Anyone who tried to come inside the house was turned away. He decided to try to get closer.

His heart pounded as he crept quietly toward the overturned couch in the back yard. A group of big men were in the kitchen with Garrett and Paul. The man who spoke had a soft voice. Such a quiet, calm voice, it was difficult to hear over the booming music blasting from the house across the street. He could just barely see Garrett through the window of the lighted kitchen. He looked scared. There was no moon out tonight.

Renly crept closer.

From where he crouched, just below the kitchen window, he couldn't see the man with the soft voice, but he heard Garrett pleading. It sounded like he was crying. Paul too. The sound of grunts and groans came to him. The soft voice wanted the money they owed him. Garrett and Paul kept saying they didn't have it, and begged for more time. The soft voice told them they would need to give something of value to hold until they paid what they owed...

* * *

He awoke before dawn, shivering in front of the cold fireplace. From a peg near the door, he slipped a battered sleeveless leather jacket over his thin shirt. Too big to be Okoro's; perhaps the fleece-lined garment had been left behind by a previous guest. No matter; at this hour in the morning, the frigid air held a nasty bite, and the heavy leather offered the only warmth.

Silverbeard stomped his feet in warning and shook his head as Renly approached the big traggah's stall. He'd asked Okoro to help him with the animal, but the old man told him he had no such powers to communicate with the traggahs; even his own. He suggested food and care as the only way to earn the traggah's trust, but Silverbeard had put his ears back when he'd fed him the previous evening. He couldn't afford to build the animal's trust over time; he needed to do something to win the animal over to him now.

He slipped handful of grain from the storage bin into each of the jacket's pockets, then gave a slight bow and gave the traggah the traditional Khirjahni greeting. "I am but one of many. I am herd."

The traggah looked away.

"You are herd to me, Silverbeard." Using a small cup, he measured out a quantity of grain and dropped it into the traggah's feed trough.

Silverbeard eagerly began to eat.

As the creature focused on his food, Renly picked up a curry brush and entered the traggah's stall. Tentatively, he began to brush the beast's broad, wide side. Silverbeard ignored him, but stomped his rear hoof as a warning, just as the horses at his parents stable had. Renly knew as long as he didn't interfere with the animal's dining, he would be allowed to proceed.

He ran the stiff-bristled brush across the traggah's close-clipped hide with firm strokes. "There you go, big guy," he spoke softly. Silverbeard seemed more buffalo than horse, more moose than antelope. More wild than domesticated. He had never had his hands on such a powerful animal.

"I need your help. We've got to go back for K'Sati. You know K'Sati?" Renly fixed a mental picture of the young woman in his mind.

Silverbeard stopped eating long enough to glance over his shoulder at him for a moment, and then turned back to the trough.

Certainly, the traggah seemed to understand, or at least respond to K'Sati's name. His ears no longer lay flattened against his skull. K'Sati had been convinced he could communicate with the traggahs. If ever there was a time to do so, now was it. He leaned against Silverbeard and spoke softly, echoing the words he spoke in his mind. "We must to go back to the temple and find K'Sati. We must go now. Will you allow me to ride you?"

The traggah backed away from the empty trough, snorting, and shaking his head. He pawed at the hay on the floor. It didn't take an empath to figure out what he meant.

Renly sighed and shook his head. He couldn't understand why these creatures were so difficult to control; especially since they adapted so easily to racing. They were intelligent, he knew. They were herd animals; K'Sati said they naturally *wanted* to bond. Maybe she was right; it wouldn't hurt to try. He remembered what Rima told him about calling the wild traggahs and decided to try.

He took a handful of grain and backed into the far corner of the stall, and eased himself down into the straw. He closed his eyes and breathed deeply; each exhalation emptying his mind of thought, using the same technique he'd used as a kid when he was looking for Garrett.

He opened his mind.

I am Renly. I am but one of many. My herd is far away, and I am alone. I would bond with you, Silverbeard, if you allow it. You carried me to help when I was poisoned and in return, I pledge my friendship to you. I will feed you and care for you and warn you of danger as long as I am able. You are herd to me, Silverbeard.

A moment later, he felt the warm breath of the traggah along his cheek. In his mind, a bright light flared, like the flame of a single candle. A voice that was not a voice, but more of a feeling resonated within him.

I am Silverbeard of the stripe-legs clan. You protected me from the Rahgs in the forest. You have fed and cared for me. I will not leave you, through the Rahgs may chase us through the trees, the longteeth may surround us on the steppes, and the craggons may seek to snatch us into the sky. You are herd to me, Renly.

With a start, he remembered the animals tracking them through the forest the previous evening. Whatever Rahgs were, he was certain he had done nothing intentional to drive them off, but if Silverbeard thought so, he wouldn't argue the point.

The traggah bowed his head to eat the grain from his hand. He caressed the sides of Silverbeard's huge head, gazing into the creature's intelligent eyes. *"We must go back to the temple and free K'Sati. She is our friend."*

The light in his brain flared a moment, and the image of K'Sati's traggah came to him. "You're right," he whispered. "We've got to get Neatfoot, too."

The traggah let out a huge shuddering sigh, and shook himself. As Renly got to his feet, he noticed the change in Silverbeard's demeanor. The resistance between them was gone. Tension disappeared from Silverbeard's expression. As if there had never been any distance between them at all. And he knew, without a doubt, that the traggah was bonded to him.

In a way, the bond went in both directions.

* * *

He made a gift of one of his burins with a vee-shaped diamond tip to Okoro. In return, the old man let him keep the jacket and gave him a length of stonewood with a loop of leather on one end for his wrist, and a rounded burl at the business end, like a shillelagh.

"Use this to fend off lizards or other predators," he warned Renly. "Much better than metal, because the rockpies and craggons aren't attracted to wood."

Renly hefted the club in his hand. The grip was comfortable, the balance good. He shoved the handle end beneath his belt. "What's a rockpie?"

Okoro grimaced. "Big lizards. Not poisonous, but they are persistent. They live in the rocks. They will attack anything that looks like metal."

Silverbeard stood gentle as a pony as he swung himself astride his back. The second sun peeked over the horizon as he said his goodbyes to Okoro and Rima. Ten minutes later, the cottage was lost behind them in the trees, and they trotted purposefully toward the Temple of the Mother.

SEVENTEEN

Renly waited impatiently in the woods until full dark. He watched the lights of the Temple come up as full darkness set in. Silverbeard had been able to sniff out the room where K'Sati was being held at the far end of the dormitory wing. All the windows in that wing were barred, and none were large enough to squeeze through, but none of that mattered. For perhaps the first time in his life, he felt eager to take action.

He waited until the stable master went off to his hut before venturing into the barn. The only light came from a shielded lamp at the workbench. He searched for a tool or saw for cutting through the bars, but found nothing suitable. A couple of stout woven ropes would have to do. Neatfoot whistled softly to him, and came to the bridle; almost as if she recognized his new kinship with Silverbeard as a shared bond as well.

As he led her out of the barn, one of the other traggahs whistled after them. Renly froze, but the lights in the stable master's cottage remained dark. He waited in the shadows with Neatfoot for a few long minutes, waiting for his vision to adjust to the starlight. Neatfoot was eager to join up with Silverbeard, and he had to hold her reins tight to keep her subdued.

With both traggahs in tow, he made his way to the end window of the dormitory wing and caught K'Sati's attention by throwing pebbles into the narrow window.

"Renly, what are you doing here?" she hissed.

"They told me you and Paul went back to the coast and at first, I believed them. Come on, let's go."

"The door is locked."

I knew it! Satisfaction flooded through him. "Why?"

There was a pause. "It is a long story; too long to explain now. K'Takiweah will not allow me to leave."

"Hang on." He maneuvered Silverbeard closer to the window. The metal bars seemed to be set solidly, as far as he could tell. He doubted they would break under pressure, but the brick and mortar walls were another matter. He wove and knotted one end of the rope through the bars and told her to stand back.

He made a large loop at the other end and slipped the rope around Silverbeard's neck; settling it at the tops of his shoulders.

The traggah seemed to understand what he wanted. Silverbeard strained at the rope, but the bars held. Neatfoot became very excited, and positioned herself at Silverbeard's side, as if to help, so he tied a second rope around the bars, and looped it over Neatfoot's head as he'd done for Silverbeard.

They strained against the ropes and large cracking sounds echoed across the grounds. A light went on in one of the dormitories. And then another.

They were running out of time.

"Come on," he urged the traggahs. "Go, go!"

With a loud crash, the wall collapsed into a crumbling cloud of debris, leaving a gaping hole. The shouting of panicked women reached him, and the lights in the stable master's cottage went on.

"Where are you?"

She emerged from a cloud of dust and rubble, and grabbed Neatfoot's reins. "Follow me!"

He swung up onto Silverbeard's back and they raced toward the blackest part of the forest.

EIGHTEEN

Only the thinnest sliver of moon hung in the night sky above them as they raced through the darkened woods. K'Sati impatiently wiped her tears of against the fabric of her shirt. She was glad for the darkness; awkward in the presence of the Terran who just saved her life.

Why he would return for her, based only on the slightest of introductions, and bring down the wall of the dormitory to help her escape the temple made no sense. No Khirjahni would do such a thing.

The sacred temple trained priestesses to serve the Spirit of the Mother. It mattered not that under K'Takiweah's leadership, the temple philosophy had become twisted. Much had changed since she fled the temple seven years ago. K'Takiweah had the orphans and acolytes locked into their cells at night. Dedication to the Mother of All was no longer a choice for the girls raised within the temple; they all served K'Takiweah now.

To her horror, one of the younger acolytes explained that any who did not fervently and wholeheartedly worship K'Takiweah as the living Mother of All were culled from the herd in a ritual purification sacrifice.

K'Takiweah had obviously gone completely mad; but no one in the temple dared to question her. Only the moon's position in the sky had spared her from the purification rites. Only one night remained until K'Takiweah would have cut her still-beating heart from her chest on the now desecrated altar of the Mother. She never thought she would leave the temple alive. Never in her wildest dreams would she have imagined a rescue by the off-worlder.

He had no idea what he'd done.

She halted several times to listen for the sounds of pursuit, but heard only the sounds of the night forest. She wanted to stop and talk to the Terran, but they would have to wait until she was certain of their safety.

Renly, she reminded herself. *His name is Renly. He came back for me. No one has ever come back for me. Not my father. Not my mother.*

She did not remember her mother, and the priestesses only knew her father was a dirt-eater; one of many disillusioned Terran miners who had gone into the Forbidden zone to look for gold and never returned, but not before he'd impregnated her mother.

The Temple of the Mother did not turn away orphans or babies born out of wedlock, but there had always been a bias against mixed race offspring, especially the children of dirt-eaters. The other children treated her badly, and the priestesses ignored her, but she never knew any other way.

She leaned low against Neatfoot's neck, avoiding the low-hanging branches. Behind her, Silverbeard struggled to keep up, handicapped by the ridiculously heavy bag Renly insisted on keeping with him.

The traggahs became her family. She understood them, and they her. They accepted her unconditionally as a member of the herd; in turn, she trusted them with her life. Until the age of five, she spent all her time at the stables, even sleeping in the stall with the old grey patriarch of the temple herd, Momo.

At five, she was initiated as an acolyte, the priestesses moved into her small cell in the temple dormitory. She spent her days in school, but all her free time, she spent among the traggahs, cleaning the stable, feeding them, tending to their needs, or, as she grew older, riding them into the forest or into the rocklands.

Behind her, Renly grunted and fell from Silverbeard's back. She reined in Neatfoot and circled back to them. He lay unconscious, his pulse strong and steady. Exhaustion, probably. Earthlings were such fragile creatures. She never expected him to survive the tree lizard bite. He was certainly the most surprising Terran she had ever encountered. She'd been only ten when she'd been bitten, and still remembered feeling weak for a long time afterward.

She got her shoulder under him and half-led, half-dragged him off the trail to a copse where the trees grew closer together. He his bare arms and face felt cold as death. After the traggahs bedded down to sleep, she helped him to a spot sheltered between their warmth, just as she'd done so many times herself when she'd followed the herd out on the plains. Their bodies blocked the wind, and radiated enough heat to keep out the worst of the wind and cold. When she'd travelled with the herd as a runaway, she slept snuggled up beneath the long strands of their shaggy coats, but the coats of racing traggahs were clipped short. She worried he might freeze to death. Even asleep, he kept a tight grip on his pack, so she curled herself around him and allowed the warmth of their shared body heat soothe her to sleep.

* * *

The next morning, his color and vigor returned. As the traggahs made their breakfast on the forest vegetation, he asked her why she'd been imprisoned, and why the Temple Mother had lied to him.

"You must understand. Traggahs are the sacred ancestors of the Khirjahni people, but my father was a dirt-eater. My mother abandoned me at the temple as a baby.

"They locked you up because your father was Terran?" He sounded incredulous

She shook her head. "This is difficult to explain to off-worlders, and even more difficult to explain to you. In days before the off-worlders came, Khirjahni tribesmen were able to mind-speak with their traggahs, but this ability has been lost by all but a few blessed by the Mother of All."

"I was born with this ability. I recognized the same ability in you at the stable that day. I now believe my empathy for the traggahs might be something I inherited from my Terran father. Are here other Terrans blessed with the gift of mind-speak?"

He shrugged. "It's not common, if that's what you mean. Most people don't believe in it. My brother and I; well, we share a connection like you said. I don't remember ever attempting to communicate with an animal before. I didn't know it would work on Terran animals. Some Terrans claim they can communicate with animals. Nobody gets locked up for it, though."

"Had I not been raised in the temple, my gift would not have been such an issue. But the priestesses all decided I had the favor of the Mother of All. It marked me as the Queen Mother's successor. Only the chosen of the Mother of All are blessed with the gift of her visions.

"I was brought before K'Takiweah and forced to admit the traggahs spoke to me every day. I protested that I did not receive visions from the Mother of All, but K'Takiweah would not listen. She felt threatened by my affinity for the traggahs. This was something she did not have. For the daughter of a dirt-eater would have this ability, where she, the Queen Mother did not, was an insult to her personally, and a grievous affront to the sanctity of the temple.

"She claimed the Mother of All spoke to her, and demanded I undergo the rites to become a priestess. I did not want to do this, but I had no choice but to obey. My days were spent in forced meditation, education, and prayer; at night they locked me into my cell. They forbid me to leave the temple.

"I decided to run away when I heard the other girls whispering about how K'Takiweah was not ready to step aside. She told her inner circle that I was an abomination; a false oracle. No child of a dirt-eating off-worlder would live to become the Queen Mother.

"In the temple, the Daughters of the Herd are taught herb lore and healing, but only the Queen Mother knows how to use the poisons of our world for pain control and healing. She alone knows how to cure the deadly tree dragon bite. As the time for my initiation into the temple neared, I heard rumors that I would be poisoned before I ever took my vows. I feared for my life.

"Two nights before the initiation, I pretended to be sick during Morning Prayer, and instead of going back to my cell, I escaped on the back of the old traggah, Darkwind. After many hard days travel, we rejoined Darkwind's herd out on the steppes. For the rest of the summer and fall, I lived the life of a solitary nomad; following the herd by day, sleeping in the warm shelter of Darkwind's thick plush coat at night. In my temple training, I learned which herbs and roots to eat, and the herd accepted and protected me from the wild animals of the steppes as they would one of their clan."

The memories of Darkwind and her simple life with the herd pulled at her. "Off-worlders do not understand the Khirjahni concept of family. For us, it means not only the family of our birth, but also our natal herd clan and their home range. Darkwind's herd was my also my birth mother's herd clan. They accepted me as family. The lands of the clan territory became my home. I feared K'Takiweah, and vowed never to return."

"Until I got bit by that lizard."

"I see your eyes are now marked like mine. I did not think a Terran could survive a tree lizard bite." She smiled ruefully. "To be honest, I did not want to take you to the temple at all. Even after so much time had passed, I was afraid. But when we arrived, I saw Golden Boy in the corral. While they were attending to you, I tried to sneak out with him. K'Takiweah recognized me, and made me her prisoner."

She took his injured hand. Although still swollen, his hand had returned to normal size, the marks left by the lizard's sharp fangs had blackened and the skin started to slough off. "Why did you come back for me?"

"I had a lot of time to think before I got to Okoro's house. I couldn't understand why you and Paul would return to the coast without sending someone back for me. I told Okoro about it, and he said he hadn't seen you. He also told me that some Arkady men had come by asking questions. At first, I thought you had sent someone back for me after all. I figured one of the men had to be with the barn manager Wayne Strickman. He'd been my escort while I was looking for Garrett."

K'Sati felt faint. If Wayne found her...

"But Okoro said they were only looking for you and Golden Boy. They didn't mention me at all. It didn't make sense, if you'd already left the temple, like she told me. That's how I figured out she'd lied to me." His eyes bored into hers. "I don't like being lied to."

"She has lost her senses." Her lips trembled. "She would have killed me, and no one would ever know. Thank you."

"No problem." He looked away, as if uncomfortable with her

gratitude. "So where do we go from here? I'm still looking for Garrett, and you're still looking for Golden Boy. Seems to me we're both looking for Paul. Do you have any ideas?" He hefted his pack over his shoulder.

The realization hit her hard. She could not return without the traggah, and had nowhere else to go. The stable had been her home for nearly four years. "The final race is in a few days. If I can return him before then, they will slip him into one of the other preliminary qualification races. I must convince Paul to trade Golden Boy for Silverbeard. Or Neatfoot. I am certain he does not realize what he has done."

"And I just want to talk to him; so we're together in this, right?"

She nodded.

"How are we going to find him in all…this?"

The after-effects of the tree lizard toxin had left deep purple bruises beneath his eyes, and his face still bore deep lines from the seams of the pack he'd slept on. He did not look strong enough to accompany her, but she could not bear to tell him so.

"All the traggahs in the stable are bonded as a herd," she explained. "As you now bonded with Silverbeard, you can sense his bond with Neatfoot, and her link with me. I can sense all the presence of all of the Arkady racing traggahs, and to a much lesser degree, their natal clans. The closer they are, the stronger their presence feels to me. Golden Boy feels very, very close. He is less than a mile or two ahead of us."

Renly's gaze sharpened. "You think he's still with Paul?"

She nodded. "I cannot understand why they are so near." She gathered up Neatfoot's reins, and using the traggah's flexed foreleg as a step, climbed onto her back.

"I'm going with you."

"Transport ships will begin departing from Aurum in the next few days. The last of them will leave in less than a week. If you miss your ship, you will be trapped here for another four Earth years."

He stared down the road ahead of them. "I came here to find my brother. Paul is the only person who can take me to him, and I'm pretty sure that's where he's headed. That's why he didn't want to talk to me. Where does this trail go?"

"Ahead of us are the Rocklands, where a mob of rockpies can strip flesh from your bones in minutes. Once they clear the Rocklands, they will be out on the steppes, where we will not be able to catch him on Golden Boy. The best we will be able to do is follow him to wherever he is going. We have no food or water or shelter with us, and without the protection of a herd, we will be targeted by predators." She stared down him. "Leave now, and the coast is a two day ride."

"How do you expect to get Golden Boy back by yourself?"

She had no answer. She hoped to approach the pair while Paul was asleep, and counted on the presence of Neatfoot to tempt Golden boy into coming with her, but she knew her odds for success depended on luck. The time for luck had passed. In a few hours, they would be through the rocklands, and the opportunity to catch up with them would be gone.

"That's what I thought." He scrambled clumsily up onto Silverbeard. "Look. You can sense Golden Boy and he's with Paul. I'm looking for Paul, and you'll need my help to get Golden Boy back. We're in this together, right? Come on, we're wasting time."

* * *

By mid-morning, the forest had thinned and K'Sati spotted the Rocklands just ahead of them; a stretch of boulders and broken rocks broken only by a rough game trail. Steep, treacherous footing and the scavenging rockpie lizards living amongst the rocks and crevices created a natural barrier between the forest and the high plains of the steppes.

She could sense Renly's anxiety escalate with every step; even the traggahs seemed nervous. Several times she asked if he would rather return to the coast, but he merely shook his head. She eyed the heavy pack he carried across his shoulder, and reined in Neatfoot to match Silverbeard's pace.

"Those metal buckles on that pack will attract the lizards. You should leave it here."

He paled when she mentioned lizards, but shook his head. "No way. This is my life. I'd as soon leave my legs behind." He shifted the pack around to a position on his hip.

"If the rockpies mob you, you will leave more than your legs behind. The extra weight affects Silverbeard. Maybe you could hide your pack someplace off the road and pick it up when we return."

He gave her a tight-lipped glare. "I'm not leaving it, and I'm not going back."

She urged Neatfoot into a trot. "As you say. Keep close and whatever you do, do not fall." She kicked Neatfoot into a lope, and they galloped up the rising trail into the Rocklands.

NINETEEN

Stiff winds buffeted Wayne and his men as they struggled to control the battery-powered sleds out on the prairie. Corey rode up in front vehicle with Lyle, while he and Nevers each piloted their own. The sleds weren't designed to operate in these conditions, but they had nothing better. No wheeled vehicle could get through the rocklands, and no other transport had enough payload to carry a full-grown traggah; even an unconscious one.

The black mood that followed him from the coast seemed to get blacker with every passing moment. His orders to bring back Golden Boy and whoever took him carried a dire threat he took seriously. Wayne gritted his teeth against the stinking gale. The reek of sulfur was always stronger out on the plains; the prevailing winds blew from the interior, where the volcanoes in the Forbidden Zone belched their flatulent gasses.

Every time one of them inched their sled up a bit in elevation for a better view of the empty landscape, a gust of near hurricane-force winds swept up beneath the transport platform and threatened to tip the pilot and all their gear. They lost one sled that way, when Corey got careless, and the wind slammed the heavy sled against a stony outcrop; one of many which dotted the landscape. Luckily for Corey, he walked away without a scratch. Idiot luck.

For the first time since he'd been sent to prison all those years ago, Wayne worried about his future. Not scared, but rattled. The meeting in the boardroom caught him flat-footed with neither a friend to back him up, nor a plan to save himself. Richard Blaylock somehow discovered he'd been betting on the races; something Arkady prohibited out of concern for conflict of interest, even though everybody did it. And they forced him to stand there and take it while red-faced Ed Duprees and the rest of the board laid into him.

They piled the conference table high with the gold and credits they'd confiscated from his so-called private apartment in the executive housing. The assholes stole his money, and then claimed it for themselves!

Lyle waved him over, shouting something, but the wind whipped the words out of his mouth. He steered the sled over to the tracker stood.

"We're not going to find anything in this wind, Boss." Unlike the rest of them, Lyle had the sense to wrap one of those woolen scarves around his head and over his mouth. "Fifty to one they're laying up behind one of these outcroppings, and there are millions of square miles of 'em. We don't have a chance in hell of finding 'em until the winds let up and we can get these sleds more than four inches above the ground. Not even the wild traggah herds move around much in this weather."

Lyle was one of the few Arkady men who familiar with the Khirjahni terrain beyond the coast. He guided the teams into the steppes to capture the yearling traggahs for the gold races.

Nevers had been part of his crew back in prison, and then in the mines. Wayne knew he and Nevers could easily handle K'Sati and whoever she had with her. Nevers suggested bringing Corey along to help with Golden Boy. Corey was a big, dumb, strapping kid who did what he was told.

"And what are these doing in your possession?" Blaylock tossed a few packets of the dream dust he'd taken from that damn junkie, Jason. Of all the bad luck. He didn't remember pocketing them. "You're under house arrest until we can arrange transport for you back to the mines."

Wayne clenched his fists, ready to take a swing and anybody who dared to lay a hand on him, but Ed Duprees stepped in just in time. "Hold on, Richard. This is not your call."

Blaylock looked as if he might have a fit, but kept his mouth shut.

Wayne went on the attack. "Those don't belong to me. I confiscated 'em from a guy hanging around the stables. Claimed to be a friend of the blacksmith's, but I told him he was on company property. I made him turn out his pockets. Musta forgot about 'em. If you'll give me a chance to speak, I can explain all of this. I got a plan to get the traggah back, but we're losing time here, Mister Duprees. Every minute counts."

One of the board members, Kenson, interrupted. "Mr. Blaylock told us the Khirjahni stable girl who stole Golden Boy is your girlfriend. Is this true?"

Wayne fought to keep his temper. The look of distaste on the faces of the men in the room told him exactly what they were thinking. What a bunch of hypocrites. "She's half Terran. And she's not my girlfriend. She's a nut job."

"Careful, Strickland," Blaylock gloated. "We have security camera footage of you and her together."

Damn! A trickle of sweat rolled down the side of his face. He hadn't decided what to do about K'Sati yet, but when he did, he would find a way to make it painful for her and satisfying for him.

Danby Coles, the Chairman, twisted the knife in his ribs. "I've heard from two other stable owners who tell me one of our stable girls came to them and begged them to hide two of our traggahs until after the final race. She claimed you instructed her to have them destroyed."

After that, everyone turned a deaf ear to his explanations, and even Duprees refused to look at him, even as he argued he hadn't done anything they wouldn't have done. They were looking for a scapegoat.

"Boss?" Lyle caught his attention. "What you want to do?"

Black clouds obliterated the suns. Probably less than an hour until first sunset, anyway. "What's the forecast?"

"Winds expected to drop off sometime by midnight. Should be clear tomorrow."

Damn. If only they'd left a day earlier. He'd pulled out every trick he could think of to persuade the board to let him go after Golden Boy and the thieves who took him. This was his only chance at getting his money back. If they hadn't spent nearly two whole days making up their minds, he would have had this mess cleared up already. And now they'd wasted two more days with only a wrecked sled to show for it. At most, they had three days left to find Golden Boy and get him back to the coast in time to qualify for the final.

He horked up a lungful of dust and spat disgustedly. "All right. Find us a place to camp out of this damn wind."

They came equipped with enough provisions for a ten-day search. In addition to the tranquilizer guns for the traggah, they had plenty of firepower and ammunition. Lyle warned them about the long teeth and the wolf-like rahgs, which patrolled much of the temperate zone. Wayne had never encountered any of the planet's apex predators, and had no desire to do so.

But wild animals aside, Dupree told him if he didn't bring

Golden Boy back in time for to run the qualifier for the final, he would personally deliver him to the ice-mine pitmaster in chains, and he would never take another breath as a free man.

Wayne was not about to let that happen.

TWENTY

Silverbeard pounded up the slope, while Renly gripped the crest of his mane in both hands. The forest road they'd been following had disintegrated into a two-foot-wide dirt track running between shoulder-high boulders. Now that they'd left the canopy of open forest, the weak suns warmed the morning air to something above freezing, barely. The air felt drier here; the sounds of traggah hooves beats echoed eerily off the rocks, like drums all around them. The winding trail rose steeply as they gained altitude.

From the top of nearly every boulder, reptilian heads turned to stare at them. A sea of lizards surrounded them. Rockpies, K'Sati had called them. These things were as big as dogs. Big dogs. Big, grey, crusty dogs, yawning in the morning sun, their sweet pink tongues belying the sharp-looking serrated teeth. They must have weighed seventy or eight pounds each. He dug his heels into Silverbeard's ribs, urging the traggah to catch up with Neatfoot. Instantly, every head turned toward him, and the lizards scrambled over each other; their attention immediately focused on the jingle of the buckles on his pack.

A fat lizard launched itself off a boulder at them. Silverbeard whistled an angry warning and sidestepped to avoid the attack, nearly unseating Renly, but the steep rocks lining the narrow trail made it difficult to evade the attack. More lizards surged forward, crowding onto the boulders closest to the path. K'Sati and Neatfoot were already a hundred yards ahead. The road reminded him of a gauntlet, as lizards climbed on top of each other for the best vantage point to launch themselves.

With a handful of Silverbeard's mane in one hand, he clamped his legs to the big buck's side and slowly eased the stonewood club out from beneath his belt. When the next lizard launched himself at them, he swung hard, and the creature went down with the satisfying sound of a crushed skull. Silverbeard's ears perked up.

Again and again, the lizards lunged at them from the boulders, and as the traggah eluded them on the right, Renly beat them back with the stonewood club on the left.

Up ahead, Neatfoot whistled loudly. Silverbeard answered, and surged ahead; Renly heard shrill, angry whistles and squeals coming from the somewhere ahead of them. The lizards too, turned toward the sounds, and as he rounded a turn, he understood why.

At a wide spot in the trail, Paul and Golden Boy were surrounded by rockpies. Paul lay trapped beneath the traggah he'd been riding. The downed traggah, was in an absolute state of panic; lathered and stinking, the whites of his eyes wide and staring, unable to rise. At his throat, swarmed five large lizards. Their jaws clamped to the poor traggah's airway, while Golden Boy fought off the encroaching tide of lizards with his hoofs; trampling as many as came close.

Renly sensed Silverbeard's outrage as the traggah leapt into the fray, stamping lizards to death beneath his feet in his determination to reach Golden Boy and Paul. Paul lay unmoving in the dirt, his filthy clothes shredded, bloody, and torn.

Time slowed, even as everything seemed to happen at once.

He slid from Silverbeard's back and began bludgeoning the lizards at the fallen traggah's throat, but realized almost at once that the poor thing was dead. Neatfoot joined Silverbeard and Golden Boy in attacking the lizards, whose attention was now focused on snatching quick bites from the dead traggah.

K'Sati knelt at Paul's head, her hand on his pulse. "He's alive, but we've got to get him out of here," K'Sati said. "There are too many of them!"

Paul's eyes fluttered. Renly pulled open the lid, noting the pupil's slow response to light. His eyes didn't look normal. Given his history, drugged, probably.

Disgusted, Renly motioned to K'Sati to help him drag Paul clear of the dead traggah. If they hadn't come along, when they had Golden Boy would probably have battled those lizards until he had no more strength left. Anger raced like fire through his veins.

All three traggahs were covered in blood; mostly lizard. They screamed furiously as they stuck at the lizards, stomping them wherever they could. The attack began to falter, as the lizards seemed somewhat reluctant to continue their suicidal charge in the face of such an array of deadly hooves. They turned their attentions to the fallen, and the feeding frenzy began; both on the dead traggah and the trampled and mangled corpses of their own kin.

K'Sati helped him get Paul's unconscious body tied to Golden Boy's saddle, and swung himself up on Silverbeard. As the rockpies feasted on the dead, they made their escape from the rocklands.

* * *

Minutes later, they emerged onto the high prairies of the steppes. The magnitude of the expanse of the open landscape around them made Renly uncomfortable. An endless sea of grey-green vegetation stretched before them, broken only by scattered islands of crumbled stone. Great fangs of distant purple mountains framed the horizon in nearly every direction, reaching such heights as if to bite the sky itself. The wind buffeted them in an invisible, malevolent force, as if to say, *go back; you are not welcome here.*

K'Sati led them to an outcrop; a jumble of wind-sculpted stones rising above the grassland. One the lee side, they found a shallow cave, not much more than a crevice, which sheltered them from the worst of the winds.

"What is this place," he asked, warily.

"Do not worry. No lizards can survive here. We are on the Plains of the U'Nui-ah. This is a safe place." She dismounted and led Neatfoot and Golden Boy toward the back of the cave.

The inside of the blackened crevice smelled like old smoke and charcoal. Renly helped her untie the still-unconscious Paul from the back of Golden Boy and lay him against the back wall. He searched through Paul's saddlebags and pockets. To his relief, one of the saddlebags was packed tightly with dried meat, fruit, a hard cheese and a wineskin filled with water. In the other, he found a heavy blanket of rough-spun traggah wool wrapped around a dozen or so of the same brown powder packets he'd seen at Paul's place.

K'Sati was busy checking the bloody traggahs for injuries. Renly admired her quiet ease with them. The traggahs seemed grateful for her presence, and leaned into her touch. Silverbeard seemed embarrassed when as she ran her hands down his legs, and gave Renly a rather sheepish look as if to say, *I'm only being polite.*

"Are they alright?"

She nodded. "I think so, but with all that blood, I wanted to make sure." She wiped her hands on her pants. She noticed the packets in his hand. "Is that dream dust?"

"I think so. He had a lot of these empty packets back at his place."

He started to open one of the packets, but K'Sati stopped him.

"Dream dust carries the disease you Terrans call dragon pox."

He dropped the packet as if burned. "I don't understand. What the hell is he doing with that stuff?"

"Surely you have seen the mandragons."

"Yeah."

"The soil in craggon caves has hallucinogenic properties which are highly addicting to Terrans. Once addicted, few Terrans ever leave the forbidden zone. Even when they come to the coast for the Gold Festival, they must bring dirt with them, or else they go into withdrawal. They can die."

Paul moaned and stirred, but did not awaken.

"Paul is no mandragon. What's he doing with this stuff?"

She gazed at him evenly. "The most likely explanation is that Paul is heading for the forbidden zone. He stole two traggahs, and has more food than he needs. He must have a partner prospecting in the Crags of Corrah. Perhaps your brother has been supplying him with dream dust in exchange for supplies."

The explanation seemed reasonable, given Paul's history. "If dream dust is full of the pox, why would any Terran consider taking it?"

Her eyes narrowed. "As the disease progresses, mandragons become increasingly paranoid. They don't dare leave their claim, but they need someone they can trust to bring them food without leading anyone else to their camp. So they get someone close to them hooked on dream dust. This is how most Terrans become dirt eaters."

Heat rose in his face. "That's barbaric. You're saying my brother would do something like this? You don't know him. He would never--." His voice cracked.

"When the mandragon dies of the pox, the new mandragon takes over the claim. This is what happened to my father."

He took a deep breath. If true, Sully and the other mandragons at the gold ball had all done the same thing. *Not likely.* "I'm sorry about your father, but you must be mistaken. Paul has always been a junkie, a liar, and a low-life. He'll do anything for a high. He probably bought this stuff off one of the mandragons."

"The addiction is specific to the particular craggon den. Once the pox has takes hold, the user is hooked on dirt from that particular claim. No other dirt will help."

He didn't want to believe her. *Couldn't* believe her. "When he wakes up, he can tell us and we'll both know."

"Get up." He shoved Paul's inert form with his toe. "I know you're awake."

Paul did not respond. Outside the shallow cave, the wind howled. An old ring of blackened stones and charcoal stood at the very back wall, but they had no fuel to start a fire. He used a strip of leather he found in Golden Boy's saddle to bind Paul's hands behind him.

K'Sati took a long swallow from the water skin and offered it to him. "Why are you so angry at him?"

He shook his head. "I don't like being lied to. I don't like being tricked. He sent me off to buy him drugs by saying he would die without them. On Earth, we have drugs like that, so I believed him, but as soon as I left, he ran. He knows where Garrett is, he just doesn't want to tell me. He's a liar and a manipulator, and he always has been."

"I do not understand. Why would he not tell you where your brother is?"

The memories flooded though him. It wasn't just his own childish jealousy of Paul that made him distrust Garrett's best friend. Their parents banished him from the house and grounds for stealing and instructed Garrett not to associate with him. But it made no difference.

Every moment Garrett spent outside the house, he was with his best friend, Paul Hite.

Much of his childhood memories were of trying to keep up with them. Part of it, he admitted, was the fascination every younger brother has to tag along after his older sibling, and part of it was to see for what Garrett and Paul did when they were off doing those BAD things; but some of it was curiosity about what those BAD things were...

"They always covered for each other when we were kids. Once, the police came to our house looking for Paul, and my brother told them they weren't even friends anymore, which wasn't true. And he would never tell me where Garrett was when I asked him. He's just always been that way."

Truth was, he resented the hell out of Paul, and always had.

Strong arms grabbed him from behind. He squirmed and yelled and kicked, but was hauled into the unfamiliar bright kitchen and dumped like a sack of garbage on the floor.

"I found this kid peeking in the window."

Garret cursed and shouted at him for spying on them and ruining everything. They taped his hands and legs together and taped his mouth shut. His heart pounded so hard he could barely breathe,

The quiet man had gold teeth and black eyes. He looked like the devil. Even afterward, his eyes and hands were the only features he ever remembered about the man who abused him. The quiet man pulled Renly onto his lap.

"I won't have the money until Friday," Garrett said. His empty face held no emotion. It was like he didn't even care. Renly knew instinctively that this must have been Paul's doing.

Garret would never leave him with this awful man. Renly closed his eyes in shame against the warm wetness spreading across his thighs. No one said anything. It couldn't be real.

But it was. They put a hood over his head and took him with them. They put him in the transport and drove around for what seemed like hours. Shielded behind the smoked glass privacy windows, the man ran tore his soiled clothes off of him. After he was naked, the man's iron hands wouldn't stop.

"Are you alright?" She was looking at him expectantly, twisting her neck scarf between her fingers.

"What?"

"I said I must get Golden Boy back to the Arkady Stables as soon as possible."

He took a step back. "Oh. Of course." He'd forgotten. Or maybe he just hadn't thought through what would happen once they caught up with Paul. "You mean now?"

"No, in the morning. First sun has already set."

"What about the rock lizards?"

"I know another way. I will take Golden Boy at first light. With his speed, we will be back in time to for him to run his qualifier." She smiled, but her eyes looked worried. "I will leave Silverbeard and Neatfoot with you and Paul."

He'd never even considered she would leave him alone out here. Well, not exactly alone, but the idea of following Paul out into this lizard-infested wilderness seemed like suicide right now. But of course, she had her own life to worry about.

"If you bring him back alone, won't they think you stole him?"

She paled. "Getting him back in time for the race is the most important thing. I will be…fine.".

Paul opened his eyes and rolled to his side. A smile curled at the edges of his mouth. "Not if that big boyfriend of yours has anything to say about it. I wouldn't want to be in your shoes when Wayne finds you."

She blushed and looked scared.

He shoved Paul roughly with his foot. "Nobody asked you. You're the reason for all of this mess." He turned to her. "Does he mean Wayne Strickland?"

She nodded. "He's responsible for stable security. I will be fine."

She didn't sound at all certain.

Paul finally seemed to notice his hands were tied. "Hey, cut me loose; you can't do this!"

The quiet man with the devil eyes took him down into a filthy basement and chained him to a bolt set into the cement floor. There was a wall sink and a filthy mattress and bucket. No windows. No way to tell the passage of time. Renly tried to guess how long it would be until Friday.

The quiet man with the hard hands and black eyes told him to call him Papa. They only brought him food after he'd done what Papa wanted. Every time he came to the basement, it seemed like he stayed for hours. Every time he left, Renly vowed he would kill himself rather than let that man do those things to him again, but he was naked, chained, and helpless. And what could a ten-year-old boy do against such a hard, bad man?

She moved as if to untie Paul.

"Don't!" He debated what to tell her. "You don't know him like I do. He's dangerous."

Paul managed to squirm into a sitting position. "Come on, K'Sati.

You know me. Not a mean bone in my body. I've never raised a hand against anyone."

Anxiety gripped Renly like a vise. "Shut up!"

K'Sati stared at him as if he'd lost his mind, and Silverbeard whistled nervously.

He took a deep breath. "When I was a kid, Paul got involved with a loan shark, and dragged my brother into it. When he couldn't pay, the loan shark kidnapped me." He shrugged at the shocked expression on her face. "Paul knew who did it, but he never said a word."

Her hand went to her mouth.

He had no memory of the rescue. His parents told him later, he'd been unconscious, emaciated, and severely dehydrated when Garrett led the police to the place where he'd been buried alive. His parents told him Garrett had dreamed of him calling out to him. In the dream, he recognized the place where his kidnapped younger brother had been buried inside an old packing crate. If not for the brothers' psychic connection, Renly would have died in that crate. Garrett was a hero, they told him

The police asked him questions, but months passed before he regained his ability to speak. He would nod or shake his head, or write the answers to questions, but the therapists said his own fear and anger were blocking his speech. A police sketch artist came and worked with him to come up with a picture of the man, but never got it right. Unable to explain himself, he took the pencil from her and drew the image of Papa himself. He tried to show the hardness of the man's face; the blackness of his eyes, the cruelty in his mouth, but he did not have the skills to capture the devil's image on paper. His drawings were not good enough.

His parents had been so proud of Garrett; Renly could not say anything to destroy his brother's new-found favor, and after all, he had saved him. He convinced his parents to send him to a private art school, and focused all his efforts into becoming an artist. In the beginning, he only wanted to learn to draw an image of Papa; something good enough to get him identified and arrested. His teachers told him he had real gift, but no matter how hard he tried, the image of Papa on the page would not come. In time, the joy of creation took over and he realized he had discovered his true calling, but he never spoke to Paul again. Until today.

"I was rescued after two weeks, but the police never caught him." *He stole my childhood. I was never the same.* He could see the distress on K'Sati's face. "I'm sorry. I didn't mean to upset you."

"It's not true," Paul said. "He doesn't remember any of it, but blames me anyway. I had nothing to do with it. Look at me! I'm the one who's a prisoner here. Come on, Ren. This isn't right and you know it. Cut me loose."

"Where's Garrett?"

"Cut me loose."

"Tell me where he is, damn it!"

"Please, stop it." K'Sati pushed him out of the way and kneeled beside Paul to untie him. A moment later, he was free.

"Thanks." Paul massaged his wrists. "Okay, you win. Garrett's prospecting a gold claim up in the Crags of Corrah. Are you happy now? He was supposed to meet me at the Gold Ball, but didn't show up."

Renly bit his lips to contain his emotions. Somehow, he already knew. Garret would be drawn to gold like a bee to honey. Neither dragon pox nor the forbidden zone would have stopped him.

"Why didn't you just tell me?"

Paul snorted. "I saw you arrive at the ball. You must've seen the nuggets up for auction. Garrett planned to be there too."

"You're saying he's one of those blasted mandragons?"

"What do you think?"

He was too late. "Take me to him."

"He doesn't want to see you, Ren. He won't leave; you couldn't pry him out of there with a crow bar."

"I don't believe you. He'll listen to me." He turned to K'Sati. "I told you he's scum. He knows exactly where Garrett is."

"He is not a criminal."

"He stole two traggahs, remember? One of them was Golden Boy." His own words sounded bitter to him.

She leveled her lovely gaze at him. "He didn't know it was Golden Boy."

"That's right, I didn't," Paul chimed in. "It was just bad luck."

"Funny how your bad luck always ends up as someone else's problem."

TWENTY-ONE

The next morning, the three of them set out before second sunrise, heading south. K'Sati agreed to ride with them on Golden Boy for an hour before leaving turning toward the coast. The traggahs loped easily across the prairie in a ground-eating lope, but they were skittish this morning. Silverbeard, especially, shied at every pile of boulders and bit of shrub. Ahead of him, Paul appeared to be having the same problem with Neatfoot.

Renly sensed the traggah's agitation, but could not understand the nature of the animal's alarm. All three of the traggah seemed jumpy. No sooner had he decided to ask K'Sati about it than Paul flew backwards off of Neatfoot.

The crack of a high-powered rifle echoed off the rocks.

K'Sati was already sliding off of Golden Boy and racing after Neatfoot. He sawed at Silverbeard's reins, and slid to the ground. Instinctively keeping his head low, he raced to where Paul had fallen, dragging Silverbeard along behind him. He grabbed Paul by the shoulder of his jacket and dragged him over to the boulder where K'Sati held the agitated traggahs.

"I'm hit." Paul held his hand tightly to his jaw. Blood dripped freely from behind his bony fingers. "Where did that come from?"

Renly reached into his pack and grabbed a sterile pad out of his first aid kit. "Here." He caught a quick glimpse of a deep, blood-filled furrow along the jaw line as he clapped it to Paul's jaw.

"They're coming!" K'Sati shouted.

He peeked over the rock to where she was pointing. In the distance, three great clouds of dust rose from the steps like dust devils; directly ahead of them.

"That has to be Wayne," K'Sati eyes gleamed with unshed tears, but she sounded calm. "Only hovercraft sleds kick up that much dust. They must have camped at the trailhead leading back to the coast. They were waiting for me."

He stared at her. She seemed unsurprised; resigned. "Why are they shooting at us?"

She shook her head. "They want Golden Boy. If I bring him out, I think they will let you go."

"Are you kidding, *they just shot Paul!*"

She continued as if he hadn't said anything. "The sleds are slow. The traggahs can easily outrun them." She gave him a steady look. "The sleds cannot follow you into the mountains."

She was talking about the forbidden zone. He tried to judge the distance peaks on the horizon. "You can't be thinking about going out there. They'll kill you."

"I'm with Ren on this, K'Sati." Paul pulled a packet of dream dust out of his pocked and shook it onto his tongue. He made a face, but did not spit it out. "Those boys are playing for keeps."

"Not if I have Golden Boy with me. He is the one they want. They will not shoot if he is standing next to me."

Renly ran his hand through his hair. He couldn't just let her face them alone, but they had no weapons. There had to be something they could do. "Come with us. We'll leave Golden Boy tied up here."

Her eyes met his for just a moment. She gave him a puzzled expression, but nodded.

They wrapped Golden Boy's reins around a heavy stone; not enough to hold him for long, but just enough to keep him there until the sleds got close enough to see him.

He helped Paul to his feet. The man wasn't much more than skin and bones. "No tricks, man. Take us to Garrett or I'll leave you here for them."

"Yeah," he muttered through clenched teeth. "But I'm telling you, he won't leave."

"Doesn't matter what you think."

He helped Paul up behind K'Sati on Neatfoot.

The traggahs all tensed, their ears perked at the approaching group. Neatfoot stamped and snorted, shaking her head. "If we are going to leave, now is the time," K'Sati warned.

The angry shouts of the men grew closer.

He swung himself up onto Silverbeard's broad back; noticing as he did, how quickly he'd gotten used to riding this strange alien beast.

As one, they raced across the high plains toward the distant crags of the forbidden zone. Two shots rang out behind them, but Renly kept his head low, pressed to Silverbeard's powerful neck. He heard Golden Boy's shrill whistle call after them when he realized he was left behind. A moment later, they heard nothing but the emptiness of the prairie.

TWENTY-TWO

The wind rose steadily as the morning progressed. By mid-day, sand-toothed winds buffeted them with enough force to abrade even the toughest bare skin. They cut strips off the blanket Paul had brought, and wrapped them around their knuckles and faces for protection.

A quarter of a mile ahead of him K'Sati and Paul rode Neatfoot; their heads swathed in a bit of blanket to fend off the worst of the biting winds. The two of them together probably weighed less than he and his heavy pack. He knew he was putting Silverbeard at a disadvantage, but Renly could not bring himself to discard it.

Silverbeard alerted him to the group of three wolf-like creatures tracking them. The traggah's ears went back, and he gave an angry squeal, as if to challenge them to attack. Renly spotted two apace just behind them, while a third moved up quickly on the left.

Reddish-grey, with dark mask and a thick coat, they looked a bit like a cross between a short-legged German shepherd and a badger, but bigger. Much bigger. With a cunning, toothy grin and surprising speed. He guessed them to be the rahgs K'Sati had told him about. He hunched tight as a limpet over Silverbeard's neck. K'Sati and Paul were too far away to hear him, even without the blowing gale. The traggah seemed more angry than afraid; bucking a bit and shaking his head, he gave a high-pitched squeal, as if to say, *you want a piece of this, come on then!*

Renly eased the stonewood club out from beneath his belt, and gave it a few experimental swings. While he'd never played polo on a team like Garrett, he'd fooled around with the game enough to have a feel for using a mallet while riding at a fast gallop on horseback. The club was heavier than a polo mallet, but on the other hand, the rahgs were a lot bigger target than the little wooden balls he'd played with as a boy.

A rahg darted in, snapping at Silverbeard's foreleg.

"Easy boy," Renly gripped the traggah's mane tightly in one hand, and raised the club into the strike position; with the business end of the club at the top of the arc. He felt Silverbeard tense beneath him. If the traggah stumbled and he fell off, he had no doubt that the three rahgs would tear him to pieces. He had no idea how Silverbeard would react to the swinging of the club, but he had no choice. "Steady."

He spun his wrist forward, letting the burled weight at the end of the club do the work. Silverbeard veered to the right as the club swung past his head, but he kept his seat. A miss.

Their attacker dropped back, wary of the club now. All three rahgs moved a bit further away from them, but maintained their pace; neither gaining nor losing ground. Beneath him, he Silverbeard's pace flattened out as the traggah relaxed; his ears swiveled alertly.

A mile or so later, the game changed. This time, the rahgs switched position, and the attack came from the right, almost as if they'd figured out he was left-handed.

This time, he twisted himself across Silverbeard's back, bringing his head and shoulders to the right side, holding the club vertical, but out of the way of his mount's head. The rahg raced in low, his yellow teeth looking to slash at a foreleg. Renly leaned as far as he dared, and lowered his head directly over the rahg as he dropped the knotted club and followed through with the shot, being careful to keep the club clear of Silverbeard.

The rahg yipped and peeled off, but he knew he'd missed him again.

A moment later, the rahg was back. He darted in again without warning, but this time, Renly didn't miss. He swung the club and was rewarded by a satisfying crunch of bone. The limp body of the dead rahg went tumbling behind them.

Silverbeard whistled and squealed, and the other two rahgs immediately gave up their pursuit. An hour later, a pack of five more rahgs approached, but quickly faded away into the grass when he shook the club at them.

* * *

By late afternoon, the wind changed direction again and came howling in from the north. The traggahs slowed to a trot, and squinted against the gale, their long eyelashes effectively serving to protect their vision, even as Renly was forced to cover his with the woven scrap of blanket.

Paul and K'Sati had stopped, and as he rode up, she told him they were going to make camp in a shallow basin for the night. The traggahs slaked their thirst from a tiny spring, they quenched theirs from the wineskin of water Paul had brought. While the traggahs grazed, oblivious to the near-hurricane conditions, they ate a cold meal of dried food from Paul's pack. The winds made a fire impossible, so they huddled together for warmth.

He changed the bandage on Paul's jaw, although the sight of the wound made him queasy. Paul didn't even flinch. Although the wound did not appear to be deep, the bullet appeared to have been deflected by the lower jawbone, a portion of which was now visible through the skin. The resulting scar would no doubt be disfiguring, even if the wound healed without infection.

As the darkness descended, he noticed lights on the far horizon and asked K'Sati about them.

She paled. "Two sleds. They have sensors on them. In the traggah roundups, they use them to find the herds, but I think they are using them to track us."

"They've got Golden Boy. Why are they still coming after us?"

She began to tremble. "They must have sent Golden Boy back to the stables on one of the sleds. Those two are hunting us. Me, at any rate."

His stomach lurched. "Why?"

"Because Wayne Strickland is not the forgiving type." Paul emptied another packet of dream dust into his mouth. In spite of his revulsion for the man's addiction to it, he didn't have the heart to take his drug from him. The dust seemed to alleviate most of his pain. "His bosses probably blamed him for this little fiasco. He knows they'll send 'im back to the mines if he doesn't fix it. He's not going to let K'Sati get away from him."

"You're the one to blame, not K'Sati!"

"Paul is right." K'Sati wrapped her arms around herself. "I should have known that turning over Golden Boy would not stop Wayne from coming after me. Those sleds run on battery. They are not fast, but we will never hear them coming. Distances are deceiving out here on the steppes. "

"How long until we reach the mountains?"

K'Sati didn't know, and Paul was too looped to answer.

As exhausted as he was, Renly volunteered for the first watch. Both Paul and K'Sati looked worse off than he felt. Beating off the rahgs had given him a second wind; a sense of pride. It wasn't much, but he felt stronger than he had since arriving on this godforsaken planet.

The traggahs bedded down on either side of them, further sheltering them from the howling winds. While Paul and K'Sati slept, Renly leaned up against Silverbeard's snoring back and stared at the lights in the distance.

Sometime later, he was startled awake by a warm breath on his neck. He scrambled to his feet. An entire herd of shaggy-coated traggahs surrounded them. The curious sniffer was a youngling; his breath still sweet with the milk of his mother. Silverbeard and Neatfoot gave a low gurgle of sleepy recognition, and the entire herd settled down to sleep around them. Several other traggahs sniffed him over carefully as well, before finding a place to settle. This must be their ancestral clan, he realized.

The wind dropped, and the air was heavy with cold, but surrounded as he was by the heat and security of the long-coated herd, Renly slept.

* * *

The next morning, the herd moved toward the mountains, and they followed. Renly worried about the lack of water, but K'Sati assured him that the traggahs would lead them to water before the end of the day.

Unlike their flight the previous day, the herd moved at a leisurely pace; grazing every step of the way, while the younglings gamboled and played games of tag, never straying far from their mothers and aunts. The young traggah who had woken him the night before seemed especially curious. She butted him playfully with her nubby forehead, licked his skin and nibbled at whatever bits of clothing she could sample. The younglings, with their soft grey fuzzy coats, blended perfectly into the grey-green grass when they lay down to sleep.

Renly pulled out his sketchpad. The sight of the younglings sleeping in the feathery grasses without a worry in the world touched him. As they slept, he sketched them and observed the behaviors of the herd. He noticed how every member of the herd casually edged close to the sleeping babies at one time or another and carefully sniffed the sleeping calves. Even Silverbeard seemed fascinated and took deep snuffling breaths of each of the sleeping younglings.

He had never been interested in the outdoors; nor had he ever attempted an animal portrait, but he was well-pleased with this pencil sketches. When K'Sati commented on his drawing of Silverbeard, he blushed at the compliment, as he had not done since art school days.

A little after noon, the herd led them to a low rock formation, which had been invisible until they were almost on top of it. Jagged black stones overhung the small pool where a steady burble of water seeped to the surface. K'Sati told him the traggahs used their sense of smell and something called herd memory to find water.

Once they'd filled their skins with the icy water, Renly was eager to move on, but K'Sati forestalled him.

"The herd is good camouflage for us. From a distance, they look like another stone formation. Wayne and his men will never think we are travelling with a wild herd."

Renly stroked the long matted coat of Silverbeard's mother. There had been no introductions, and he didn't know her name, but there was a, un-nameable *shape* of her name in his head. Her youngling was the curious, friendly one. Clearly the dominant female of the herd, she had somehow adopted him. The idea charmed him.

As they travelled, she took up a position just forward of Silverbeard's left shoulder, and thus, walked right beside them. At night, when she bedded down, she made sure Renly and her youngling were both sheltered between her and Silverbeard. He didn't understand it, but knew, somehow, that he had been accepted into the herd by way of his bonding with Silverbeard. Again, no words had been exchanged, but the feeling of belonging to this extended clan was undeniable. K'Sati was right. There was a sentience about the traggahs that transcended what he'd experienced with animals, even horses and dogs, on Earth.

Paul, however, was itchy and restless. "I thought you guys were in such a hurry to rescue Garrett," he whined.

He must be running low on dust. "K'Sati's right. As long as we're moving in the right direction, it makes sense to use the herd as cover."

Paul shook his head. "We could have been there already. At this rate, it'll take us two more days. The longer we're out here, the better chance Wayne and his men have of catching us. Of course, if you two want to turn back now, you'll still be able to make it back in time to catch the last transport off this bucket."

"I'm not leaving without my brother."

He shrugged. "Don't say I didn't warn you."

* * *

When the herd turned south the next day, they continued east. Some of the young males whistled forlornly after Neatfoot, but she did not seem affected. Without the herd to set the pace, they made better time, and by nightfall, Paul told them they were within a few miles of the Crags of Corrah.

The relentless wind buffeted them all day long. No matter how much water they drank, the cold, dry wind seemed to suck the moisture out of them. Renly could not remember ever being so thirsty. By noon, they'd finished the last of the water. Renly ran out of clean bandages. Paul's face remained wrapped in the same brown-stained dirty dressing they'd applied two days ago. All of them had chapped and bloody lips.

Paul, of course, blamed the traggahs. "If we hadn't a wasted time poking along with the herd, we'd be filling our skins at the base of the mountains by now."

Renly shared a glance with K'Sati. There would be no point in arguing. The herd had not only led them to water, but protected them at night from the rahgs and longteeth, the apex predators of the steppes. Every night, the sentries formed an armed ring around the herd; their impressive and dangerous horns facing out, creating a protective barrier that not even the most persistent predators dared engage.

K'Sati told him the Khirjahni feared the longteeth of the Lekhulu even more than the craggons of the forbidden zone. Longteeth possessed an excellent sense of smell, and the ability to smell blood over long distances.

"At the temple, the priestesses would tell us stories about leaving us outside at night for the longteeth if we weren't good. I used to have nightmares about them." She shivered. "Without the herd, we are extremely vulnerable."

"I've never had a problem with them," Paul bragged. "The secret is to keep moving. Anyway, we're almost there now. They won't follow us into the mountains."

Neatfoot gave an unhappy whistle and shied. K'Sati had to grab her mane to stay seated. "What's wrong?" Renly asked.

Paul pointed skyward. "Craggons." High above them, almost too high to see, two winged figures wheeled overhead.

K'Sati whirled Neatfoot around, trying to coax her into moving forward, but the traggah had other ideas. Stubbornly, she kept her head turned south.

"From now on, no shouting. Once we're in the mountains, we'll have to whisper," Paul said. "We're entering craggon territory."

Both traggahs began to fidget and pull against the reins. The circling craggons weren't much more than dark specs in the lavender sky, but Silverbeard had his ears laid back. Neatfoot, too.

"Ignore them." Paul dug his heels into Neatfoot's side; hard enough to make her grunt. "They always make a fuss like this when they get too near the mountains. They don't like being here. We'll have to blindfold them when we reach the first peak."

Renly checked the stonewood club beneath his belt. "They won't attack, will they?"

K'Sati looked extremely pale. "They're carrion eaters."

"Speaking from experience, I can tell you they *will* attack, if only you make enough noise or they catch you near their dens. The traggahs are too heavy for them to carry off, and no predator has a chance against a herd; they can stomp even an adult craggon to death. But without the herd behind us, it's a bigger question. If you catch their attention, they'll come after you. They're eyesight isn't much better than ours, but they have extremely sensitive hearing. No yelling or clanging. It makes them crazy mad. Understood?"

Renly nodded.

"And keep your eyes sharp for longteeth. Craggons often feed off their kills, and they get more common the closer we get to the mountains. We won't be safe from the longteeth until we're in the mountains; that's craggon territory." He gave them a mirthless grin. "Craggons won't tolerate anything but prey in their territory."

"Where exactly are we going?"

Paul looked away. "I don't know the name of the place, but Garrett and I call it the Yellow Chimney. We should be there day after tomorrow."

K'Sati finally got Neatfoot headed in the right direction, and with a little coaxing on his part, he got Silverbeard to follow them.

TWENTY-THREE

They reached the foot of the mountains at the end of the day, hunched over their tired mounts; parched and battered by the incessant winds. The ground rose quickly from the plains; the transition from flat grassland to chaparral to broken woodland a matter of only a few hundred feet. Here, within the mountain shadows, the angry air finally stilled. In the waning light of first sunset, Paul pointed out a game trail. Both traggahs appeared reluctant to move forward. Seated behind K'Sati, he urged the parched and now exhausted Neatfoot forward with vicious kicks to her ribs. Renly pressed Silverbeard forward as well, offering reassurance to the reluctant animal.

The trail led to a spring. Unlike the surface springs they visited out on the steppes, a mist of fog hovered over the surface of this pool. A faint mineral odor hovered over the water, but once they caught sight of the still water, the traggahs didn't hesitate. They waded in up to their knees and drank in great gulping breaths. Renly threw his leg over Silverbeard's head and slid into the pond. Using his hands as a cup, he drank until his stomach could hold no more. K'Sati and Paul followed his example.

A copse of low trees surrounded by thick brush sheltered the pool.

After sleeping exposed the last several nights, the idea of sleeping under a canopy of trees appealed to him.

"We can't stop here." Paul whispered. "Don't even think about it. We've got to keep moving."

Paul jerked on Neatfoot's reins, dragging her back toward the trail. In spite of the chill bite in the air, Paul's face and hair were damp with sweat, his eyes glassy.

Withdrawal symptoms, he guessed, although he hadn't seemed nervous earlier. Here, at least, they had water and shelter from the wind. "Come on, it's getting dark. Let's camp here tonight."

Paul wouldn't hear of it. He pointed to a myriad of animal tracks in the mud around the edge of the pond. "This is a watering hole. Every predator in the area hunts here at dusk. We don't want to be anywhere near here when they come through. There's a safer place three hours up ahead."

"We cannot travel in these mountains at night," K'Sati protested. "The traggahs are not sure-footed on rocky trails."

Dark bruises circled beneath K'Sati's beautiful eyes. She looked exhausted. Renly didn't want to keep going either, but for once, he agreed with Paul. "Three more hours? Isn't there someplace closer?"

"This is also one of the few known watering holes on the edge of the forbidden zone. You can bet Wayne Strickman and his crew will head this way," he hissed. "So will any --." Paul froze; his eyes fixed to a spot behind them.

Renly followed his stare. Two mandragons stood amid the shrubs on the far side of the spring. One of them held a laser weapon pointed in their general direction.

Instinctively, he grabbed K'Sati's arm and pulled her behind him.

The mandragons edged their way clumsily around the pond, the darker of the two keeping his weapon leveled in their direction.

Both of them seemed even more reptilian than the mandragons he'd encountered thus far. Their legs barely supported them. They wore no shoes; their claw-tipped, elongated toes gave them a ponderous, lumbering gait.

Paul swore quietly. "Keep your mouth shut and let me do the talking. They're claim jumpers. They want us to lead them to our claim. Once we do, they'll kill us all."

The one with the gun spoke first. "Where y'all heading?"

With a pang of homesickness, Renly recognized the Maryland accent. Somehow, it seemed wrong, coming from the lizard-man.

"Thank god you found us," Paul stepped forward, as if to greet them, but the mandragon with the weapon motioned to him to keep his distance. "We ran into a bit of trouble out on the plains with a posse of Arkady men. They robbed us; tried to take our woman. We were lucky to get away. Can you help us?"

The one without the gun snorted. "Yeah, right. Cut the crap. We've got you dead to rights. You're going to take us to that camp of yours."

Paul grinned and shook his head. "Oh we don't have a camp. We're just looking for a safe place to hide until they give up. Check our packs, if you want. They've taken everything."

Renly admired Paul's coolness. But then, Paul had always been a cunning liar.

The mandragons shared a glance, and nodded. "Oh sure, we'd be glad to help you out." One of them pulled a length of stout cord from his pack.

Neatfoot whistled a shrill warning. Beside him, Silverbeard began to buck. He looked to K'Sati, but she didn't have a clue, either. Only Paul seemed to understand; he grabbed the reins of both traggahs and ran up the trail, dragging the terrified traggahs right behind him.

The mandragons seemed uncertain.

The underbrush around the pond seemed to explode with rahgs. As their closest target, the heavy-footed mandragons stood no chance against the pack

K'Sati froze; petrified by the sight. Renly grabbed her by the hand and dragged her from the carnage. She fought him; mad with panic. Unable to calm her, he picked her up and threw her bodily over his shoulder, while behind them, the hoarse growls of the mandragons gave way to the sounds of tearing flesh and the crack of bones.

* * *

She recovered a short while later, but they'd lost valuable time. They raced after Paul and the traggahs as twilight deepened around them. The steep trail hampered them, but after hour, they still hadn't caught up to him. Frightened as he was of the predators behind them, Renly began to wonder if Paul was deliberately trying to lose them. As the light faded to full dark, the traggahs tracks became impossible to follow. He was no longer sure they were on the right path.

K'Sati must have been thinking the same thing. "We cannot find him in the dark." She dropped to the ground, panting. "I can go no further."

He dropped next to her, exhausted. "He's gone. He's got the traggahs, all the water, and the supplies. He doesn't need us anymore," he added, bitterly.

A sliver of moon peeked over the mountains, revealing the dark tumble of a rock formation about thirty yards off the trail. He pointed it out to her. "What do you say we wedge ourselves into the rocks for the night? Just in case those rahgs come looking for us?"

She shivered against him. "I am too tired to care anymore," she said.

He heaved himself to his feet, regretting for the hundredth time the weight of his satchel.

They found relative safety in a niche beneath a massive overhang of rock.

She curled herself against him, and fell asleep almost at once. In spite of his own exhaustion, he found himself unable to do the same. The temperatures had been below freezing since shortly after second sunset. He envied her lack of sensitivity to the cold. Even the traggah-wool-lined craggon vest couldn't stop the stone's bitter cold from seeping painfully into his bones. His face felt hot; feverish. He wondered if he was coming down with something. He realized that as soon as they left the steppes, they'd entered the forbidden zone; the one place he'd been so determined not to go.

He groaned inwardly. How had this happened? Not even K'Sati had ever been here before. Of all the places... *What am I doing here?*

He massaged the pounding headache at his temples with his fingertips. He never imaged he'd have to go through all this to find Garrett. Never thought he'd end up running away from nightmare creatures who wanted to eat him and mining executives who wanted to shoot him. What the hell?

He sighed and shook his head at the irony. Garrett and Paul came here for the gold, just like the Arkady Universal Mining Corporation and all the festival visitors. He reached into his pack and fingered the heavy bars of precious metal he'd brought with him. He was probably the only person in the universe who'd actually *brought* gold to Aurum. They had no water or food, and since Paul took the traggahs, their only way back was through a predator-infested wilderness. They could be shot by Wayne and his men, or freeze to death, or get eaten by any number of wild beasts, but by golly, he had a bag full of gold. *Isn't that just great.*

At this point, the likelihood of them surviving the freezing temperature and predators to find Garrett seemed impossible. Death now seemed to be the most likely outcome of this trip. *I do not want to die here.* All his fine posturing about owing Garrett his life seemed stupid now. A nagging little voice in his head kept whispering that Garrett would not have come this far for *him.*

He huddled closer to K'Sati's sleeping form. *I'm done with it.* It wasn't fair to drag K'Sati along with him, and he couldn't bear the thought of continuing on alone. Tomorrow they would turn around and head back down the trail and toward the coast. At least he was certain of *that* direction. He'd catch the last transport and be rid of this planet for good.

But what about Garrett?

The guilt left a sour taste in his mouth. He would never forgive himself if he left without Garrett. Or at least did everything he could to find him. He tried to remember the last time he'd felt Garrett's presence. At the race track. Maybe he really was dead. Paul didn't even know for sure. None of them would know until they reached his claim among the Crags of Corrah.

He reached for his brother, but felt only Silverbeard's sleeping presence somewhere ahead of them. Again and again he opened himself mentally, straining to detect any sense of his brother, but there was none; there was only the traggah. It was almost as if Silverbeard had taken up residence in his head, usurping Garrett's position. How odd. Even now, with Paul and the traggahs somewhere ahead of them, he could feel Silverbeard sleeping inside his head. The traggah had no worries or strong emotions as he slept; yet his mere presence seemed to block his ability to sense Garrett.

Neatfoot was there too, he realized. Fainter, but a separate, recognizable presence. Somewhere below them, out on the windswept plains, he could sense the peacefulness of the herd bedded down for the night. In fact, it seemed as if his head was filled with the gentle presence of all the traggahs. Even K'Sati was there.

She sighed in her sleep; her comforting heat warming him where their bodies touched. If Wayne and his men caught them, they would not treat them kindly, yet she had not really said anything about her relationship with Wayne or why she was so afraid of him. Paul had called Wayne her boyfriend and she had not denied it. But it seemed an odd pairing. Wayne had seemed entrenched in the Arkady hierarchy; on the other hand, her whole world seemed to revolve around the traggahs. While K'Sati's humble origins and her job at the stables made sense to him; Wayne had made his contempt for the native Khirjahni, especially the women, quite evident.

What did she see in that guy? She was nothing like Terran women he'd known. Strong, but reserved. Childlike, but not foolish. Sensitive but practical. She'd been confused by the purpose of the antibacterial wipes he'd packed in his satchel; then laughed when he ran out of them, rightly pointing out that after surviving a tree lizard bite, he was probably stronger than anything he would encounter on Aurum.

She smelled of sweet grass and dirt and tired woman. A warm scent, like horses after a good run, or the traggahs when they bedded down for the night. Every Khirjahni he'd met on this planet had been a surprise; K'Sati in particular. Independent, proud, responsive people with a sense of honor and the ability to laugh at themselves and others without spite. K'Sati's ability to connect with the traggahs, even the wild ones, seemed almost magical to him. On Earth, they called them horse whisperers.

His ex-girlfriend Sumi had been strong-willed too, but her idea of an 'outing' involved a trip to a day spa; she'd been about as natural as halogen lighting. Sumi ran their relationship like she ran her consulting firm, and he'd let her. She'd imposed strict rules on the relationship, his behavior, and their time together. Now that he thought about it, his phobias had gotten worse during their time together. If she hadn't already left him, one look at him right now would have clinched it.

They were so different; no comparison really. Of course, K'Sati was only half human; raised in a matriarchal society. Compared to the often belligerent behavior of the Arkady executives and other Terrans he'd encountered on Aurum, the Khirjahni seemed almost passive. But based on what Okoro had told him of the Khirjahni battles against the warlike Th'Dorrans, he understood that they were not pushovers. They were willing to fight, whatever the odds, to preserves their homeland and culture. Not even the Arkady Mining Corporation had managed to wrest away all the Khirjahni mineral rights.

He yearned to sketch her, but didn't trust himself.

TWENTY-FOUR

The scream of a craggon high overhead brought K'Sati out of a deep sleep. She struggled briefly, until she realized she lay wrapped in the arms of the Terran, Renly Harkness, in a shallow rock crevasse in the forbidden zone. The idea that a craggon could be hunting for them terrified her. She'd never seen one, but the sound of its screams...

She buried her face into Renly's neck, breathing deeply to distract herself from the invisible predator soaring high above them. The smell of him, mixed with the scent of traggah calmed her. He smelled different from the other men of Earth.

There were other differences, too. He seemed uninterested in gold; he did not gamble, or speak endlessly of his job or investments as did so many of them. A strong, brave man, he did not share the off-worlder fear of traggahs, and she'd never known of a single Terran who survived a tree lizard bite. And although he'd initially worn the gloves all Terrans wore to protect themselves from the native virals, he stopped wearing them completely after making friends with Silverbeard's youngling brother. The sight of the youngling sleeping in the grass while Renly sketched him brought a lump to her throat. At times, the Terran would even run his hands through the baby's plush coat, something both of them obviously enjoyed.

She thought of Wayne, who had no such tender qualities. The men were as different as two *kinds* of men. Perhaps among Terran men there were also clans such as Khirjahni and Th'Dorran.

Given that, Renly would be descended from traggahs, like all Khirjahni, and Wayne would be Th'Dorran. The revelation both pleased and shocked her. She would never consider giving herself to an arrogant, aggressive, warlike Th'Dorran, but she had. Until she met Renly, she considered all Terrans alike: Wayne, Mr. Duprees, horrible Mr. Blaylock; or even Ruben, the stable master. They all used their power and position to get what they wanted. Wayne seemed unable to speak with her without leaving painful marks on her flesh.

Renly, on the other hand, did not use physical force or coercion. Renly was more like the herd; something she'd not experienced with any being other than the traggahs. It made sense, she supposed, that she felt comfortable with him. He too, was an empath. Whether he believed it or not, he could not hide his intentions from her.

She knew he was attracted to her, and that the idea bothered him. In those moments when Renly's regard for her began to warm, she would see him glance at her horns and look away. He made no effort to seduce her, in spite of their nightly sleeping arrangements, even as she thought she might like it. She'd seen him watching her, when he didn't think she was looking. It thrilled her, just a little. But Wayne had given her similar looks in the past, and look at the trouble she was in because of it.

The sky took on the deep violet hue, which announced first dawn. She missed the comforting presence of Neatfoot at her back; they'd been nearly inseparable for the last four years. K'Sati had never been in the forbidden zone before. After losing her parents to this place, she ever, ever wanted to come here. And now, the worst had happened.

They would no doubt be torn apart by wild beasts.

She could not return to the coast. Mr. Duprees would no doubt blame her for the theft of Golden Boy and throw her into the company prison. And if Wayne ever got his hands on her; well that was something she didn't dare consider. She could not return to the temple, either, not that she ever would, but her choices for the future were limited.

She rewrapped her scarf around her and eased herself out of Renly's sleepy embrace. The faint scent of woodsmoke came to her as she stepped out from the shelter of the rocks. No doubt Wayne and his men were still tracking them. No way to tell how far away they were, but there was no wood to burn on the steppes. Perhaps the men had left their sleds at the base of the mountains and were pursuing them on foot. If true, their only way forward was through the mountains. She knew of no one who had done so and returned.

Another craggon scream broke the dawn stillness. She could sense Renly's rise to consciousness. As soon as he awoke, she would have to tell him that Wayne was still hunting them. If he found them, he would kill them; she had no doubts about that. How did everything go so wrong so quickly?

Renly ducked out from the rocks and shouldered his satchel across his shoulders. He gazed at the sky, his glance captured by the tiny form of the craggon circling high above them. He shoved the ironwood club into his belt and nodded, as if satisfied.

"We're turning back," he murmured.

"We cannot. Wayne and his men are right behind us. Can you not smell their campfire?"

He paused to sniff the air. "You're right." His eyes scanned the mountain behind them. "There."

A wisp of smoke curled above the trees. So close! "They must have a tracker with them. We must leave now."

"You don't have to do this, K'Sati. I mean, you could hide in the rocks until they pass and then head back the way we came."

She could sense the despair in him. No one could feel strong without their herd. "Come." She began to climb the steep trail. "They must give up eventually. The only way they will catch us is if we stop."

* * *

Their fear kept them moving; they climbed steadily throughout the morning. Renly no longer felt the chill in the air, even as they continued to climb. The way was steep, but the footing was good, if uneven, and he was sweating beneath the leather vest. At times, K'Sati stopped to listen, as if she thought she heard the sound of voices echoing across the hillside. He'd come to trust her superior hearing, and resented their self-imposed silence, but the wheeling of craggons overhead was a constant reminder.

The trail, or what there was of it, was scant even in the best conditions. Every time he caught sight of a traggah print, he silently cheered that they were still going in the right direction, even as he realized their pursuers probably felt the same way. When he tried to rub out their tracks, K'Sati stopped him; pointing out that his clumsy efforts only made the tracker's job easier, not harder.

In his head, he sensed Silverbeard up ahead of them, neither closer nor more distant than last night. This morning, he thought he had felt Garrett's presence, but wasn't certain. He suspected that his connection to Silverbeard was somehow masking his more distant connection with Garrett.

Twice, they spotted traggah prints leading off the trail and followed them to caves. The first cave was too small even for K'Sati to squeeze into, the second was large enough to walk in, as long as they hunched over. From the entrance, they heard the trickle of water coming from the depths. Their thirst made them braver than their fear of what might be inside, and using one side of the tunnel as a guide, they moved blindly toward the sounds of water dripping. After a quick sniff, Renly scooped out handfuls of the warm, mineral-tasting water. They drank as much as they could, knowing they had nothing in which to carry more with them. But as they continued, they found plenty of streams and water, although some of it was too hot to drink. The mountains seemed to be riddled with caves and caverns, many of which were warmed by geothermically-heated reservoirs inside.

The brush thinned out as they climbed ever higher. They reached the peak in mid-afternoon. Renly stifled a groan as he scanned the endless range of mountains. The Crags of Corrah stretched before them like fangs; each looming larger and steeper as they faded into the distance.

The trail before them quickly disappeared as they re-entered the tree line. Renly searched for any sign of Paul and the traggahs, but the trees here grew thick and dark. He scrutinized the nearest peaks, his eyes sharp for any movement. Paul and the traggahs couldn't be more than a few hours ahead of them. They should be able to spot them. The deep forest litter hid all signs of traggah tracks. He stared across the vista, looking for anything that would give them a clue as to which way Paul was heading. He reached out mentally, seeking Garrett's presence, but felt nothing. He closed his eyes, turning in every direction. Nothing.

He'd been staring at it for several seconds before he recognized what he was seeing. *There.* He pulled K'Sati close and pointed a slide area on the side of a crag just south of where they stood.

"Right there," he murmured. "See that bare strip of yellowish rock along the side of that mountain? I'll bet that's the place Paul is heading for. The Yellow Chimney, he called it."

At that moment, a great yellow craggon launched itself from a ledge half-way up the buff-colored gash in the slope. They shrank into the shrubs around them, as the huge creature soared directly overhead; so close, Renly could count the scales on its stomach; each as large as the coronation medal he'd designed for Queen Fabienne a lifetime ago. The craggon's filthy black talons looked as long and presumably every bit as sharp as one of his gravers.

As he passed overhead, the beast flapped his wings awkwardly to gain altitude. Renly allowed himself to breathe again. He disentangled himself from an equally frightened K'Sati. Not daring to even whisper, he pointed at the ledge and she nodded; her eyes wide with a silent fear that mirrored his own.

They waited until the craggon disappeared over the summit of a nearby mountain, and edged their way down the backside of the mountain. Renly silently cursed Paul for misleading him about how far they'd have to go into the mountains to find Garrett. Renly began to think that Paul would have stolen the traggahs and made off in the middle of the night, even if they had not had the run-in with the mandragons.

His heart pounded. "Garrett's got to be over there somewhere."

She nodded, her eyes glued to the yellowed ledge where the craggon had just launched himself. She said nothing; merely pointed.

It was Paul, on foot, dragging Silverbeard and Neatfoot behind him. The traggahs were blindfolded, and Paul was limping. They were too far away to see the expression on his face, but he looked determined. Renly guessed he must be very close to his destination.

The group moved into the trees again and was lost from view. "You're not part of this" he told her. "You can still turn back."

She shook her head. "I am Khirjahni." She put her hand on his arm. "I will not allow harm to come to my herd."

"That's crazy," he hissed. "You're willing to go into a craggons lair to rescue the traggahs?" He shook his head.

She pulled her hand away and stared at him. "You still do not understand. Neatfoot and Silverbeard are herd to me. The traggahs *are* our people. We are born of the same clan. Surely you can understand. As you feel the bond with your brother, you also feel the bond you have forged with Silverbeard. You swore an oath to protect them both, no?"

"Yes, but..." *I never thought I'd have to face off a craggon for him.* "Come on, you're half Terran. We're descended from apes but that doesn't make us willing to sacrifice ourselves for some chimpanzee."

The anger in her face stopped him. "You are herd to me as well, Terran.

Too late, he understood her meaning. He had just insulted her. His face grew warm. "All I'm saying is, you don't need to go after Garrett with me."

"I cannot go back." She turned her back to him and began to make her way down the mountain. Ahead of them lay the larger peak with the yellow chimney. He wondered how long she would stay mad at him, but the challenges of the trail soon had both of them sweating and cursing under their breaths.

If anything, the downhill track was tougher than the uphill. The shadows of the circling craggons overhead carried a constant reminder not to go too fast or make too much noise. But at the same time, they dared not stop until they found decent shelter. The trail was too narrow to sleep on, and too exposed. With Wayne and his men so close behind, they needed to find a shelter somewhere off the trail. Renly had marked a spot on the next mountain, but wasn't sure they'd make it before dark.

They didn't.

The bottom of the canyon between the mountains was deep in shadow by the time they reached it. They turned south, following a tiny stream as it flowed between the rocks. K'Sati found a number of thorny bushes with blue-black berries which she declared edible. They stuffed themselves on the ripe fruit, their hands and lips quickly becoming stained purple with juice. The food put them both in better spirits, and when K'Sati suggested spending the night in the branches of a large tree, he didn't argue. But as he settled himself into a less uncomfortable position, he knew he would miss more than her sleeping warmth beside him.

Her half-human heritage did not matter; she had never been to Earth, had never been exposed to Terran culture. Her beliefs were as alien to him as his were to her. Yet she no longer seemed alien to him. He hated seeing that stricken expression on her face, knowing he had caused her pain. She had risked everything to save him, and he his thoughtless remarks had wounded her deeply. As the sounds of predators sniffing at the base of the tree carried up to him, he vowed to keep her safe and make it up to her.

TWENTY-FIVE

Wayne Strickman and his Arkady crew of three smelled the carnage at the spring well before they arrived, but the sight of the mandragon carcasses brought a smile to Wayne's face. He'd been terrified they would find the corpse of Golden Boy.

All that remained of the former Arkady miners was a pile of heavy bones, bits of scales and rotting skin. No way to tell who they might have been.

The hunter, Lyle, knelt to examine the tracks. "Longteeth." He touched one of the prints. "Check this out."

"Whatcha got?"

Lyle showed him traggah and human tracks leading away from the spring. "Three sets of footprints. Your friends have split up. One of 'em has the traggahs; the other two are on foot. Less than a day ahead of us."

"Is Golden Boy with them?"

Lyle shook his head. "Traggah won't willingly go into craggon territory, or anywhere near the mountains. These two resisted. You can read the panic in their short, choppy prints. No man is a match for an unwilling traggah, unless he's got a bridle on 'im. These other two were also stolen from the stable. Their hooves are shod."

Corey, who had been making pointed suggestions about returning to the coast, lost what little he had in his stomach. "We've gotta go back," he choked.

"Shut your hole. Ya got no say here." The kid had been nothing but trouble; he should not have let Nevers talk him in to bringing him. The kid was like a bad luck charm. First the sled, and then Golden Boy. He should have brought one of those damn Khirjahni groomsmen.

None of them had any experience in handling a traggah, and all of them, even Lyle, were terrified of catching something if they came in contact with it. After Lyle darted Golden Boy with tranquilizer dart, they managed to get the unconscious traggah onto one of the sleds. Corey pulled first watch, but fell asleep. Golden Boy apparently woke up and walked right out of camp while they slept.

The next morning, Wayne would have killed Corey with his bare hands, if Nevers hadn't stopped him. Lyle pointed out that Golden Boy would go after the other traggahs, and if they followed Golden Boy, they would likely catch up to the thieves who took him as well.

"Ya said Golden Boy would follow them."

Lyle shrugged. "Not into the mountains."

Wayne took a handkerchief out of his back pocket and covered his nose as he passed the corpses and approached the mud around the watering hole. A cloud of grey carrion moths flew up from the death scene in a frenzy, bushing against Wayne's face and clothes in a furry, putrid panic. He swatted at them, then turned away in disgust as several of the soft-bodied creatures burst open on contact. The stink of death grew even worse.

He studied the tracks Lyle pointed out at the waterline. Three distinct sets of human prints were evident in the mud. He recognized K'Sati's immediately by their small size.

"I'll bet you anything these two mandragons were lying in wait for some other mandragon on his way back from the Gold Ball," Nevers offered. "They woulda followed him back to his claim and killed him. Instead, our little thief K'Sati and her gang showed up."

Wayne considered the implication. "You think that's where these guys are headed?"

"It's the only thing that makes sense" Lyle agreed. "The guy with the traggahs has a destination in mind. I'd say, he's heading toward a prospector camp; probably with a load of supplies. K'Sati and whoever she's got with her are following him."

How can I use this? Wayne surveyed the scene from upwind. *If I go back without Golden Boy, I'm done, even if I say predators killed him. Especially if I say he was killed predators. It's back to the mines for me.*

"So where the hell is Golden Boy?"

Lyle made a face. "I'd have to backtrack to see where he turned off. Since he's not following them anymore, I'd guess he's searching for his herd. He could be anywhere."

"Can ya find him?"

"Probably."

But Lyle didn't look convinced. No. Golden Boy was gone, which meant his relationship and any possible future with Arkady Universal Mining Corporation was terminated. If he showed up now, they'd slap him in chains and ship him back to the mines, big time.

Nevers leaned in to say something so the others couldn't hear him. "You know, if we find that mine, we're set for life. We'll never have a better chance to go for the gold than right now."

Wayne pressed his lips together. The sleds would be useless on the mountain. They would have to stash them somewhere. They had weapons and food enough for another week in their packs. His decision, either way. He cocked an eye at Lyle. "You think we can catch up to them?"

"Check this out." Lyle pointed to a dimple in the dirt beside the man's footprints. "This guy's wearing city shoes. They're not made for hiking, and it looks like he's using a cane or walking stick. I'd say he's an off-worlder. Probably here for the festival."

The pieces to the puzzle finally slipped into place.

Wayne clapped him on the shoulder. "Hey, I know this guy! Name's Harkness. Came here looking for his brother; probably thinks he's out here. Maybe he met someone who said he knew where to find him. Either that, or some smartass conned him into bringing him out here. Whatever." These mountains had chewed up far tougher men than Renly Harkness. Either way, no one would come looking for him.

With any hope of returning with the traggah in time for the race and salvaging his career at Arkady, Wayne decided to settle for revenge. K'Sati, she was dead the minute she took Golden Boy. She and Harkness whoever they were with would pay. Big time.

Corey wiped his mouth on his sleeve. "You can't be thinking of going after them."

Wayne ignored him. The idea of catching up to K'Sati and Harkness had driven all other thoughts from his mind. Golden Boy was beyond salvage, he could see that. He could turn this to his advantage and walk away with another man's gold in his pocket. Enough gold to buy a ticket off this stinking planet, and a whole new life.

"I say we go after them." He glanced at Nevers, who immediately understood his proposal.

"I'm in."

"Me too," Lyle agreed.

He knew Corey didn't want to come, but wouldn't dare say it. "You can stay here and wait for those longteeth to come back or come with us. What'll it be?"

TWENTY-SIX

Renly.

He jerked himself awake and peered around in the pre-dawn darkness. Garrett's voice sounded so close, so clear. He could almost feel the vibration hanging in the air. *Garrett was still alive!*

The twin suns shone directly overhead when they reached the mining camp. Renly frowned, unable to correlate the refuse heap and scattered rock piles with any sort of order he would associate with a real camp. Only the presence of the dejected-looking, blindfolded traggahs told them they were in the right place.

They trotted across the packed dirt clearing to the picket line. K'Sati called softly to them, and both traggahs whickered softly in recognition; even before he reached them, he sensed their change in spirit.

Silverbeard shoved his head blindly into his chest, taking great snuffs of air as if to reaffirm his presence.

"Take it easy, boy." He rubbed his hands over the eager traggah's snout and the soft plush of his neck. He reached to untie the blindfold, but K'Sati stopped him.

"No," she murmured. "We do not want them spooked if the

craggon comes back. We must wait until after we are well away from here."

He nodded. He hated seeing them so helpless, but the stink of craggon pervaded the air around them. The entrance to the craggon's cave had to be close; the air was thick with the ammonia and the fetid reek of shit. Paul and Garrett couldn't be far.

But where?

He asked K'Sati to stay with the traggahs, and set out to inspect the clearing, which was only about sixty feet across. He found no tent or shelter of any kind; only trash. Bits of charred wood and the remains of prepackaged Terran food littered the clearing. There were no metal tools of any kind; only some pointed sticks and bits of filthy canvas. Four large empty water skins lay near a wooden trough for the traggahs.

K'Sati caught his attention and pointed toward a narrow pathway leading between a cleft in the rocks. He motioned her to wait, and started down the track.

He froze. Coming toward him were two figures. In the lead, was a mandragon; behind him, was Paul.

The mandragon appeared more man-like than those he'd seen at the Gold Ball. His cranial features retained a recognizably humanoid shape, although his skin had thickened and hardened into scales.

The mandragon turned and their eyes met.

It was Garrett.

They'd come to a standstill, some ten feet apart. He didn't recognize his brother by his features; the dragon pox had already robbed Garrett of his expression, but his complexion had not yet acquired the dark bronze color or the reptilian sheen. His jaw line, once heroically square, had not yet achieved the unnatural length of a full-fledged mandragon, but would never be mistaken for human.

Only his body posture and his brother's distinctive bow-legged walk made him recognizable. That and the fact that he returned Renly's stare with an air of aloof disbelief..

Even from this distance, the stench of dragon feces hit him like a blow.

Renly coughed. "You saved my life once, Garrett. I'm here to return the favor."

"I didn't believe Paul when told me, but here you are."

Only the barest trace of Garrett's remembered voice remained. His frozen lips bore the teeth-baring grimace of all mandragons. Renly wanted to say or do something to break through his brother's cold demeanor, but didn't know what to say.

He tried again. "I, I came because you called me," he stammered. Garrett's eyes had changed, too; they were yellow now, just like Sully's. Even now, as they stood face-to-face, he couldn't believe he was speaking to Garrett. His brother's gnarled deformed hands and blackened, eagle-like talons bore no resemblance to human hands. "I'm here to rescue you, Garrett."

Garrett laughed broadly, showing off his lower tusks.

Revulsion filled him. Something was wrong with Garrett. Something more disturbing than the physical changes. More than anything, he wished he'd never found his brother.

"I don't need rescuing, Renfield. I need strong backs. But since Paul didn't bring any, you'll have to do."

The words hit him like a slap. He'd forgotten about his brother's way with words. *Renfield.* He'd forgotten that hated childhood nickname, too. And how he'd earned it by doing by doing anything and everything his brother wanted; *anything*, just to be allowed to tag along with his brother and his friends. *Garrett's little Renfield,* Paul and the rest of his brother's friends called him.

"Let's go. I'm taking you back to Earth. If we leave now, we can make it back to the coast before the last transport leaves. "

Garrett's eyes flicked to a movement behind him, and Renly felt K'Sati's hand on his arm. "Is that him?"

He nodded, not liking the gleam of interest in Garrett's eyes.

"Welcome." Garrett nodded his head in Paul's direction. "You must be the lovely K'Sati. I approve, dear Renfield. Heartily so."

Renly fought to control his reaction. He was embarrassed for K'Sati; that his brother would leer at her, but then of course he'd always been that way, hadn't he? Always the one with the pretty girl on his arm? Always the guy who...

K'Sati gave his arm a small tug. "The traggahs have been watered, but there's no food for them. We cannot stay much longer."

"I'm not leaving, little brother. And if you want to go, you'll have to walk. We need those traggahs." The old arrogance in Garrett's voice came through loud and clear.

"What are you talking about? You've got the dragon pox, Garrett. The sooner we get you back to Earth, the sooner you can get your life back."

Garrett's lipless grin widened in a cruel approximation of a smile. "Oh look who's talking. What a hypocrite. You've got a blue ring around your iris, just like hers. That's what you get from sleeping with the locals. I'd guess you'll be sporting horns before long, *Renfield*."

He shoved his hands into his pockets to keep from checking his forehead. He'd felt the knots forming beneath the skin, but refused to consider the possibility. He realized Garrett was deliberately baiting him; just as he'd done when they were children. Of course, the ten-year age difference between them had always favored Garrett. For the first time in his life, he saw his brother as a manipulator. Coldness seeped through him, washing away the sting of his long-forgotten childhood humiliations.

"You've insulted K'Sati, and you're doing a pretty good job at embarrassing me. I came halfway across the galaxy for you. What the hell do you want?" The sight and smell of him bore little resemblance to the witty, urbane brother he'd so loved.

Garrett's yellow eyes narrowed. "You're right. I do need your help. And your girlfriend's too. Come with me and I'll show you." He turned back the way they'd come, and he and Paul set off down the trail

With a swift motion, Renly ran his hand across his forehead. Of course there were no horns there. Just those tender, itchy spots beneath the skin. He made a silent appeal to K'Sati and saw the truth in her eyes. She knew. His stomach lurched. *Oh god.* But now was not the time for self-pity.

"I'm sorry about that. He's not himself." But it was Garrett. Unmistakably so. How could he have forgotten his brother's sneering condescension? His bullying? That hadn't changed a bit. "He's sick."

"What are you going to do?"

He sighed. "If I had an ounce of smarts, we'd leave right now."

"He doesn't care about you, Renly. Let's go."

He shook his head. "Take Neatfoot and go. I don't like the way he looked at you, but he won't hurt me. I'll help him out with whatever he needs, and then I'll catch up to you." He turned to follow his brother down the trail, but she grabbed his arm.

"He is not bonded to you! He is not bonded to anyone. "

"He's my brother."

"You mean nothing to him. How can you not feel his contempt for you? If you get in his way, he will hurt you."

"You're wrong. He'd never hurt me." But even as he said it, he wasn't so certain. For the first time in his life, he felt uncertain about his own feelings for Garrett.

"He is not the brother of your childhood. He is mandragon now. You cannot save him. In a few more weeks or months he will be like those pathetic creatures at the spring."

"I'm going after him."

"No, you have to listen to me! My father was Terran; he also went into the Forbidden Zone for the gold and became a mandragon."

He hesitated, watching the retreating backs of Paul and Garret as they made their way down the trail.

She tugged on his vest. "You know the Khirjahni traditional greeting, right?"

The words came out automatically. "I am but one of many. I am herd." Saying the words aloud brought him a curious sense of comfort. He felt rather than heard Silverbeard's whicker against his mind. K'Sati and Neatfoot were there, too.

"Remember that, Renly. We are herd, you and I." She stared into his eyes, her face rigid with intent. "As the Khirjahni are to traggahs, the Th'Dorrans are to the craggons. They have a traditional greeting too. They say, *'are you predator or are you prey?'* And the ritual Th'Dorran response is, *'when I taste your blood, you will know.'*

"So?" He wrenched himself away from her.

"Think about it," she said. "He will take as he will from you by whatever force is necessary. It is his nature. Your brother is a predator now. You are herd. He will use you for whatever he needs from you, and then he will find a way to trap you or kill you, because otherwise, you will try to take his gold from him."

"Don't worry." He caressed the side of her sweet face. She had been orphaned at a young age. She'd never known a family; she'd never had a brother or sister.

"You don't know him. Not like I do. He knows I don't care about his gold. Once I help him out of this jam, he'll come back to Earth with me." He started down the trail after his brother. He glanced back at her, but she hadn't moved. He hated seeing that look on her face. Like he was abandoning her. "Take Neatfoot and go," he added, lamely. "This shouldn't take long."

TWENTY-SEVEN

The stench intensified to eye-watering levels once they entered the lava tube. Renly held a bit of flannel from his pack up to his face, but his eyes streamed tears from the heavy concentration of ammonia in the air. Garrett handed him a flashlight, but told him to be careful not to knock it against anything.

"The sound of metal against stone drives them crazy. They can hear the sounds of metal against stone from miles away."

The walls of the tunnel were smooth from centuries of craggon hide scraping against stone. The packed earth beneath their feet was uneven and slippery as wet tile. Garrett explained the mixture of lava powder, craggon feces and urine baked in the steamy heat of the cavern into an impermeable, stinking adobe-like surface. At one point, the tunnel sloped so steeply, they simply sat and slid into the main cavern. Paul eagerly raced ahead of them and disappeared, but Renly didn't like the being here one bit. The slickness of the slope would make it impossible to get out the same way they entered. If the craggon came back, they'd be trapped. Claustrophobia and panic churned his gut. Beneath the craggon-skin vest, his shirt was already damp with sweat.

"How do we get out?"

"This lair is riddled with lava tubes; there are a couple smaller tubes that lead to the surface. Too small for the craggon to get out through, but this is the fastest way in, as long as she's not home."

Garrett flashed his blue-tinted lantern around the cavern, which was a good forty degrees warmer than the outside temperature. At its widest point, the cave stretched sixty feet across and perhaps fourteen feet high. In a grotto to the left, near the back, and Renly their lights reflected off a steaming dark pool of water. A slow plink dripped; echoing softly across the darkness. Mist rose from the superheated pool and filled the cavern with a foul-smelling fog. The walls wept with dank sweat, and the thin film of moisture on the floors made them slick and treacherous. Like the tunnel, the sides and floor of the cave were smooth-packed with centuries of fossilized urine and feces.

"This is his where she sleeps." Garrett's ghastly face appeared even more monstrous by lantern light. "This way."

Renly fought back a gagging reflex, and followed his brother around the edge of the cavern, around the worst of the piles of fresh dung. They passed through several smaller caverns. In one, a filthy straw pallet, wads of old clothing, and the remains of food packets stacked in one corner gave evidence that Garrett had been spending a lot of time down here.

"Don't tell me you live here," he said.

"Better here than freezing to death topside." Garrett actually sounded offended. "After a while, you get used to the smell. Besides, down here, every day is like Christmas." He kneeled beside a rough-hewn wooden chest, approximately the size and shape of a child's coffin. "Check this out." He lifted the lid.

A mother lode of gold nuggets filled the sturdy box. Solid gold nodules, from the size of his big toe to as large as a tangerine, gleamed in the dim light. He ran his hand across the surface of the trove and whistled softly.

"Okay, you've made your point; that's a lot of gold. But what about the craggon? *What about the pox*, Garrett?"

Garrett closed the lid. "The advantages of the pox is it makes them think you're one of them. They don't see you as prey anymore. The body's chemistry changes, and they think you're some kind of youngling. So long as I keep real quiet and stay out of her way, she doesn't pay any attention to me. So I sleep when she sleeps, and as soon as she leaves, I go back to work."

Renly flashed his light over the filthy bedding and empty food packets. "How can you live like this?"

"Don't judge me until you see what I've got to show you. Then you'll understand. Come on."

With a growing uneasiness, he followed his brother deeper into the maze of tunnels until they rounded a curve in the rock and reached another cavern. He stopped, stunned by the sight before him.

Paul lay on the fetid floor, his body curled protectively around a huge, partially exposed boulder of what appeared to be solid gold. Paul had his eyes closed, as if in some sort of trance.

Renly frowned, unable to make sense of what he was seeing. Like a cat cleaning itself, Paul was licking and gnawing at the filthy, feces-hardened clay that encased the nugget. The partially-exposed surface of the gold nugget protruded some twelve inches from the crud. Like an iceberg, there was no way to tell how much more of the nugget was beneath the surface, but it looked far too big to be called a nugget. The entire surface of the gold had been scored with marks. Teeth marks.

Garrett and Paul had both gone mad. He was filled with a despair unmatched by anything except that horrid time of his childhood. Living down here in this filth and darkness had affected their minds.

The fumes alone were probably toxic enough to kill brain cells. He fought to control his growing sense of panic. He had to leave this place as quickly as possible.

Garrett knelt down and caressed the exposed gold like a proud papa. "What do you think?"

"You've already got more gold in that box back there than you'll ever need. Let's take it and get out of here!"

Garrett shook his head. "There's a lot more than one box, little brother. You don't get it. The craggons have been using these lava tubes as lairs since forever. These mountains are chock full of gold and precious metals. When the craggons enlarge and extend the lava tubes to make their dens, they uncover the gold. Don't you see? They do all the work! This gold has been here for a couple million years, just waiting for someone like me to come along. I'm not leaving without it."

"You're talking crazy." Renly snorted in disgust. "Think about what you've done to yourself. And Paul. I want no part of this."

Paul grinned woozily up at them. "Hey, this is top grade dream dust. You should try it."

Dirt eaters. The term was an apt one. "You're both sick. You tricked me into coming here. And now you want me to, what, become like *you*?"

Garrett's eyes glittered in the dim light. "You were always such a prude. Renfield."

"You don't need me. I'm leaving." He shook his head in disgust, the bad taste in his mouth grew worse. He'd given up his home planet for this? He stared at Garrett's monstrous face. "I'm leaving."

"Oh contraire, dear brother," Garrett's tone oozed sarcasm. "I need you to help me get this gold to the surface. I figure this baby is going to run at least three hundred pounds. It'll break every record at the Gold Ball. We've only got a couple days before the end of the Festival. The nugget I sent back with Paul was supposed to buy traggahs and a carry pack. Unfortunately, things didn't go quite as planned, but now that you and the girl and the traggahs are all here, I think we've got a chance."

His heart skipped a beat. "No." He would not let them touch her. Garrett always had an ability to coerce others into doing what he wanted. And he always ended up taking more than they were willing to give. In a flash, the memory, long forgotten came back to haunt him.

The housekeeper's young niece. Sweet, but not too bright. He had watched Garrett and Paul flirt with her, tease her, and then lure her back to the barn one night with the promise of a party. The police had been called. No, she couldn't remember which boy had touched her first. But she looked at Garrett with great tear-filled eyes as she spoke. In the end, no charges were pressed against any of the boys in the crowd, and the housekeeper had been dismissed. The incident hadn't been the first time, nor would it be the last.

How did I forget about that? Leo tried to tell him; tried to talk him out of coming. How could have forgotten how self-centered and lacking in empathy Garrett really was?

Garrett poured a cupful of cloudy water over the cement-like earth clinging to the edge if the gold and began licking and scraping at it with his tusks.

Renly's lip curled back in disgust. He dug into his pack and pulled out his chasing hammer and one of his burins, and held them out to Garrett. "This should make quick work of freeing that nugget."

Garrett slapped away the proffered tools. "You don't get it, Renfield. Beneath that slick surface, the dirt is hard as a rock. We can't use any sort of explosives or metal tools. If we do, that craggon and all her angry relatives will be down on top of us in no time. They're like sharks sensing prey struggling in the water. Any rhythmic sound or metallic noise makes them crazy. The only thing to do is get down here in the dirt with us and ease it out with our fingernails, tongues and our teeth. Come on, try it."

"I don't care how much gold you've got there. I am not going to help you dig it out. Neither is K'Sati. In fact, we're leaving. Right now. Last chance, Garrett. Are you coming or not?"

"You aren't leaving, Renfield."

"Like hell you say." He'd already made up his mind. He slipped his tools back into his satchel and turned to go.

Garrett's attack came from behind; without warning.

TWENTY-EIGHT

K'Sati stared after Renly as he followed Paul and Garret down the trail and out of sight. Not for anything in this world would she willingly follow him into the lair of a craggon, but at the same time, she was certain those two men would do something terrible to Renly. How could he not sense their intentions?

She mistrusted Garrett on sight; he seemed nothing like Renly. And Paul was not the easygoing Terran she thought she knew. The two of them together, in the craggon lair, might very well decide to hurt him. She glanced in the direction of the blindfolded traggahs.

I should leave. Now. She glanced back down the trail. She could not shake the sense of foreboding she felt from Renly's brother. *I cannot leave him; he needs me.*

High above, the distant specks of craggons circled, sending prickles of fear down her spine. Until yesterday, she had never seen one, and she never wanted to get so close to one again, but Renly and those men were marching right down into a craggon lair. If she left without him, she might never see him again.

If she left now, something bad would happen in that cave, she was certain. What if they'd already hurt him? She could not let that happen.

He is herd to me.

She started down the trail toward the craggons lair.

A familiar voice sounded behind her. "Hold it, girl. What's your hurry?"

She jumped. Wayne had three men with him: his scary friend Nevers, and two strangers. The dark expression on Wayne's face and Never's cruel grin told her everything she needed to know. *I am dead already.* They stood between her and the traggahs. Her only chance of escape was to follow Renly into the craggon's lair.

She ran.

Wayne caught her fifty feet from the entrance to the cavern. He tackled her in mid-stride, growling like a rahg as he took her town.

She grunted under his weight and butted him in the face with her horns, but couldn't shake him loose. He cursed her, and wiped his bloodied nose on his shoulder, but held on until Nevers and the others caught up.

They grabbed her by her arms and jerked her to her feet. Wayne ripped the front of her shirt to her waist.

"You want to play rough, well ya bloody well asked for it this time, *bitch.*" He grabbed her by one horn and shook her nearly senseless.

"Forget about her," one of the men she didn't know interrupted. Don't you know what this is?"

He wasn't dressed like the Arkady men; he wore rugged, oddly-pattered canvas clothing. The tracker, she guessed.

"Worst stink I ever smelled," Wayne answered. "We've got the girl and the traggahs. Let's go."

"No, wait. This is the craggon's den. This is what those mandragons were looking for. Don't you get it? It's a gold mine. We just hit the jackpot, gentlemen. We can't walk away from this."

"Lyle's right," Nevers said. "This is the chance of a lifetime.

Forget the girl. We gotta check this place out."

"She was going into the cave," the bearded one never took his eyes off her naked breasts. "

Wayne licked his lips and shook her by her horn again. "You're right. How many are down in that mine? And don't lie to me."

Tears streamed down her face. If only she hadn't waited so long to decide. If she'd gone after Renly two minutes earlier, they might never have found her. They might have walked right by.

"Three."

Wayne held her by her horns while Nevers handcuffed her.

"I'm not goin' in there," the bearded one said. "What if the craggon comes back?"

"Fine Corey, have it your way." Wayne grabbed shoved her toward the bearded man. "Stay here and keep an eye on her."

She didn't like the leer on Corey's face. She did not want to be left alone with him. "Take me with you, Wayne. I can call to them. They will listen to me."

"Yeah, right. And warn 'em," The one called Lyle answered. "I say leave them both here. More gold for the rest of us."

"Hey! Just 'cause I' don't want to go into that stinkhole doesn't mean I don't get my share of the gold," Corey protested. "Somebody's got to stay up here and warn you guys. What if that craggon shows up?"

"He can snack on you and the girl while we fill our pockets with gold and sneak out the back." Nevers grinned as he pulled a flashlight out of his pack.

"Give him your sidearm, Lyle," Wayne ordered. "I don't much relish going in there, but if craggons caves are as full of gold as I've heard, we ought a check this out. At the same time, I don't' want to get trapped down there if that craggon comes back." He gave her naked breast a squeeze. "But don't worry, bitch. I'll be right back. You and I have plenty of unfinished business to take care of."

TWENTY-NINE

Garrett's fist slammed into the back of his head, just behind the ear, sending Renly sprawling forward and down to the slippery floor. He struggled to keep his feet under him, but Garrett was on top of him, reaching his arm around his neck. He hardly had time to think, but jerked an elbow back instinctively. The satisfying crunch of bone and his brother's loosened grip told him he'd tagged Garrett good.

He whirled to face his attacker, and whipped the flashlight around for a blow, but Garrett parried with his forearm, and the flashlight went flying. In the dim light of the single lantern, Renly saw Garrett open his arms wide and lower his head to grapple him and take him to the ground.

The slick surface beneath his feet betrayed him yet again, and Garrett flattened him; pinning him to the floor again by virtue of his height and greater weight. As Garrett panted into his face, Renly used the slick mud slime to his advantage and twisted; squirming onto his side.

His brother dug his blackened talons into Renly's shoulder. He grunted in pain as the image of millions of aggressive black viruses swarming into his bloodstream sent him into a panic. His brother's hot sour breath enveloped him, and from the depths of his subconscious rose another forgotten memory of childhood.

"You little sneak," Garrett hissed furiously, just inches from his face. He jerked Renly up by his shirt, tearing the sleeve. "It's about time you learned a lesson or two about life." Garrett held him above his head, to the amazed stare of the dozen big men in the kitchen. "Here, take him! He can be my collateral!"

The man with the quiet voice nodded. "Bring him into the light. Let's take a look at him."

He struggled against Garrett with all his strength, but his brother was ten years older and ten years stronger. Once they bound him with duct tape, he was helpless.

"Your young brother here will be your marker until you pay me the money you owe me, Harkness," he said. "You'll think twice about ducking out on me again, I promise." As he spoke, he stroked Renly's hair as he would a cat.

Renly screamed, but no sound escaped him. He stared desperately at Garrett, but his brother wouldn't look at him. The quiet man tightened the grip around his throat with his hard, hard hand. Renly remembered the feel of hot tears tracking down his face. No one in the room would look at him; not even the big bodyguards the quiet man had brought with him. He felt invisible. Helpless.

Renly's heart pounded in terror. In a flash, everything came back to him. No wonder he could never remember his abductor. *There had never been an abduction.* It was Garrett. His brother had given him willingly to the pedophile with the hard hands. The police and everyone else hailed Garrett a hero, but it was all a lie.

Garrett smashed his hand into his face, but Renly felt nothing but his own rage.

All those years of pent-up guilt. Of feeling helpless and stupid that he couldn't remember, when all along it had been Garrett who betrayed him, Garrett who gave him to that horrible man. The kidnapper was a myth, a lie. A lie that kept him hiding behind the walls his studio, afraid to face the outside world. Afraid of everything. His inability to remember the incident fueled his determination to become an artist; he remembered how desperately he wanted to become a police sketch artist like the one who tried so hard to help him remember his kidnappers face. But there had never been anything to remember; Garrett's face had been right in front of him every single day. And then, when Garrett's face became the only face he could draw, he never made the connection between his own brother and the abuse he suffered at the hands of that pedophile. And Garrett had known all along!

He brought his knee up hard between his brother's legs. Garrett howled with pain and curled into a fetal position. Renly rolled away from him and scrambled to get his bearings. At the foot of the far wall, the light from his flashlight illuminated one side of the chamber.

He stumbled to his feet. Carefully, he skidded over and picked up the light, relieved it still worked. Garrett still lay moaning on the floor like an animal.

"I remember now, Garrett. You lied about everything, didn't you," he panted. "We never had a psychic connection between us. You made that up. Every word that comes out of your mouth is a lie."

A low growl was Garret's only response.

If he stayed any longer, Garrett would try to kill him. The anger he felt toward his brother was rapidly fading to a numb disgust. Garrett had made his choice; he preferred to live in the filth and slime of the craggon den and seek his pathetic dreams of gold. Up on the surface, K'Sati was waiting for him with Neatfoot and Silverbeard.

"I'm done here. You are no longer my brother. You lost that privilege twenty years ago." He wiped the blood from his face and without a backward glance, set about finding his way out of this hell hole.

He found his way back down the tunnel to Garrett's sleeping cave. For a moment, he considered taking the casket of gold with him, but it seemed pointless. This gold was tainted; just like Garrett and Paul and every other mandragon who had ever hoped to pull gold out of a craggons den. The gold on Aurum only led to madness.

He noticed a smaller tunnel leading from the back wall of Garrett's sleeping quarters. The tunnel was lower and narrower than the main lava tube. The surface texture in this tunnel was coarser; the air cooler and less feculent. Forced by the low ceiling to walk hunched over, he braced himself against the sides of the tunnel and instinctively made his way toward the surface. The lack of guano in the narrow tunnel reassured him.

His thoughts were consumed by Garrett's betrayal. The string of lies his brother told everyone had stolen his childhood from him. His parents must have known something; or guessed. They'd been so agreeable when he told them he wanted to attend that private art school in Boston. They never invited Garrett home for the holidays. It was almost as if they suspected Garrett's involvement.

He'd been so stupid. So willing to believe Garrett when he said they shared a psychic connection. That he'd made such a massive fool of himself burned deep. He readjusted his pack in the narrow tunnel and moved forward. His hands shook badly. When the icy chill of fresh air hit his face, he welcomed it. It smelled as sweet and fresh as any he could remember.

He wondered if K'Sati had already left. She'd sensed Garrett's true nature almost immediately, but he'd refused to listen. She was so sweet; so unassuming and quiet, it was easy to overlook her quiet strength. She'd only had his best interests at heart. He could trust her. She was herd to him. He hurried forward, eager to reach her; hoping he wasn't too late.

THIRTY

At a narrow crevice near the entrance to the mine, Wayne motioned for silence. Someone was coming; they heard muttering and the sounds of footsteps before they saw him. Renly Harkness came into view.

He paused, as if temporarily blinded by the light, and Wayne motioned to Lyle and Nevers to grab him. Second later, they had him cuffed and helpless, not that he put up much resistance. He'd obviously been beaten badly.

"Thanks for makin' this so easy for us, Harkness." Wayne squinted at the man, so changed since he'd last seen him as to be nearly unrecognizable. Blood poured from Renly's nose and a cut on his lower lip. He wore a pair of badly scuffed Italian leather dress shoes and the clothes and sleeveless battle vest of a Khirjahni tribesman. Wayne recognized the heavy-looking satchel he wore across his chest.

Living rough on the prairie had made him nearly unrecognizable. He'd acquired a certain weathered toughness. Lean and wiry, he glared at Wayne with a dangerous expression.

Wayne frowned; there was something else, something different about his eyes. A pale ring of blue circled the brown iris. *Just like…*

The answer came to him like an explosion. Heat roared through him. With a wordless cry, he launched himself at Harkness, pounding him with his fists. Harkness went down like a stone and curled into a ball.

Wayne kicked him again and again.. "Ya fucking animal! What gave ya the right put your hands on her? I helped you look for your damned brother and this is how you repay me? Ya go behind my back? Take this, asshole!" He kicked Harkness again and again, as each blow brought a satisfying grunt from Harkness.

"Easy, boss," Lyle held him off. "Gotta keep the noise down, 'member? Don't want to bring those craggons down on us now."

He delivered a final vicious kick to the head and allowed them to pull him away. He choked back bitter acid at his throat. "He's been sleeping with that bitch; don't tell me ya haven't," he hissed. "We can all see it. Ya got the same blue ring around your eyes she does."

Harkness groaned, but didn't say a word.

That K'Sati would let this piece of shit touch her made him sick to his stomach. He'd spent months trying to seduce her. "The local cuisine is off limits without a condom, idiot. Otherwise you'll end up just like 'em. They're all diseased, get it? Ya just lost your passport off this hunk of rock. Federation rules. No transport captain will touch ya now. Gotta protect the masses. Was it worth it?"

K'Sati's recent reticence toward him suddenly made sense. She'd been avoiding him, even before the Terran arrived, but he probably wasn't the only guy she'd been playing games with. He'd been worried she'd taken a shine to the stable master, Ruben, but no; she'd taken up with this pathetic piece of shit. Or maybe the both of them.

Harkness heaved and spat up a gob of blood. Good. This guy wouldn't be a problem much longer.

Nevers squatted down beside Harkness and pulled up his head by his hair. "How many more down there?"

But Harkness was too far gone to answer. "Doesn't matter," Wayne replied. "Come on, we'll leave him to Corey. The bitch will tell me what I want to know."

They dragged him back up the trail to where they'd left Corey and K'Sati. Neither of them looked happy. K'Sati sat huddled on the ground, clutching the tattered remains of her shirt to chest, a mutinous look on her face. Corey had a bloody lip. As soon as she saw them, she scrambled to her feet.

Wayne ran his hand through his hair. The sight of her changed the heat of his anger. Seeing her like this, handcuffed and shirtless, stirred something primal within him. His body responded, thick with desire. He had never seen her angry like this; her eyes flashing, her face flushed with heat. He wanted to strip the rest of her naked and beat her into submission with his bare hands, like he'd never dared do before. To punish her; to make her cringe and beg him for forgiveness. For mercy.

He forced himself to look away. Not now. For what he had in mind, he wanted privacy, and this wasn't the time or place. No matter how much he wanted her, the gold had to come first.

She wouldn't look at him. Her eyes were only for Harkness. "What have you done to him?"

"He just tried to talk a little sense into your lover boy," Nevers retorted.

"Can it." Wayne motioned to them to drag Harkness's limp form over to Corey. "Got another one here for ya, Corey. You sure you don't want to come along?"

He didn't like the way Corey was looking at the girl. That he'd tried to claim her as soon as his back was turned. Bad enough that she had something going with Harkness, but at least he wouldn't be pulling any funny stuff in his condition. It still bothered him that he'd so underestimated both the bitch and the Terran.

Corey shook his head. "Nah, you guys go ahead. The little girl and I were having a discussion."

"I wouldn't if I were you," Nevers chimed in. "The girl belongs to Wayne and he doesn't like to share, isn't that right?"

"I said shut your fucking trap, Nevers." He turned to Corey. "Ya lay a hand on her and I'll take you apart with my bare hands and leave you in that cave for craggon fodder. Understand?"

Corey nodded, but he didn't look happy.

Wayne grasped the K'Sati's arm until she winced. "Who else is down there?" He shook her. "And don't lie to me because I'll know."

She stared at him, her eyes flat. "Where's Golden Boy?"

He backhanded her; savoring the satisfaction as she hit the dirt, even as he rubbed his hand in pain. He'd forgotten those damn horns kept him from really getting a good lick in. Like as broke a bone or two in his hand. "It's too late for Golden Boy, and it's too late for you, bitch."

But even as she scrambled to her feet again, she had that same mutinous look in her eyes. He laughed. "Hoo, look a you, girl. I bet ya anything she'd love to kill me right now, wouldn't ya?" He gave Corey a final warning. "You touch her you're dead."

He turned and led the way back down the trail. It no longer mattered whether Corey would ignore his orders or not. Not one of the three one of them would be coming back with them. People disappeared into the forbidden zone all the time. It's not like anyone was going to come looking for them. And if the gold in the cave was as plentiful as everyone said, he'd be set for life. More than enough to pay for his ticket off this planet and away from Duprees and Arkady forever.

The idea appealed to him; his conviction grew with every step. Of course, everything depended on how much gold they found in the cavern, but Nevers claimed that the dream dust junkie, Jason Brown had brought a six-pound nugget to the assayer's office earlier in the week. He'd gotten that nugget from somewhere, and Wayne was willing to bet this was the place. A hundred to one, junkie Jason was a buddy of the Harkness brothers. It was the only explanation that made sense. He had to have a regular supplier somewhere, and mandragons were the only ones with access to both gold and dream dust. Jason Brown had to be the guy K'Sati and Harkness were following. He was one of the men in that cave; Wayne was certain. That made the mandragon, Harkness' brother, the only other person down there. He remembered his encounter with Jason in the stables. The guy was a lightweight. The three of them would have no problems dealing with the junkie and a mandragon.

He paused just outside the entrance. "Way I figure it, we're facing a mandragon and that pathetic little junkie, Jason Brown. I want to go in real quiet and if we can, sneak up on them. If they hear us, they'll assume its Harkness coming back. They won't be expecting three of us at all."

Each of them had the laser lights they'd brought with them from the sleds. "I don't know what it's going to be like down there, but I expect there will be at least a lantern or two will already be lit. If they spot us first, follow my lead.

"How we going to split up the gold?" Lyle asked. "I don't want to give any of my share to Corey."

"Far as I'm concerned, we gave Corey every chance to come with us. I think a three-way split of whatever we find works good for me." Wayne studied men's faces for their reaction. They were taking all the risk, and the stink wafting out of that hellhole was the price of a share.

The men nodded in solemn agreement. Each of them covered their nose and mouth with their shirts and descended into the craggons lair.

THIRTY-ONE

Renly lay still, waiting until Wayne and his men were out of earshot. K'Sati kneeled beside him, hovering over him, her warm breath soft on his face.

She murmured into his ear. "Are you alright?"

Her hands cupped his face and he leaned into their roughness. Warm, capable, trustworthy hands.

He kept his eyes closed. No, not right. Not right at all. All the unspent fury he'd walked away from when he'd left Garrett to his stinking gold had been snatched away when he saw K'Sati.

It didn't matter anymore that his long-cherished beliefs in his brother the hero had been based on one big fat lie. The lie had not been of Garrett's making. Not completely, at any rate.

The bigger lie had been that he'd allowed fear to take over his life. *Don't go out, bad people are out there. Don't eat that, it can make you sick. Pain is a symptom of illness. You. Might. Die.*

All bullshit. Like now. He could barely catch his breath. He had at least two broken ribs and his mouth was full of blood, but he knew with absolute certainty that whatever was broken or battered or bruised right now didn't matter. Pain would not kill him. Wayne would. Wayne would kill them both.

He opened his eyes. Her lips were smeared with his blood. "Where's the guard?"

She glanced across the camp. "Twenty feet. Between us and the traggahs. He has a gun."

His pack was beneath him, where he couldn't reach it. "Help me up."

She tensed. "What are you going to do?"

"I'm going to distract this guy. While I do that, I want you to release the traggahs."

"No! He will kill you."

He shook his head. "We're already dead. Maybe this won't work, but we've got to get out of here." She'd been right to fear Wayne. No doubt he planned to kill them both in the most painful way possible. Their only chance lay with the guard. There was no way of telling how much time they had before Wayne and the others came back. "I'll be okay. Get out while you can."

He reached for her, but she was already gone. Over to where the guard with the gun was standing.

Oh no. She was trying to help him by distracting the guard. He rolled over to his stomach, and got to his knees. The guard gave him a brief glance, but K'Sati smiled and touched the guard's arm, keeping his attention riveted on her.

She was flirting with him! He had never seen her act like this. She lowered her hands, giving the guard an eyeful of her naked breasts. Unsurprisingly, she he had the guard's complete attention.

He turned his back to them, and slipped the stonewood club from beneath his belt.

With her hands cuffed, she was helpless to resist the guard's attentions. The horror-stricken look on her face and fixed grin revealed to him how hard this was for her, but the guard wasn't looking at her face.

He used the club as a brace and pulled himself to his feet. Gripping the club in both hands, he hefted it. K'Sati had the guard turned to that his back was to him. The guy was three big strides away.

He took a deep breath. He would only have one chance at this.

The guard must have seen something in K'Sati's face, because he turned before the blow connected, and managed to grab the club by its length. The guard was burly and able to twist it out of his grasp with ease.

Renly didn't hesitate. He lowered his head and used his momentum to shove the man off balance with his shoulder. The both of them went down and the club went flying. K'Sati screamed.

Renly struggled to get to his feet, but knew he was too late.

The guard reached for his gun.

THIRTY-TWO

Wayne flashed the laser's narrow light beam around the main cavern. The air was warm here. Warmer than anything they'd experienced since setting out on this blasted expedition, at any rate. The reek of ammonia and feces had tears streaming from their eyes, but he was pleased to note Nevers and Lyle weren't put off by a little stink. Nevers pointed his light along a two-inch wide crack in the cavern wall gleaming with a rich vein of gold. Holy crap.

The sounds of voices reached them and they followed the sounds into a smaller cave; this one with a bed and crude furniture, then on through a short tunnel toward a light shining from a cave ahead of them. He didn't have to say a word as all three of them stalked silently toward the sounds of quiet scraping.

The sight of Jason Brown and the mandragon chewing at a massive chunk of gold both disgusted and thrilled him. They were both high; nearly oblivious to everything around them. And subduing the both of them had been ridiculously easy. They handcuffed Jason, but the mandragon's thick arms were too thick for cuffs. Wayne instructed Nevers to watch him with his gun.

Jason was wacked out of his skull. The mandragon appeared

coherent, but obviously not too happy about their presence. The gold gleamed bright as the sun in the laser light.

"Damn sweet. Will you looky here," Lyle's voice carried a reverent tone.

"No shit." The sight of such a treasure took his breath away.

"What's wrong with them," asked Nevers.

"They've got the pox," Lyle answered. His eyes never left the gold. "In another few months, Jason will be a mandragon just like the other one. Makes you sick, don't it?"

"His name is Paul. Paul Hite." The mandragon's voice reminded Wayne of a talking crow he'd seen once back on Earth.

"You must be Harkness. We got your brother right outside."

The mandragon didn't respond.

"What do we do?"

Lyle's eyes had gone glassy. Whether from the ammonia fumes or the allure of the gold, Wayne couldn't tell. "Find us some tools we can use to dig that big chunk out. Come on, anything."

He gave Nevers his gun and told him to keep an eye on them, while he and Lyle searched the place. They went back to the sleeping quarters and found four wooden crates filled with gold nuggets.

He let out a low whistle. None of the nuggets was bigger than his fist, but the chests were full and more importantly, portable. They could take the crates with them and leave immediately.

Wayne grinned and reached into the crate for a few heavy nodules. "There must be a hundred pounds of nuggets in each one of these." Most looked like solid gold; only a few carried any sort of quartz or inclusions. The weight felt good in his hand.

Lyle grabbed a handful as well. "We've got to take these with us."

Lyle began to fill his pockets with nuggets, but Wayne stopped him. "No, wait. We'll take these chests with us. Load 'em on the traggahs. Divvy it up when we get back to the sleds."

"I'm not leaving without that big rock back there," Lyle warned.

"Suit yourself." Wayne flashed his light around the squalid cave. "I don't see anything here we can use to dig with, and there's no telling how big that gold rock is. I don't want to spend any more time down here than I absolutely have to, especially since these crates are already packed and ready to go. And I'm not waitin' around for the resident craggon to come back."

Lyle nodded noncommittally. "Let's go talk to Nevers."

They trooped back to where they'd left Nevers watching over the mandragon and Paul.

He frowned at them. "Where are the tools?"

The mandragon's fixed smile widened. "You're the only tool here, civilian. You want to call down the craggons? You use a metal tool in here and they'll be down on you quicker than lightning. This is how you do it." Using his lower tusks, the mandragon gouged a bit of dirt away from the nugget and ate it.

Wayne's stomach lurched in disgust. This golden boulder was covered with similar marks, just like the big nuggets at the Gold Ball. He'd always wondered about the marks. The longer they stayed down here, the greater their chances for catching dragon pox grew. Oh god, he did not want to be down here one minute longer than absolutely necessary.

He turned to Nevers. "If you and Lyle want to risk catching the pox to stay down here and dig that nugget out, you've got my blessing. I'll take the crates and go."

"Like hell you will." The mandragon leapt at him, but Nevers used the butt of his gun to knock him back. "This is not your gold; it's mine."

"You don't get a vote here, Harkness." Wayne took his gun back from Nevers. "The way I see it, you can keep quiet and stay out of my way or I'll just shoot you now and let you rot down here where you belong. You're nothing but animals, the both of you." He glanced at his men. "You guys coming? No amount of gold is worth risking the pox for. There's more than enough in those crates for each of us." He nodded toward the mandragon and Paul. "Is that how you want to end up?"

"Wait," Lyle said. "There's a hot spring in the main cavern. We can use the water to dissolve this crap." He poured water from his water skin over the nugget and pawed the mud away from the edges. "See? We've got other skins we can fill from the spring; once the water penetrates the dirt around that thing, it'll pop right out. Take us a day, at most."

Wayne wiped his sweaty face. Lyle was a pretty smart guy. With the three of them working, it probably wouldn't take long at all.

The mandragon made a rasping sound deep in his throat. Wayne realized it as laughter.

"What's so funny?"

"You can't work while the craggon's here."

"Ah shit, he's right." Lyle shrugged. "So, we'll work around 'im. Isn't that what you do anyways?"

Wayne didn't like Lyle making assumptions about what they were doing. It wasn't right. He was the one in charge here, not Lyle. He made his decision.

"Do what you want. I'm taking those crates and leaving."

The mandragon's laughing croak sounded again. "Not so fast, big guy. Craggon's coming."

THIRTY-THREE

K'Sati tripped and skidded on her hands to reach Renly's club. The stonewood was heavier than it looked, and the handcuffs restricted her movement, but she scrambled to her feet, determined. She ran toward Corey's back; the club raised over her head, ready to strike. Behind her, the blindfolded traggahs whistled a warning. Corey already had his gun out. Great stars, he was going to shoot Renly!

She swung the club at the back of his head with all her strength, but struck only a glancing blow off his shoulder. He grunted with the impact and the shot went wide.

Renly lowered his head and plowed into the man's stomach. They rolled in the dirt, but handcuffed as he was, Renly was no match for the bigger man. She brought the club down into the middle of Corey's back with everything she had.

Corey grunted and his whole body stiffened into a spasm. He dropped the gun

Renly shouted at her, "Go, K'Sati! Get out of here!" He squirmed out from beneath Corey's dazed form.

But she would not leave without him. As she raised the club to strike Corey again, a large shadow passed overhead. Instinctively, she ducked; then froze.

In a whoosh of air, a yellow craggon landed in the middle of the camp its attention riveted on Corey, as he convulsed helplessly in the dirt. She tossed the club toward Renly, then raced to the blindfolded traggahs. She *had* to free them. She opened the gate and reached for Silverbeard's reins. In a single motion, she slipped off the bridle and whipped off his blindfold. The traggah bucked once at the sight of the craggon, then laid his ears back and took off at a dead run.

The craggon already had Corey trapped beneath one claw. It made a half-hearted snap at the traggah as he raced by, but was more interested Corey. And Renly.

K'Sati stood frozen, staring at the huge winged monster, helpless to do anything. Each one of its deadly curved black talons was as big as her whole hand. With Corey in one claw, the craggon hopped at Renly, who scrabbled away in the dirt, trying to reach the gun. She remembered craggons were carrion-eaters, but this one looked keen on killing both men.

Finally, Renly got his hands on the gun. He tried to run, but the craggon managed to snag the strap of his heavy pack in its claw. Renly was dragged off his feet, unable to flee. As the huge beast snaked in to deliver a killing bite, Renly fired a shot directly at the craggon's face.

The bullet glanced off the craggon's thick scales.

Another craggon screamed from close by, galvanizing her to action. Fueled by adrenaline and fear, she slipped the blindfold off Neatfoot and swung herself up onto the mare's back in a smooth motion. She grabbed a handful of mane, and dug her heels into the Neatfoot's side.

Two more shots rang out; this time the yellow craggon bellowed in pain and anger as loud as anything she'd ever heard in her life. Neatfoot whistled in terror, and they raced away. Her last glimpse of the camp showed a second craggon landing beside the big yellow, blocking her view of Renly.

THIRTY-FOUR

The mandragon's jaws widened. "Prepare yourselves, boys. We are about to have company."

"Yeah, right," Wayne smirked. "I don't hear a thing." This guy was nothing like that wimp brother of his. He'd seen other mandragons before, but always made sure he kept his distance. This creature's frozen expression made him impossible to read, but he had a crafty gleam in his eye. He would have already figured out what they were planning to do to him and his little junkie pal.

"Oh, right. I keep forgetting how bad human hearing is. Somebody upstairs just fired a shot." He cocked his head for a moment, as if listening.

"Shut your trap." But he tightened his grip on his the handle of his holstered gun. Nobody ever told him mandragons had better hearing than Terrans. He was pretty sure this guy was playing them for fools, but not absolutely certain.

"Craggons are very territorial, you know. She will hunt and eat anything down here that doesn't smell like craggon." The croaking laugh sounded again. "You're welcome to help yourself to all the mouthfuls of dirt you want. Of course, it takes a few days for the pox to take hold and cover that Earth stink you're wearing."

Wayne wiped the sweat off his face. The humidity in this stinkhole was getting to him. And this unnatural creature's smart mouth gave him the creeps. Like talking to a damned animal!

The sooner he got out of this place the better. He should just take the gold and leave now. He could probably load two chests on each traggah without much trouble, and fill his pockets with as much as they'd hold. He could out of here in less than an hour still be filthy rich. "You guys do what you want. I'm getting out of here."

He made a move as if to leave, but Lyle barred his way. "What are you doing? We're all together on this. You agreed. Look at the size of that rock over there. All we have to do is play it smart and we can get out with both the nugget and the gold. We're talking about a fortune here!"

Sweat trickled down the side of Wayne's face, but he resisted the urge to wipe it away. Lyle was becoming a real problem. "Weren't you listening to him? There's a fucking dinosaur outside. And in a few minutes, it'll be coming *inside*."

"Oops," the mandragon interrupted. "Two more shots. Sounds like more than one craggon is screaming up there." He shook his head theatrically. "Can't you guys hear any of this? Who's the idiot firing a weapon, anyway? You can't kill a craggon with a gun. Bullets can't penetrate their hide. Shooting at them just makes 'em madder."

"Gotta be Corey." Even Nevers looked spooked.

"I said shut up," Wayne hissed. He clenched his fists. "One more word out of you and I swear I'll shoot ya in the face," He cursed himself for letting Nevers bring Corey along in the first place. Well, maybe Corey could kill the thing; or better yet, the thing could save him a bullet and get rid of Corey. K'Sati and Harkness were already good as dead; but they wouldn't be able to get out with the gold with a bunch of craggons running around up there. There had to be another way out.

"You're the brother, right? Garrett Harkness?"

The mandragon rose clumsily to his feet. "In a former life."

"Your kid brother is up there with them craggons. Came all the way from Terra to find you. Seemed to think you needed rescuing."

The mandragon snorted; he helped his bleary-eyed friend to his feet. "We aren't close. Took me awhile to explain the concept to him."

Animal. Wayne shook his head. Nugget or no, they had to get out of here before the craggon came back. He had no doubt the craggon would kill them if he found them.

"Fine." Wayne leveled his weapon at the mandragon. "Show us the back way out of this trap and we'll be on our way."

"What if I don't?"

Lyle grabbed Never's gun from his holster and shoved it into the mandragon's ribs. "You die."

"Easy, pal." The mandragon, with Paul in tow, moved to walk past them. "You can't threaten me. I'm family to that big lizard out there. You guys came here to rob me of my gold. Don't expect me to help you."

Lyle's shot echoed loudly in the cavern, and Paul sagged to the floor, black blood pouring from the point-blank chest wound.

"You idiot!" Wayne snatched the gun away. "You want to get us all killed? You're going to bring that beast down here on all of us."

The mandragon knelt over Paul and checked for a pulse. He shot Wayne and accusing look. "He's dead."

Wayne felt his control slip away. In the ghastly light of the lanterns, the thing that had once been Renly Harkness's brother gave him an utterly reptilian stare.

"Once old Yellowsmoke gets a whiff of you three Terrans, she'll tear this place apart trying to kill you. In fact, I have no doubt she's whetting her appetite on my brother and your friends upstairs right now."

A rumbling roar echoed across the cavern.

Wayne froze. Nevers and Lyle looked like they were about to cry. The mandragon Harkness dragged Paul's body out of the cave, and out to the main cavern. "You better hope she finds his body and forget about looking for you, but I wouldn't' count on it." He rose and crossed the cave to a narrow passageway and paused. "Paul had the pox. She's gonna come looking for the intruder who killed her baby, and she won't be looking for me. I'd kill those lights if I were you," Garrett whispered. "Mommy's home."

THIRTY-FIVE

Renly estimated the yellow craggon's leathery wingspan spanned at least forty feet from tip to tip. The creature clutched the big guard in one powerful claw while it snapped at Renly with a hooked, eagle-like beak edged with pointed teeth. Encumbered by his heavy pack, he scrambled backwards, but the craggon had the strap of his pack snagged on one claw. Being cuffed, he couldn't get rid of the pack now, even if he wanted to.

The guard struggled weakly. He didn't know how the man could still be alive, but was too busy trying to get in a position to shoot. He caught a glimpse of first Silverbeard, then Neatfoot with K'Sati on board as they charged past, momentarily distracting the craggon's attention.

He scrambled to his knees, being careful not to drop the gun. He managed to get to his feet, only to fall again as the craggon lunged at the escaping traggahs, dragging the pack with her.

Overhead, a smaller, greyer version of the great yellow swooped down to investigate. The yellow craggon, infuriated by the smaller trespasser, lunged at the grey.

Leathery wings buffeted him from all sides. The yellow roared and leapt into the air at the smaller craggon. With a sharp jerk, Renly found himself suddenly freed from the craggon's grip on his pack. He ducked low, then rolled away from the battling lizards. He scrambled beneath the shrubbery at the edge of the camp and tried to make himself inconspicuous, even as he gripped the pistol in both hands.

The smaller craggon twisted out of the talons of the big yellow and screamed a challenge, but the yellow wasn't going for it. She dropped the guard; and began scratching furious gouges into the dirt, as if to claim her territory. The grey rose higher in the sky.

The guard landed in a bloody heap, less than a dozen feet away. Their eyes met. The guard screamed, but before Renly could react, the great yellow craggon bit him in two. He heard the crunch of bones and saw the guard's eyes dim. He remembered Okoro telling him how young Khirjahnis were able to kill craggons with a single spear to the eye

A shot rang out from inside the cavern. The craggon heard it, too. She paused to listen.

The grey pounced on her from above.

Quick as a cat she whirled and slashed out with her deadly claws. The thin membrane of his wing shredded, and he went for her throat. They rolled, each seeking to eviscerate each other with their deadly talons. Closer and closer they rolled.

The yellow managed to grab the grey by his neck and trap him beneath her, using her superior size and weight. They were so close, he could almost touch them. The grey's yellow eye faced him at point blank range.

He pulled the trigger. Nothing happened. He pulled the trigger again, but the gun was empty. The yellow delivered the killing blow to the grey with her wicked beak.

He shrank back, but she was too busy to notice him. She continued to pound at the unlucky grey's skull in a fury of blows, until she reached the brain. Finally, she seemed to realize that the grey was no further threat. She carefully sniffed the corpse, as if to assure herself he was no longer a threat.

Renly waited, his heart in his throat, for her to notice him. His stonewood club lay on the other side of the dead craggon. The empty gun would not help him, and neither weapon would help him get the cuffs off. He was utterly defenseless.

From the lavender skies above, other craggons screamed their challenges. Finally satisfied that the grey was truly dead, the yellow bellowed her answer at the circling intruders. The flyers retreated to tiny specs high in the sky.

Renly waited in the dense brush, holding his breath, too terrified to move. Gradually, the yellow seemed to satisfy herself that there was nothing else to do but return to her cave. He watched her move down the trail leading to the cavern until the rocks hid her from view.

He waited as long as he dared, but heard no more shots. Wayne and his men must be dead; Garrett and Paul too, probably. He would not mourn his brother's passing. Garrett had chosen his life's path; time to leave him to it. He would not risk his life again for his brother. He needed to find K'Sati now.

Cautiously, he edged his way out from the cover of branches, leaving the useless gun behind him. His club lay in the center of the clearing, twenty yards away. As he debated whether to go after it, two craggons landed in the middle of the camp. He withdrew, working his way deeper into the underbrush. Even as they began tearing at the corpse of the grey, he knew he would have to leave the club behind.

Weaponless and handcuffed, he didn't dare stick around. Maybe one of the tools in his pack would be able to break the cuffs, but first he needed to get as far away as possible from the camp.

The pain in his ribs made breathing difficult, but not impossible. Grimly, he headed down the trail, realizing as he did, that he was all alone, wounded, and lost. Up ahead somewhere, he sensed K'Sati, Neatfoot, and Silverbeard, but they couldn't help him. First sunset was less than an hour off; he was covered in blood, and the predators would be waking soon. Gritting his teeth against the pain, he began to jog.

THIRTY-SIX

K'Sati clung to Neatfoot's back, her heart hammering in her chest. In Neatfoot's panic to escape the craggons, the traggah raced down the trail at breakneck speed. Low branches scraped at them as they flew by, and K'Sati feared the terrified traggah would stumble and kill them both in her frenzied escape, but Neatfoot never faltered. The traggah's acrid sweat soaked her clothes; it seemed like hours before the traggah's hysteria began to fade.

By the time they reached the bottom of the trail, they both trembled with fatigue. Neatfoot made her way unerringly to the spring she and Renly had found two days before, and plunged knee-deep into the shallow water to drink. K'Sati slipped off her mount's back and did the same. The cold water slaked their thirst, but now that they had outrun the immediate danger, both of them needed food.

Neatfoot grazed hungrily on the tender grasses surrounding the spring, while K'Sati searched the lhossa bushes for berries; each a sweet explosion in her mouth, but not enough to sate her hunger.

She kept her attention focused on the trail behind them, alert for any sound. Any moment, she expected Renly to appear, but as the minutes stretched, she began to fear the worst. The idea of traveling alone at night terrified her, but if he did not show up soon, she would have to leave without him.

The thought that he might not be coming haunted her.

He was not dead. She sensed his presence miles behind her, but not clearly. She sensed Silverbeard too; ahead of them, all alone, and desperate to find them. His forlorn unhappiness pulled at her; calling to her like a desolate beacon. She sensed Neatfoot's anxiety-ridden longing for him as well. Traggahs did not belong in the mountains; they were children of the open spaces. She added her assurances to Neatfoot's soothing thoughts; they would be herd together again soon.

But none of them would be safe until they reached the herd out on the steppes. She took pity on hungry Neatfoot and curled up beneath the fronds of a large fern for a quick nap. In spite of her hunger, she fell asleep quickly.

When she awoke, the deep violet of the sky told her true sunset was less than an hour off. She did not dare waste a minute more. After another deep drink of water from the spring, she swung herself up onto Neatfoot's back, and they followed the game trail leading up and out of the mountains.

The trail grew steeper in the fading light. She dismounted to walk beside the traggah, fearing the animal would stumble in the darkness. They settled into a mindless rhythm; of moving forward, ever upward. Sometimes she grabbed at branches to help her pull herself forward, at others she gripped a handful of Neatfoot's mane and let the traggah pull her. With only the stars to light their way, she had no idea if they were still on the trail. She trusted Neatfoot's sense of direction, and knew the only way out the mountains was up and over.

Neatfoot began to huff and snort nervously. She skittered at shadows within shadows; sometimes dragging K'Sati with her as she shied. K'Sati began to hear small yips in the underbrush. At first, she thought they were the startled cries of awakened treboos, but before long, the calls were all around them.

Her blood ran cold. Hunters had found their trail.

She had no idea what kind of creatures these were. All she knew was that they were outnumbered. At least four, she thought. Maybe five. The darkness and rough terrain made it impossible to outrun them; they needed to find some sort of shelter.

Panic sapped her strength; the darkness made her footing unsteady. She panted; sweat ran into her eyes, making it even more difficult to see. They'd seen a cave as couple of miles back; they should have stopped there for the night. It would have been safer than scrambling around at night. But it was already too dark to see if something hadn't already claimed the shelter for the night. She'd hoped to walk all night, and escape the mountains in the morning, but realized neither she nor Neatfoot would be able to keep going much longer.

The terrain began to level out a bit, and the brush thinned and gave way to boulders and rocky soil. Her spirits soared as she remembered the place. The dim light of the stars illuminated a clearing full of hulking forms; the boulders would protect their backs.

She patted the traggah's neck and led her across the clearing, toward the largest clump of boulders. Behind her, the yips became calls. She urged Neatfoot forward, sensing their pursuers were about to attack.

They reached the sheltering rock formation and whirled to face their attackers. Neatfoot whistled a challenge.

There were five of them.

She couldn't see them clearly in the dark, but they were light-colored and furry, with long tails like rahgs, but about half their size. Too small to threaten a traggah alone, but as a pack, she had no doubts as to their intentions. These were predators. Even in the dim starlight, she could see the gleam of their teeth as they paced nervously; looking for an opportunity to attack.

The boulder at their back towered at least ten feet above her head, and smaller boulders flanking them on either side protected them from anything but a frontal assault. Neatfoot snorted and pawed the ground while she scrabbled around in the scree for fist-sized rocks.

The first darted in, quick as lightning, but wary of Neatfoot's hooves. She threw every stone with as much power as she was able. They dodged quickly, but she caught one with and it yelped sharply before limping away. The other four didn't seem to notice.

They had a strategy where they took turns darting in to bite at the traggah's legs. She sensed Neatfoot's anger, but her fatigue, too. Already, Neatfoot had taken several deep bites to her front legs, which bled black in the starlight.

It seemed to be a coordinated, practiced attack. She recognized their affinity for each other as something similar to the traggah's herd instinct. If she could wound more of them, she was pretty certain they would give up. She began pelting their attackers with rocks as fast as she could. Each time she scored a direct hit, she was rewarded with a sharp yip and cold satisfaction. Her arms ached. The pack grew bolder. She got one of them in the face, and another in the leg; hard enough so that he limped away on three legs. After they left, the final two disappeared into the darkness.

Neatfoot trembled beside her, her head hanging dispiritedly. She ran her hands down the traggah's injured forelegs. The wounds had bled freely, but weren't deep. It was too dark to see the damage, but Neatfoot did not appear to be limping. She coaxed the traggah to bed down in the shelter of the rocks, and sent her mental images of watching over her as she slept. Finally, the injured traggah snorted a long sigh and fell into a deep sleep.

Exhausted as she was, K'Sati could not close her eyes. What if those things returned with the rest of the pack? She did not believe they would last the night if they did. Alone, they were a target.

She hoped Renly was safe. She reached out with her gift, searching for him, but his presence did not feel as close as Silverbeard. Renly felt faint in her head, but alive.

As Neatfoot's breathing slowed, her head began to droop. She leaned against the traggah's broad, warm side, watching in case their attackers returned. She fought to keep herself awake and alert, but in spite of her fear, sleep overtook her.

THIRTY-SEVEN

Another roar rumbled through the outer cavern. "Cool the lights, guys," Wayne whispered. He snapped off his flashlight and Nevers followed, but Lyle had other ideas.

"Are you crazy? There's only one way we're going to get this gold out of here without ending up like that damn lizard-man. We've got guns, man. We've got to kill this thing, and we can't do it in the dark."

Wayne edged away from them, and picked up one of the blue-shielded lamps the mandragon had used. The guy had to be smart, to live with a craggon all this time. He wouldn't be using a blue light if it hadn't given him some kind of advantage. He switched on the lantern.

And if craggons could be killed with basic Terran hand weapons, they would have been wiped out decades ago for the gold. Lyle was a hunter by trade; he liked to shoot stuff. But Lyle had never faced a craggon. If they listened to him, they could all end up dead. Let Lyle deal with the craggon, if that's what he wanted.

Wayne flashed his blue lantern toward Garrett's retreating form. He was headed toward his personal sanctuary, where the gold was already packed up and ready to move.

"Give me back my gun," Nevers said to Lyle.

"It's mine now."

The craggon stink cranked up about a hundred notches as the beast circled the outer cavern. The creature sniffed noisily, searching for the intruders. He weighed the odds: take the risk that Lyle could kill the craggon, or hole up with the mandragon until things quieted down. To hell with it. Let the craggon take care of Lyle and Nevers. Once they were gone, he'd take care of the mandragon, take what he could carry and come back for the rest of the gold in his own time. He handed his gun to Nevers.

"Here. Take mine."

"You're not coming with us?"

Wayne eased his way over to the muddy area surrounding the giant nugget. "I'm no hero. I'm gonna find me a place to hide, until that thing calms down."

Lyle snickered, but Wayne didn't care.

After Lyle and Nevers moved into the outer cavern, he scrambled over to the massive nugget. He choked back his nausea as he grabbed handfuls of the fetid mud and slathered the muck all over his pants and shirt. Let those two idiots feed the monster, and it would be far less interested in looking for anyone else; especially if he smelled no different from the guys who were already living here.

In only a few minutes, he'd coated his clothes in reconstituted craggon shit. If that didn't protect him from becoming craggon fodder, he figured the stink would probably kill him.

He grabbed the blue lantern and moved down the passage toward the mandragon's sleeping quarters. Garrett Harkness would be his ticket out of here, and he did not intend to let that guy abandon him to the craggon.

A shot rang out. The craggon's scream echoed through the narrow passage like a physical presence.

Two more shots rang out, and he heard someone's scream abruptly cut off.

He listened to the sudden silence. Had the scream been Nevers or Lyle? Or both? Wayne decided it didn't matter. He wondered if he ought to risk a peek. If the craggon was dead, he'd have heard from his men already. If Nevers and Lyle were dead, well, too bad. Every man for himself.

He thought about trying to retrieve one of the guns, but quickly decided against taking the risk. No guarantee the craggon was really dead. The risk wasn't worth it. All he really needed was for that Garrett Harkness creature to show him the other way out. And there *had* to be one.

Wayne knew lots of ways, quiet ways, of convincing the mandragon to tell him what he wanted to know.

And then all that gold would be his for the taking.

More than he ever expected to win betting on Golden Boy. Getting the load out of the mountains might be dicey, but the traggahs would be able to carry more than half of it. Whatever they couldn't, he'd leave. No point in getting greedy, but long as he didn't have to share, he'd still be richer than Midas. He would just have to make sure there were no survivors.

Once he got the gold back to where they'd stashed the sleds, it would be easy to get back to the coast and arrange passage off Aurum. But the Gold Festival was nearly over. Figure two days to get back to the sleds, and then another two to get back the coast. Tight, but doable, if he pushed it. And for that kind of payoff, he would.

He wiped his hands on his pants and drew his Bowie knife from the sheath on his belt. The entrance to Garrett Harkness's living quarters was just ahead of him. He picked up the blue lantern and headed after the mandragon.

THIRTY-EIGHT

The next morning, K'Sati ran her hands down Neatfoot's swollen and enflamed legs. The traggah stood stoic, her head low, her nose close to K'Sati's cheek, blowing little puffs of breath as if to say, *ouch ouch.* She winced as she probed her traggah's injuries; sensitive to the animal's pain, unable to ease her misery.

Renly still had not caught up to them, but she could not wait any longer. They had to get out of the mountains and onto the steppes before dark, where she was certain Silverbeard and the herd would quickly find them. With the other traggahs to protect them, they would be able to wait in safety.

They started slow; as the morning progressed, Neatfoot seemed to improve. By the time the twin suns showed midday above them, they'd begin their final descent from the mountains, and were nearing the rocky zone, which bordered the high steppes. Neatfoot's demeanor seemed to improve, and her ears perked up.

The herd must be near. She reached out with her gift and called to Silverbeard.

The quiet was shattered with the piercing call traggah whistles, warning of danger. Neatfoot whistled an answer and tossed her head in agitation. Without thinking, K'Sati swung up onto her back and they raced toward the sounds of distress.

They rounded a set of low cliffs and came upon Silverbeard and Golden Boy fighting a losing battle against a pack of longteeth. Neatfoot thundered into the melee, striking out with her hooves and scattering the eight longteeth, who backed off but did not leave. K'Sati clung to Neatfoot's mane, but had little control over the furious and determined traggah.

Blood dripped from huge gashes at Silverbeard's neck and shoulders. He held his bloodied right rear leg well off the ground. Both traggahs were white-eyed and covered in a sweaty lather. They would not last much longer.

The longteeth circled closer. At the base of the cliffs K'Sati caught sight of three hover sleds tucked beneath a low overhand. This must be where Wayne and his men had cached their sleds! She attempted to coax Neatfoot back toward the overhang, but two longteeth lunged for them. In her panic, Neatfoot slipped on the loose shale and K'Sati screamed as the traggah stumbled and came down on top of her. The bones in her lower leg snapped beneath Neatfoot's weight.

The longteeth swarmed over them, lunging at Neatfoot as she struggled to rise. Trapped beneath her traggah's bulk, she could do nothing but shield her face from her attackers and wait to be ripped to shreds.

The longteeth ignored her and focused on Neatfoot.

Golden Boy and Silverbeard rushed in, their huge hooves slashing at the longteeth. One longtooth, which had Neatfoot by her throat, had his skull crushed in the melee. Neatfoot struggled to regain her feet, and K'Sati grunted in pain as her thigh snapped under the pressure.

The three traggahs faced off against the seven longteeth. Silverbeard limped on three legs and blood flowed freely from

Neatfoot's neck; only Golden Boy remained unscathed.

She had to get to the sleds. Grunting with the effort, K'Sati used her arms and elbows to drag herself across the scree toward the sleds at the back of the shallow cave. One leg was useless; the other numb and uncooperative. If she did not reach the sleds, she would die.

Outnumbered, the traggahs fought gamely against the longteeth. They were running out of time! With trembling hands, she finally pulled herself to the nearest sled, only to find her hopes dashed. The sleds were designed to be operated from a seated position; both feet were required to start the vehicle. The heart-pounding pain in her leg would not allow her to get into the seat without assistance. Even if she did manage it, she would not be able to operate the pedals.

A longtooth, one of the young ones, circled closer. She had never been this close to one. The massive skull and six-inch canines dwarfed the savage yellow eyes, but there was no mistaking the sly intelligence behind them. It darted forward and made a grab for her.

Instinctively, she kicked out with her good leg, but the longtooth grabbed her by her injured leg and began to drag her away from sleds, back to his pack. The pain in her thigh flared white hot. She screamed in agony before the darkness took her.

THIRTY-NINE

Renly gave a satisfied grunt as the chain linking his handcuffs broke apart. His hands shook so badly, he worried he would not be able to free himself. He slipped the chasing hammer back into his pack, then rubbed his bloody wrists where the tight metal cuffs remained locked in place. Getting enough leverage to pound the chisel into the metal links had been tricky, but at least now his hands were no longer bound together. He'd used the leather of his vest to cushion the sounds of the iron hammer striking steel chisel, and so far, no craggons had appeared. He hadn't held a burin in his hand in months. The weight of it comforted him. He slipped the chisel beneath his belt and felt better than he had in days.

Walking away from the stonewood club nearly broke him, but after the two craggons landed to feed off the corpses, he knew better than to stick around. He stayed off the trail, where the circling craggons might see him, and used the underbrush as a screen. Keeping to the trees and brush, it took him hours to put a safe distance between him and the craggon's den. He dared not return to the trail until after first sunset.

Worry for K'Sati kept him going. He hoped she was safe. She had no more experience in this wilderness than he, and only the traggahs to protect her. With any luck, he would find her bedded down in the same place they'd found before. But as the shadows lengthened, his hopes of catching up with her faded.

He was forced to halt at full dark. With no rocks or caves for shelter, he chose the base of an enormous cedar-like tree with a nest of roots extending from its base like the arms of a massive octopus. Cave-like crevices, big enough for him to crawl into, riddled the soil beneath the roots. He groped beneath the tree blindly; terrified of being bitten by something even worse than a tree lizard. He finally found a den-like space, barely big enough for him to curl up in. The nest-like root structure gave him a sense of safety he hadn't felt for some time. The pain in his ribs made lying down for sleep impossible, so he settled himself into a sitting position, with his back supported by the moist earth of the cave. Compared to the disgusting hellhole of the craggon's den, the clean smell of earth and tree roots reminded him of home.

Garrett was dead to him. He felt nothing; no sense of loss. Only a lingering pity for the creature his brother had become. As his memories returned, so too did the shame and pain and anger for what he'd been forced to endure. Even the bad man had been shocked by Garrett's callousness.

And as horrified as he'd had been by the mandragons, his conversation with Sully convinced him that at heart, they were still capable of human feelings and emotions. Only now did he realize that Garrett's total lack of empathy could not be blamed on the pox. Garret must have been a sociopath long before he came to Aurum. Not that it mattered any more. He'd heard the gunshot. Garrett was gone. Wayne and his men merely accelerated the inevitable. And now they were gone, too.

He closed his eyes. *It's over. Finally.* The festering wound of his forgotten childhood had been lanced. Garrett had undone himself, and could never hurt him again.

Tomorrow he would find K'Sati and the traggahs. They would head back to the coast and then…*What?*

Anything you want.

The idea was too big to contemplate. He thought of K'Sati, but would not allow himself to dwell on thoughts of her. Or Silverbeard. Enough to feel safe within his nest of tree roots, and be thankful he survived the day. No longer haunted by the ghosts of his past, and in spite of the danger and strange night sounds around him, he slept.

* * *

The shrill sound of a traggah whistle woke him in the full light of mid-day. Golden Boy stood some twenty feet outside his den, pawing and snorting. Renly winced into the bright morning, while Golden Boy snorted and bucked as if to say, *hurry up!*

Painfully, he managed to crawl out of his sleeping den and stagger to his feet. The stabbing pain in his ribs twisted like a knife with every move. Purple bruises, cuts, and scrapes covered his arms, but he felt wide-awake and alert.

"What is it, boy?"

Golden Boy sidled nearer, and held his near foreleg cocked, as Neatfoot did to assist K'Sati to mount. The traggah had no bridle, no reins, or anything to hang onto, but the message was clear.

Renly stroked the traggah's neck, and as he made contact, he sensed the animal's urgency and deep agitation. Something was wrong.

Using Golden Boy's leg as a step up, he launched himself onto the traggah's back, gasping in pain as his ribs protested. No sooner had he swung his leg over than Golden Boy took off at a dead run, and Renly was forced to grab the traggah's sparse mane to hang on.

Golden Boy was bigger and more powerfully built than Silverbeard. The traggah pounded down the trail as Renly clung to him, praying he would not fall. He murmured soothing words to him, hoping to calm the excited traggah, but even as he saw Golden Boy flick his ears back to listen, they flew down the trail at breakneck pace.

An hour later, they reached the floor of the ravine, but the traggah paused only long enough for a snatched slurp of water before galloping up the slope.

He heard the whistles of alarm well and snarling before they arrived. Golden Boy rounded the trail and burst onto the scene: three Longteeth fought over the remains of Neatfoot while Silverbeard struggled valiantly against a longtooth at his throat and another on his back. Two dead longteeth lay trampled and lifeless in the dirt.

Renly slipped the chisel out from his belt and dug his heels into Golden Boy's side.

Without hesitation, Golden Boy threw himself at the longtooth hanging from Silverbeard's neck. Renly lost his balance and allowed himself to slide off rather than fall. He stepped around Golden Boy and stabbed at the longtooth on Silverbeard's back with all his might.

The predator was quicker. It leapt out of range and circled around to join the rest of the clan dining on Neatfoot.

Silverbeard screamed in terror, but even as Golden Boy slashed out at his attacker at his throat, Silverbeard went to his knees and collapsed. Still the longtooth did not let go. Renly slammed his chisel into the top the longtooth's skull over and over until it fell senseless into the blood-soaked dirt beside Silverbeard.

He knelt beside his traggah but his friend was already gone.

"I am so sorry, boy," he choked. A great emptiness filled him. He stroked the blood-soaked fur of Silverbeard's neck. Not even Garrett's absence filled him with such as sense of grief. His magnificent protector was gone.

"*Be at peace, my friend. Ever may you run with the great herd.*"

While Golden Boy furiously trampled Silverbeard's killer to a pulp, the other longteeth fought over the remains of Neatfoot.

"K'Sati?" he called. A moan sounded from behind him. Beneath the overhang, he recognized three land sleds. He ran up the incline toward the shallow cave. At the back of the overhang, he spied K'Sati lying behind one of the sleds. "K'Sati!"

"Take a sled and get out of here," K'Sati called out weakly. "You cannot help us."

He gathered her into his arms and kissed her damp forehead. She felt cool to the touch. Too cool.

The sight of her mauled leg sickened him. So much blood.

Golden Boy edged closer to the sleds, as the remaining pack of five longteeth continued to snarl and fight over their meal.

Her pulse fluttered beneath his fingers. They needed blankets. And weapons. The longteeth would turn on them any minute. He leapt to his feet and began to search the sleds.

"There are no weapons here," she said. "I have already looked. There is nothing. Take Golden Boy and head for the coast. If you hurry, you may be able to catch the final transport leaving Aurum."

Tenderly, he lifted her head into his lap and wiped her damp hair off her face. "How can you believe I'd leave you here?"

Her eyes were dull with pain. "My leg is broken. I cannot walk or ride. If you stay they will kill us both."

Anger and frustration coursed through him. This couldn't be happening. Not after all they'd already come through. Not for the first time, he wished he'd brought the club with him. Without a weapon…

He eased her back to the ground and inspected the sleds. Any one of them was large enough for her to stretch out on the back. He'd never piloted a sled before, but the controls looked similar to the Personal Flight Vehicles on Earth. In the sleds, they could hover high enough above the ground to avoid the longteeth. The sleds would take them to safety.

His gaze rested on Golden Boy. One lone traggah would not stand a chance against four longteeth. Weariness washed over him. The traggah had brought him here to help. He'd fought so bravely, and even now, he stood before the entrance, quivering with outrage as the longteeth tore into his stable mates. His herd.

The traggahs could easily outrun the longteeth, yet Golden Boy chose to stay, even though he was not bonded to either K'Sati or himself. He had never known such loyal, noble creatures. Golden Boy should have run his race, won the richest prize in the universe, and been released to join his herd in the wild. It wasn't fair that he would die like this.

He ran his hand through his hair and stared out beyond the bloody arena to the steppes stretching wide and empty, all the way to the horizon. His lips trembled, and he shook his head.

He slipped over the barricade to stand by Golden Boy.

"What are you doing?"

She sounded so weak. "Don't worry, I'm not leaving you."

The traggah seemed to be waiting for him. He sensed the animal's demanding question in his mind. The three younger longteeth had been driven off Neatfoot's carcass; they now began tearing at Silverbeard.

Heat rose into his face. Renly shouted at them and shook his chisel at them. They startled, but continued to tear at the Silverbeard's neck and stomach, gorging themselves. Not even longteeth could easily penetrate the thick hide of traggah skin, but watching them tear into Silverbeard's soft underbelly was something he would not stand for. Something he would not allow to happen to Golden Boy.

Not if he could help it.

He turned to Golden Boy and put his hand on the brave animal's neck. He closed his eyes.

I am Renly, and I am herd to Silverbeard, but Silverbeard is no more. I would bond with you, Golden Boy, if you will accept me. I pledge my friendship and loyalty to you. I will feed you and care for you and warn you of danger for as long as I am able. You are herd to me, Golden Boy. I will protect you with my life.

The traggah trembled beneath his touch. In his mind, a bright light flared, like the flame of a single candle. A voice that was a more than a feeling resonated within him.

I am Golden Boy of the stripe legs clan. You were herd to Silverbeard, who is no more. I will not leave you, through the Rahgs may chase us through the trees, the longteeth may surround us on the steppes, and the craggons may seek to snatch us into the sky. You are herd to me, Renly. I will protect you with my life.

The traggah bowed his head and leaned into hand. He caressed the sides of Golden Boy's head, gazing into the creature's intelligent eyes. He made a mental picture of the traggah herd, as clear and as detailed as his memory could provide.

"We are herd, Golden Boy, but you must leave us. You must go, now, and bring back the herd. Only the herd can save us from these longteeth." He pictured an image of the herd moving across the steppes in his mind and hoped the traggah would understand.

The traggah let out a huge shuddering sigh, and shook himself. To his mind, the traggah seemed to give him a reproachful looks, as if to say, *Now that we're bonded, why are you sending me away?*

"Go," he said softly, and slapped the traggah on his hip for emphasis.

Golden Boy gave a snort and a little buck, then lowered his head and took off like a racehorse, making a wide berth past the dining longteeth. One of them made as if to rush him, but the traggah veered sharply, and was soon out of reach and out of sight.

Grimly, Renly reached into his bag and took out his stoutest chisel and slipped the tane into a burin handle. He took out two of his chasing hammers and handed one to K'Sati.

"What are you going to do?"

She stared him with a fevered gleam. She was bloody, filthy, and had horns like a youngling traggah. She wasn't human, and nothing in this world or the next would make her so. Yet the sight of her roused something in him he could not explain, even to himself. He would not let those longteeth get to her; but if he tried to move the sled out from beneath the overhang, they would surely attack. And if he did not get K'Sati out of there, he doubted she would last another night. He had to protect her. There was no other option.

With his chisel in one hand, and his chasing hammer in the other, he turned to face the pack of longteeth. A sense of deliberate calm settled over him.

"Don't go anywhere. I'll be right back."

FORTY

He faced a divided pack; two youngsters fed at Silverbeard's carcass while the two adults finished off the remains of Neatfoot. He told himself he wouldn't need to kill them all; the adults were the most dangerous. Each of them outweighed him by a couple of hundred pounds, and both possessed the six-inch fangs, which the smaller juveniles did not yet have.

He edged toward the two adults, keeping an eye on the youngsters, who were busy fighting over the remains of Silverbeard. The adults ignored him until he thought he couldn't take another step.

The big female lunged at him, snarling.

She flew at him from less than ten feet away. He braced himself for the impact, his hammer raised.

As he anticipated, she leapt for his throat, just like they'd done to the traggahs.

He slammed down with the hammer with all his might, right between her eyes. Her momentum carried him to the ground, but she had no thought for him; she staggered away in a half circle before dropping to the ground.

Still on his hands and knees, the male came at him from the

side. Both weapons flew from his hands with the beast's impact. The longtooth ravaged his shoulder, straining to reach his neck. Renly got his arm up to protect himself, but creature overwhelmed him.

He reached for the burin in his belt, and in one swift motion stabbed the longtooth in the side. The chisel sliced through the ribs like butter and plunged deep into the brute's chest cavity. With a yowl of pain and anger, the predator whirled to escape, tearing the still-embedded chisel from his hand.

Renly scrambled to his feet, his right arm nearly useless, and pulled the other burin from his belt. The injured longtooth rolled in the dirt, trying to dislodge the weapon; instead, he merely drove it deeper. Dark blood seeped out from around the deep wound, but Renly didn't believe he'd inflicted a fatal injury. Slowly, he backed away from the big male.

Behind him, the younger longteeth had stopped their fighting to watch the big male struggle. The larger of the two darted forward, but as it leapt, Renly stepped to the side and stabbed it high in the shoulder. The cub yowled in pain and took off running, its tail between its legs. The other youngster took off as well, trailed by the wounded adult, with the chisel still firmly embedded between its ribs.

He fell to his knees, panting in the dust and blood as he watched the retreating longteeth. *I hope he takes a really long time to die*, Renly mused. He found his chisel and chasing hammer and wiped them clean, then shoved them back beneath his belt. Covered as he was, in blood and sweat and dirt, he felt invincible. Carefully, he slipped off his leather vest to inspect his mangled shoulder. Although the bruising was already starting, the thick craggon leather of the battle vest had protected him from even the longtooth's bite. Other than a superficial gash on his upper arm, the skin wasn't even broken.

Damn right.

He slipped the vest back on and hiked back up the slope to where

K'Sati lay.

She gripped the hammer fiercely, her eyes streaming tears. He knelt beside her and she pulled him close with a strength that surprised him. "I thought you were dead," she murmured.

He smoothed her hair. "I'm a little banged up, but I'm alive. Come on, love, let's get you onto one of these sleds before they decide to come back."

He strong-armed the largest sled out from beneath the cliff face and after a little experimentation, figured out how to operate it. He loaded it up with everything useful he could find; a full water skin, several packets of dried food, and enough traggah wool blankets to make K'Sati comfortable.

Her face was still pinched and pale, her skin hot and feverish. The sled would provide a smooth ride over most of the terrain, but even if they rode all night, he guessed it would be at two days or more before they reached civilization. K'Sati pointed him in a different direction from the one they'd come; she wanted to avoid the Temple of the Mother. He hoped the woodcarver, Okoro and his wife would be able to help them. He used tent stakes to stabilize her badly damaged leg, but knew it was only a temporary measure.

Getting her onto the sled was an agony for both of them. "Alright, love. Are you ready?

She nodded bravely. "Ready."

He got her onto her feet. In spite of all his efforts, she screamed as he lowered her to the floor of the sled, then apologized for being so weak.

He got her settled made her comfortable as possible. She was trembling and far too pale when he finally took his seat behind the wheel of the sled.

"Here we go," he called out.

FORTY-ONE

Wayne Strickland set down his pack to wipe the sweat from his face. Deep bite marks along one side of his face burned like fire to the slightest touch. Infected, probably. Not surprising. He was covered head to toe in mandragon blood and craggon feces. The stink didn't bother him as much now as in the cave, but he couldn't wait to get back to the sleds. The craggon shit he used to disguise his scent had dried and caked to his clothes. The heavy pack had worn sores into his shoulders, and they looked like a bloody pulp. They hurt like hell, but he only had a little further to go, and the gold would help him forget the pain.

Somehow, Renly Harkness and that infuriating bitch K'Sati had stolen the traggahs from him *again*. Without the traggahs to carry the gold, he'd been forced to rethink his plans for leaving this stinking planet. And walking out of the mountains on foot with ninety pounds of gold on his back would keep him from getting back to the coast in time to catch the last transport. He would be stuck here another four years. Ninety pounds of gold might be worth a lot of money to some people, but it wasn't nearly enough to set him up in the new life he pictured for himself. No, he would have to come back for the rest of it. Maybe dig that golden boulder out, too.

Of course, he'd have to avoid Duprees and the rest of the Arkady folks, but after the Gold Festival, they'd all clear out and go back to the mines for two years, at least. He'd be safe enough in town. He would use the time to get the rest of the gold out and then lay low at the coast and take things easy until the next Festival.

He couldn't wait to wash the stink off him in that spring they passed on the way in. With less than a mile to go until he reached the sleds, he finally believed he was going to get out of this mess, after all. He winced as he adjusted the weight of his heavy pack and continued down the trail. His hands and fingernails were stained black from the filth of the cavern. He had never been so disgustingly dirty in his life, but he didn't regret covering himself in craggon manure for one moment. The act had saved his life.

Not only had it saved him from meeting the same fate as Nevers and Lyle, he was certain the stink of craggon kept him safe from predators as he made his way out of the mountains. He walked all night, and never heard so much as a cracked twig.

In the end, only Garrett Harkness came close to beating him. The mandragon was smarter and stronger and than he ever imagined. Harkness came at him with one of the heavy crates filled with gold, and might have crushed him right there, if Wayne hadn't already been moving in to stab him.

The knife went in just below the armpit, and punctured the creature's lung. The wound slowed him down, but didn't drop him. They went down together, the mandragon snapping at his face, as Wayne kept right on stabbing him in the chest and neck. Finally he nicked an artery, and figured the mandragon would bleed to death, but the nightmarish thing refused to die.

It bit him on the jaw and held on, grinding his pointed teeth deep into the flesh. Wayne twisted and struggled to free himself, but his attacker was heavier and stronger. Only when Wayne finally managed to slit his throat and halfway sever his fool neck that the monster collapsed.

He found Nevers and Lyle's bodies in the craggon's cavern. Nevers died of a gunshot in the back. Lyle apparently killed the craggon with a shot to the eye, but was crushed beneath it as it died. He found his gun and grabbed Nevers pack, filling it with as much gold as he could carry. He dragged the other crates of gold outside the cavern and buried them beneath a pile of rocks, not far from Corey's remains.

Corey deserved everything he got, but the fact that K'Sati and Harkness had taken off with the traggahs burned his hide. A couple of thieves, the both of them. Every step he took down the trail was another strike against them. They would pay for this. Even one traggah could have gotten him out with enough gold for his needs. He cursed the both of them with every step; promising to make them beg him for death if he ever caught up with them.

K'Sati, in particular fooled him completely. She'd seduced him; persuaded him everyone else at Arkady Mining into thinking Golden Boy was a sure thing, then stole the traggah and left him behind to take the blame for it. He wondered how long she'd planned it. She must have been stringing him along for weeks.

He recognized the final curve in the trail leading to the cliff face to where they had stowed the sleds. As he rounded the curve, the smell of blood stopped him. Wayne froze in his tracks, unable to believe the scene before him. The clearing looked like a war zone; the dirt was churned up and clotted dark with blood and animal carcasses, but that wasn't what riveted his attention.

Renly Harkness sat in the driver's seat of Wayne's personal sled, with K'Sati seated like a queen behind him.

Wayne dropped his pack and drew his gun. He had a clear shot at either one of them, but Renly's chest presented a better target.

He fired.

The Terran twisted out of his seat and crumpled into the dirt beside the sled.

FORTY-TWO

Renly coughed and opened his eyes. Something in the palm of his hand burned like fire. He dropped it.

A bullet.

The stink of craggon washed over him and he glanced up to see a wild man covered in blood and filth trying to drag K'Sati out of the sled. The terror in her face fired his anger. He got to his feet and pulled the burin from his belt. Something about the wild man looked familiar.

K'Sati screamed in agony and fear. "Wayne, no!"

That guy just shot me!

Adrenaline pounded through him. He grabbed Wayne by his shirt and jerked him off K'Sati. Wayne went for the gun at his hip.

Renly acted without thinking. He drove his chisel through the larger man's chest. Wayne gave a little hiccup. His eyes glazed over and he crumpled motionless to the ground.

K'Sati reached for him, and he went to her. "Are you all right?"

She nodded, but her expression was full of pain. "Are you? I saw him shoot you."

He rubbed his chest. "He did. Good thing this vest is craggon hide. That's twice today it saved me. Three times, if you count keeping me from freezing to death."

"Oh, look!" He followed her gaze as she a pointed at a dust cloud rolling over the prairie toward them. "We've got company."

He reached out with his gift and sensed Golden Boy's brave spirit racing toward him. "It's Golden Boy. He's bringing the herd." He gazed into her green-brown eyes. "What say we fire up the sled and ride out to meet them?"

EPILOG

The unveiling of the new Seal of Khirjah was held in the walled garden of the royal residence of His Royal Highness, King Okanga Hakaroah. It was the start of Renly's second summer in Aurum, and the twin suns Oratei and Ahipu gleamed brightly overhead amidst cloudless lavender skies. A trio of musicians played native Khirjahni folk tunes on hand-carved stonewood pipes, while the guests mingled with members of the Royal family.

Ambassador Reinhardt was in attendance of course, as well as several senior officers from the Universal Consortium of Planets. The UCP had recently declared the Arkady Universal Mining embargo around Aurum illegal, and the officers were here to redefine access and landing policies for Aurum with the Khirjahnis and Th'Dorrans. As far as Renly could tell, no one from Arkady had been invited to the celebration.

The intoxicating scent of Ungah lilies perfumed the air, and Renly inhaled deeply, savoring their delicate fragrance.

K'Sati gave him a playful nudge. "Stop sniffing my hair. You'll bruise the flowers."

A wreath of the cream-colored flowers encircled her head and horns like a halo, complimenting her lovely olive skin. She wore a simple, traditional Khirjahni *mohko*, woven of pale traggah wool, cinched at her narrow waist with a shell-trimmed belt. At her neck, she wore the small platinum locket he's given her; inside an engraved portrait of Neatfoot. She strolled easily at his side with no trace of limp.

The waiter brought around a tray of sparkling Lhossa wine and they each took a glass. The taste of the tangy berries reminded him of how much they'd been though.

A beaming Ambassador Reinhardt approached them. "Congratulations, Renly. Everyone loves the new seal. The King tells me he is well pleased."

The new seal depicted a mother traggah and her youngling standing on the cliffs overlooking the sea. Beside them, an aboriginal Khirjahni herder rested his hand on the mare's shoulder, as they watched the twin suns of Aurum rise above the horizon, and sea creatures frolicked in the surf.

"And on a personal note, I must say, it's enough to make me forget the stink of this place. Well done."

Renly made a small bow. He'd never done an animal portrait before, or much in the way of nature, for that matter. The etching he did of Neatfoot for K'Sati had given him the idea. He used the sketches he'd done of Silverbeard's mother and youngling as his models for the traggahs, and based his drawing of the herdsman on the woodcarver Okoro. He fretted for months after completing the design; worried that the King would not like it. K'Sati and Okoro both told him the Khirjahni people revered artisans as blessed by the gods, but he did not want to have his art viewed as merely an off-worlder tribute; he wanted his art to capture the heart and soul of the Khirjahni.

At the private unveiling for the royal family the previous week, several members of the royal family had been moved to tears. Okanga proclaimed him as an official citizen of Aurum and offered to sponsor him as the royal engraver. It meant a freestanding cottage in the capital, and a stipend big enough to support both his and K'Sati's modest needs.

"With the embargo lifted, I imagine you'll be heading back to Terra soon?"

Everyone else he'd met on Aurum seemed to be asking him the same question. Now that the embargo was lifted, there was nothing to keep him from returning to his studio on Earth.

K'Sati, too, had asked him the same thing. She reached up and smoothed a stray lock of hair behind the nub of his horns. He kept trying to tell her they weren't really nubs anymore. They were starting to curve backwards now. She was the only one who knew he'd already made his decision.

"There's still a question about my genetic stability, and whether Terra will accept genetically altered humans, but I'm not worried. I've got several commissions lined up, and His Highness has mentioned a project he wants to talk to me about. Besides," he gave K'Sati the smile she knew was just for her. "The place is growing on me."

END

ABOUT THE AUTHOR

Award-winning author Sharon Joss writes science fiction, fantasy and horror. She is the author of seven novels, including, BROTHERS OF THE FANG, and the alternate history thriller, STEAM DOGS. In 2015, she won the Writers of the Future Golden Pen award for speculative fiction with her novella, Stars That Make Dark Heaven Light. She lives amid a thicket of blackberry vines in Oregon and writes full-time. Find out more about her and her books by going to www.sharonjoss.com

AUTHOR'S NOTE

Thank you for giving this book a read. If you enjoyed it, please tell your friends and consider leaving a review on Amazon or Goodreads, even if it's only a line or two; it would make all the difference and would be very much appreciated.

If you'd like a quick note when I have a new release, please sign up for my new release mailing list at:

http://bit.ly/1MhS3lb

Your email will never be shared and you can unsubscribe at any time. I'll send you a free e-book right away and occasionally send out information about contests or opportunities to snag review copies).

OTHER GREAT FICTION FROM SHARON JOSS

Winner of the
2015 GOLDEN PEN AWARD

Worlds and species collide on the planet Hesperidee in this classic winning tale of love, duty, and the future of humanity.

"STARS THAT MAKE DARK HEAVEN LIGHT is an amazing story, as powerful as it is beautiful. Award-winning author Sharon Joss manages to prove herself to be one of the best writers of our time."

--New York Times bestselling author David Farland

BROTHERS OF THE FANG
THE DIRTY DOZEN WEREWOLVES MEET A HIGH PLAINS SHIFTER IN THIS SUPERNATURAL THRILLER

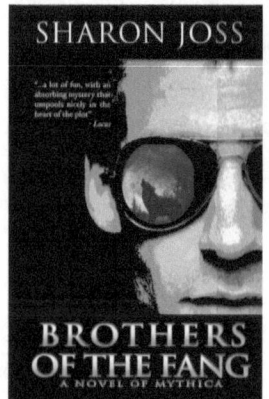

Detective Mike Bane is a shape shifter with two beasts: a 300-lb black jaguar with a taste for turtle meat, and a psychotic Olmec shaman named Tehuantl with a taste for blood.

When Mike accepts a security job at Mythica, America's only supernatural theme park, he discovers an unexpected kinship with the park's werewolf pack.

But when curiosity gets the best of him, all hell breaks loose in a centuries-old feud between Mythica's vampires and the Fae of the neighboring High Tor clan. Only Tehuantl's magic will save Mike's brothers of the fang; in return, Tehuantl wants permanent possession of Mike's body, mind, and soul.

"... a lot of fun, with an absorbing mystery that unspools nicely at the heart of the plot. "

- Locus

THE SEARCH FOR PEACE IN A TIME OF
DESTRUCTION

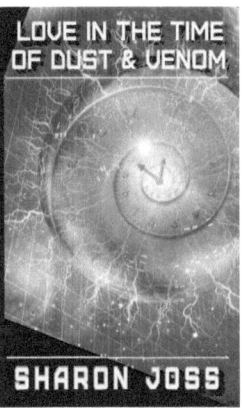

After the Fukushima Daiichi nuclear disaster, Keiko's grandfather insists on returning to his homeland to die in peace. Radiation prevents his return now, but what about the future? Time travel makes it possible, but no one can know what the future will bring…

FIVE MEMORABLE TALES OF TIME AND SPACE

From the past to the post-apocalyptic present to the future; from the planet Earth to distant galaxies, this collection of short science fiction is the first from acclaimed author Sharon Joss.

Love in the Time of Dust and Venom
Flight Risk
Memories of the Skin
Return for the Dead
A Time of Patriots